WHEN THE SUMMER'S OVER

WHEN THE SUMMER'S OVER

ANNA POLLOCK

BRASEBERRY PRESS

Cover design by Anna Pollock
www.annarbpollock.com

Cover photography by Janosch Diggelmann
www.janoschdiggelmann.ch
Cover Illustration by Olivia O'Quinn

ISBN 979-8-9875186-6-3
eBook ISBN 979-8-9875186-7-0

I want to acknowledge that Wakuta is a fictional town named after Chief Wakuta or Wacouta I of the Mdewakanton Band of Red Wing, MN, a sub-tribe of the Dakota people. Its geographical location is based on Mankato, MN, the site of the largest mass execution in U.S. history of the Dakota 38. The surrounding towns are located on stolen land.

It's important to note that even fictional places are based in real history filled with genocide and forced removal of indigenous people.

*Dedicated to my sister, Kendra, for inspiring me to tell stories,
and to KaRa Lyn for giving me the confidence to do so.*

CHAPTER 1

Ellie

Dear Elizabeth Somers,

It is with much enthusiasm that Somers Farm, LLC has been chosen as a recipient of the Tellema Agriculture Innovative Workforce Development Grant to employ a part-time graduate student through the University of Minnesota Environmental and Agricultural Sciences, Wakuta.

This award comes with an unrestricted one-time grant of $100,000. Attached is a payment schedule, along with information on our grant acknowledgement terms. Wages and taxes will be paid by the University of Minnesota, Wakuta.

Due to timing restrictions, we are unable to involve farms in the hiring process of graduate students in the program. See below information regarding the first day of employment.

Cyrus Lexington, PhD Candidate
Physiology & Ecology of Horticultural Crops
Research Term: May 16th - August 26th
Phone Number: 507-555-3500

Please reach out with any questions or concerns!

Thank you,
Josephine Robertson
Program Manager, Grant Relations
Tellema Foundation

She read it a few times to make sure it was real.

$100,000.

A farm hand.

Tingles spread from Ellie's chest to her fingertips.

No more pinching pennies and cutting corners. No more worrying if they could operate another year. She had been waiting for this email for nearly three months. After weeks of perfecting her application, proving her worth to big wigs in cities she'd never been to, she finally could exhale.

"Oh my goodness," she whispered to herself before letting her entire body burst with excitement. "Dad! DAD! We got the grant!"

She heard Doug's shuffled footsteps before seeing him. Her dad wasn't old by any means, but he was aging in a way that made this grant all the more necessary. Thirty-some-odd years of being a farmer does things to a body that time only intensifies.

"Are you pulling something, Ellie?"

"We did it. One-hundred thousand dollars for operations, plus we get a farm hand for the summer. Look!"

He bent over her shoulder, squinting at the screen. She pulled the spare pair of his reading glasses she kept at the computer for this exact occasion, and within seconds, his bespectacled eyes widened with a smile that matched. That smile was the entire reason she did this.

"Holy cow. I can't believe it, kiddo! Have you talked to Mom? What does this mean for taxes?" Of course this was the first thing he asked about.

"Mom!" she screamed, shrinking in her seat after nearly yelling into her dad's ear. He didn't mind, he was too busy laughing and re-reading her computer screen.

Martha Somers entered the crowded office with her hair pulled back and glasses hanging low on her nose. Not the most expressive of the Somers, but when it came to matters of finances, Ellie's mom was always the one to call. She provided for the family after a modest career in accounting at the Wakuta school district. Without her expertise in finance and tax law, they would have lost so much more than ninety percent of their farmland. Retirement was treating her well, and there was no one more deserving.

"We got the Tellema grant. The innovative workforce one!"

"Oh, my. Send me the details," she smiled with a pat on Ellie's cheek. "Nice work, Elizabeth Mae. Maybe now you both will stop asking me to pull weeds."

"Never!" Ellie cheered, too elated with the news to give into her backhanded remark.

It was true, things had been tight. Work had been nonstop. After the last eight years, this would finally allow some breathing room for all of them. Every season revolved around the farm. Fall consisted of Winter share prep, Winter shares lasted until Spring, Spring was busy with planting, and Summer was a marathon.

It had been years since Ellie had been able to take a breath. Vacations? Out of the question. Weekend getaways to the Twin Cities? A thing of the past. Visits to her sister, Hannah, were few and far between, completely out of the question during the warmer months. Plus, any time she came to visit, her kids stayed back in Seattle.

There was too much work to do with an extra pair of hands and the little ones weren't yet ready to be productive. She hadn't seen her niece and nephew for months, which meant Martha hadn't seen her only two grandchildren in months, too. She only complained about it on days that ended in 'y'.

It didn't matter anymore. Now it was all worth it. She'd have someone to share her life's passion with, someone who probably matched that passion with her. Someone who could teach her about everything she hadn't already learned from stewarding the land for the last twenty-seven years.

This was going to be the best summer of her life.

Cyrus

Hey Cyrus,

Might have a solution for you, but I don't know if you're gonna like it. All research spots with the CALS department in Cornell here are booked solid since the summer semester already started. However, we have a partnership with other ag-focused schools across the country, specifically one in Minnesota that's nicknamed "Harvard of the Midwest" for Ag programs. Whatever that means. It's through a workforce grant program with the Tellema Foundation if you've heard of them. Huge foundation for workforce innovation with environmental sustainability.

From what I found, this might be one of the only programs that can get you the research you're looking for and still has a spot available. Sounds like some hobby farm outside of town grows the kinds of vegetables in your line of work. Kind of makes sense to be working in the breadbasket of the country, right? Sorry again about all of this, but so it goes.

Let me know. And soon.

Cheers,
Brad Goffard, Senior Career Advisor
Cornell University Graduate School

Sorry, my ass, Cyrus thought. He'd been in Brad's office no less than twice a week for the past year, going over his dissertation, complaining about his review committee, and ultimately conceding to the fact that it was "Approved with Conditions". All he needed was one more round of research, per the board, and this might be his only shot.

Rolling his eyes, he pictured all of the ways this would be a disaster. Hobby farms weren't exactly known for their meticulous documentation, and from the looks of it, Cyrus was already behind. When did growing seasons even start in Minnesota? Wasn't it snowing there literally all year round? He'd never been. Why the *hell* would he have a reason to go to some flyover state known for cheese or something?

He considered calling his parents. Heavyweights in the world of academia could always pull strings that seemed impossible to tug, but if he was going to crawl out from under their thumb anytime soon, he had to stop asking for favors. Getting into Cornell on his own intended to do just that, until the Dean of Admissions reached out to buy him dinner with the caveat of bringing his dad. He couldn't escape his last name. Luckily Brad, his advisor, didn't bullshit him the way the rest of the world did.

With no one to tell, and the number of people he'd have to say goodbye to counted on one hand, he typed out his response, cornered without any other solution.

Ever the optimist, this was going to be the worst summer of his life.

CHAPTER 2

Ellie

Ellie popped up from where she was pruning the trellised tomato bushes, excited to take on the day. This early in the season, if she turned her back for one second they'd be growing wild. It was always keep up, not catch up with these things.

Her watch read 8:06 AM, a full hour after what she told Josephine to use as an arrival time for their new farm hand, Cyrus. *Cyrus Lexington.* What a name. She used the delay to get a head start on the chore list, knowing most of her attention would be spent training him in. Luckily, nothing could stop her mood from faltering. Their finances were looking great, the fields were planted, and they'd finally have some help starting today.

A warm, spring Minnesota morning was there to greet him. Mid-May was always a gamble in this state. A few years back, a snowstorm ravaged the county on May 3rd. Yes, *May 3rd.* The fact that it had been in the 60s for a week straight was nothing short of a miracle. Blue skies and seventy-degree weather was in the forecast for the rest of the week.

On her walk to the shed, she tried to envision the field through new eyes. The seedlings of the season didn't seem like much. Zucchini resembled the cucumber, the differences between broccoli and cabbages were hardly discernible. To the trained eye, however, it was easy to see that each row was unique, and well, whatever she couldn't distinguish was tucked away in a spreadsheet in the shed. Freshly purchased twenty-foot garden tunnels housed seeds on the cusp of germination, waiting to be transplanted directly into the soil. The weeds were a little embarrassing, but that's why they had the farm hand. It would be number one on the to-do list once chores were done.

In her mind, this was the most beautiful place on earth. Her mom's flowers lined the perimeter of the field, standing out against the lush emerald clover that carpeted the lawn. She looked up at the house, a two story cottage that sheltered three generations of Somers before her. A mammoth of a maple tree sat in the middle of the yard, a tree that felt like the center of the universe, acting as an anchor that provided shade, a swing, and hours of climbing with her older sister in their youth. Everything was familiar and well-loved by those that loved her in return. She couldn't imagine living anywhere else.

Locking the wire gate and clicking the electric fence on, she anticipated teaching Cyrus all the ins and outs of the place she loved for so long. Still no car in sight, however, she reached the shed and stalled at the workbench to scribble off the tasks completed.

Harvest list:
 ~~Lettuce (1st planting)~~
 ~~Cilantro~~
 ~~Radishes (1st planting)~~
 ~~Chives~~
 ~~Rhubarb~~
 ~~Early june strawberries~~
 ~~Asparagus~~
~~Transplant lettuces (3rd planting)~~
~~Transplant ALL peppers~~
~~Transplant bitter melon~~
~~Fertilize herbs~~
~~Prune tomatoes (cherry)~~
 ~~Check romas?~~
Lay straw over potatoes
* Khang's share (Felix wants extra cilantro)
* Loretta Cottrell share (add Mom's rhubarb jam)
* Send Cyrus home with jam!
Morning Chicken chores (Train Cyrus)
~~ORDER FEED!~~
Weed list (Cyrus):
 Strawberries
 Asparagus
 Sweet corn seedlings
 Kohlrabi

After a few more minutes of puttering about, she checked the time again. 8:33 AM. Over an hour and a half after Cyrus was supposed to arrive. If he'd worked on farms before, he would know that the earlier the better. The mornings had been consistently cool, but the high today would easily reach seventy five.

Mornings were always her favorite, though. The smell of dew and flowers opening up for the day brought back the fondness of growing up on this land, feeding the cattle that once roamed the pasture, watering the pigs, and cleaning out barns. Yes, even the foulest of smells sometimes brought back the rosiest colored memories.

She checked out the window of the pack shed and glanced at the driveway. Again nothing.

Maybe he was busy with his own morning chores. Lots of students in the Ag program had their own farms to maintain on top of their studies. All she knew about this *Cyrus Lexington* was that he was a PhD candidate at the school in Wakuta, a premiere college about forty minutes outside of Meriden.

It wasn't until after nine o'clock when a white sedan with a New York license plate pulled into the driveway. Her gaze followed the *Mercedes-Benz* up to the garage, and she wondered if this really was the farm hand, and why he was parking next to the garage when the shed was right there. He remained in the car long enough for her to walk up behind him, waving into the driver's side mirror. A turtleneck sweater and a pair of sunglasses stepped out of the car.

A turtleneck. He was wearing a turtleneck.

"Um, can I help you?" Ellie asked by mistake, thinking momentarily that this was a curious first-time customer, or someone lost on the highway. Way lost. He pulled his sunglasses down, revealing dark brown eyes that warmed the more she looked at them. He side-eyed her, running his fingers through a perfect swoop of shiny deep strawberry blond hair before answering.

"I'm Cyrus. I'm the PhD candidate with Cornell, er, the University in Whack-uh-ta?"

"Wah-*koo*-ta?" Ellie answered.

"Sure. Uh, anyway. Can I speak to the owner of the farm? My advisor said he'd be here today. Or is there someone here named Elizabeth?"

"Ellie." She crossed her arms, unimpressed with his gendered assumption. "And you're over two hours late."

"Yeah, well, I got very lost on the way here, and that highway didn't have an exit for twenty miles." Okay so he *was* lost. He turned and pulled a three-ring binder and a few notepads from his car. His nonchalance hit every nerve ending on Ellie's body. "So are you the owner then?"

"Yes." Ellie straightened her back.

"Uh, okay. I have a few things I'll need to begin my research. Do you have a spot where we could discuss my expectations, or are we just going to stand in the driveway all day?" he chuckled with arrogance.

Ass.

Without a word, she turned on her heel and led them to the shed, trying valiantly to relax her knitted eyebrows. Hopefully they could get back on track once she introduced herself properly.

"Alright, let's start over," she huffed and turned to face him. He approached the workbench hesitantly and spread open his binder, not even looking up as she spoke. "My name is Ellie, and this is Somers Farm. I've owned and operated it for about five years now, and before that, I worked as a farm hand for my father."

Silence.

"Each morning we begin with chicken chores, then move to the harvest list. Once we have everything in the cooler, we usually take a lunch." She pointed at the door of the walk-in refrigerator next to her.

Cyrus continued to look around, not meeting her eyes still.

"After lunch, we come back to the shed where we do all our washing and packing for our CSA shares. Pick-ups are usually Tuesday and Thursday, except for the Khangs, who pick up on Mondays. Thursday nights are our community nights, when anyone in Meriden can come pick up or buy produce straight from the farm, but those don't start until June. Oh, and we sell a lot of our produce at the farmer's market that happens every Saturday in Downtown Wakuta." He finally lifted his eyes to her and she noticed faint freckles across his cheekbones. "So, I can get you trained in on chicken chores, and then—"

"I'll stop you there," he interrupted her. "I was more hoping we could go over the expectations of my research on the farm."

A wave of embarrassment traveled down her neck. She hoped it wasn't turning red. "Of course. That's a great place to start. First things first, we start chores at 7 AM. It's after nine."

He scoffed, "Uh, yeah. Not really sure why I need to be here for chicken chores."

"Excuse me?"

"Look, I'm here to do research on the development of specific species of fruits, vegetables, and herbs. I'll come to take some samples, but most of them will be taken back to a lab. I *will* need a detailed description of the seeds used, date planted, potting soil used, and fertilizers after germination," he demanded, rattling off on his fingers. "Also, any pesticides utilized."

"We don't use any non-organic certified pesticides here on the farm," was all she could react with after this monologue.

He focused on the papers in front of him. "Great, well, I'll still need to know which ones you *do* use. I'm going to take a few soil samples today from the field before heading back to Whack-uh-ta, or whatever. When can you get me the information about the seeds and planting times?"

Seething, she spun around and turned on the old, dingy laptop that lived in the shed for easy access. "I have all of that information here. Do you prefer a print out or an email?"

He finally looked up, following her to the computer and looking over her shoulder. "Oh. Is it on a computer?"

"Yeah, we exist in the twenty-first century, if you can believe it. I've kept records of all seeds purchased since I took over. Brands of potting soil, dates of planting, germination, transplanting, and harvest, it's all here." The spreadsheet in front of her was too large to see on one screen. She scrolled down the rows of information as Cyrus watched on with an eagle eye.

"Nice, usually don't see that kind of tracking on a hobby farm."

"This isn't a hobby farm, Cyrus." She took a deep breath and clenched her fists, wanting to scream. "This is a for-profit LLC. It's how we make our living. And we can't do that unless we have a farm hand that will be here at 7 AM Monday through Friday. That means tomorrow."

"And if I'm not?"

"If you're not, I'm contacting my Program Manager at the Tellema Foundation about a replacement."

Her voice carried a bit more force than she meant to. Maybe it was a bit harsh, but none of this was how she had imagined it. She'd never met someone who was such a defiant asshole, let alone someone who would also be working with her on the farm. This was her baby, her pride and joy, and all she wanted to do was share it with someone. Not like this.

His eyes narrowed, and he had the audacity to smirk while he packed up his things.

"I'll see you tomorrow," he mumbled and left without a backward glance.

*　　*　　*

"And then!" Ellie practically shouted at her dad in the shed. The late afternoon sun warmed the air now that nearly all of the chores were done. "He called us a hobby farm!"

Doug laughed as he folded wax produce boxes that Ellie filled with radishes, lettuce, chives, asparagus, rhubarb, and extra cilantro for the Khangs down the road. The rest of the shares were sitting in neat stacks on the workbench. All there was left to do was grab some rhubarb jam from inside the cellar, add it to the last share, place everything in the cooler, and finally the day was done. A day that she thought would look completely different when she first woke up that morning.

"Do you think he'll eventually help at all with the market? Or harvesting in the morning?" Doug asked.

"I have no idea now!" Her dad switched from packing boxes to cleaning out the sinks they washed the produce in for the day. Ellie stopped what she was doing. "Hey, I can do that. Do you want to grab some jam from the cellar? I need two."

"Sure thing, boss," Doug nodded with a wink. It was a thinly veiled attempt to get him to slow down, but that didn't stop her from worrying about him. He didn't need to be doing manual labor six days a week at age fifty-nine.

The crunch of the gravel signaled that the Khangs had arrived to pick up their share, and Felix running into the shed moments later with his sketchbook confirmed it. His mom, Trang, followed him through the open garage door.

Felix was a lanky 15-year-old only child and had a knack for drawing and talking. With an OB-GYN for a mom and a high school choir director for a dad, he spent most of his time with adults or at the Ortegas, their neighbors. Ever since Felix was allowed to bike to the farm by himself last summer, he'd been itching to get back in the field with his sketchbook. Recently, his favorite subjects included the most brilliant vegetables and their different life cycles with picturesque detail. The more colorful the plant, the more he liked it.

"Hey Ellie!" Felix said before diving in. "We got to take home our flora projects now that school's almost done. Look!" He held up a series of drawings, all bright and full of life. The deep pink stalks of the rhubarb contrasted beautifully with the kelly green leaves, ripe tomatoes shined with juiciness, and orange squash blossoms popped off the page. "I got As on all of them. Mom said it was because your vegetables were my muse!"

"Felix, these are incredible. Wanna hang them up in the shed?" Ellie asked, still transfixed by his talents.

His eyes widened, and without an answer he reached for the wide masking tape they used to label boxes and posted each sketch side by side near the entrance. At this point, Felix knew the ins and outs of the shed as well as anyone.

"How's the bitter melon looking?" Trang asked.

"Really good finally. It definitely made a difference having the hotbeds this spring. Transplanted it today actually."

"Thank god *someone* has a green thumb. He's been asking me to make bitter melon soup and I can never find it in stores around here," Trang shared, pointing at Felix concentrating on his project. "Don't know when I'll have the time, but Lance can figure that out once school's done. Speaking of which, Felix, did you have something you'd like to ask Ellie?"

Felix finished smoothing the final piece of tape before turning around. "Oh yeah. I got a job at the grocery store when school's out. I'll be a bag boy since I just turned fifteen, but I don't work on the weekends because they already have staff that work on the weekends. It's a whole thing because they've been working there for years, and I guess the weekdays are when people with other jobs work, but this is my only job. I mean, I could work the weekends when we're back in school I guess, but I really—"

"*Felix*," Trang nudged.

He finally took a breath and rolled his eyes in the jovial way he did whenever someone cut him off. "I know, okay. So I was wondering if I could help work the farmer's market for a little extra cash or maybe I could come to the field every once in a while to draw — like I already do — but I know the summer is really busy and that you usually have so much to harvest before Saturday, and then Tuesdays and Thursdays are really busy for CSA pick-ups, so maybe I could come after work on Mondays and Wednesdays to be in the field? But only if it's okay. Oh! And there's a weekend in August I can't work at the farmer's market because of camp."

Ellie tried to find the question in there while Trang sighed and placed a hand on her son's shoulder. It seemed to be lost on both of them how he could talk for so long without taking a breath.

"Yes, Felix. You are more than welcome to work the Saturday markets and come to draw in the field whenever you want, you know that. Let's start with $15 an hour, does that sound okay?"

His eyebrows raised with a look of disbelief. "That's five dollars more than Hobern's is paying me."

"The market's only open for four hours a week, honey," Trang explained.

"But still! Okay, when do I start?"

"First market is this Saturday," Ellie replied, handing over the produce box smelling of cilantro and chives. "It starts at eight, but I'll take you at seven to help set up. Think you can make that work?"

"Do I hear the newest employee of Somers Farm?" Doug's voice echoed up from the cellar stairs. He returned with a smile.

Felix nodded violently, squeezing his fists in excitement while bringing them up to his chest. Trang watched the two of them before sharing a private smile with Ellie. After knowing the Khangs for almost a decade, they were at a point where an entire conversation could exist with a single look. She waved goodbye with a wink and they were off, leaving Ellie and her dad alone again in the shed.

"Last one for the day. Loretta is picking up her share tomorrow afternoon and the rest are for Thursday," Ellie said to her dad as he slid the two jars of jam over.

"Why'd you need two jars if that's the last box?" her dad asked, mirroring the same concern in her mind after he said it.

"That was for Cyrus. I was going to send him home with some after the day of work."

A sigh escaped her, only it was much bigger than she intended.

An hour of stewing later, she finally convinced her dad to go back to the house for the evening and finished inputting the day's harvest into the computer, already worried about the market on Saturday. It's not like Felix was a nuisance by any means, but the fact that she now had a fifteen year old to manage made it that much more important to get help. Help that Cyrus clearly wasn't willing to provide.

Day one and already he wasn't holding up his half of the bargain. The jar on the counter was taunting her, reminding her of the vision she had of the day, a tour of the farm, talking about planting schedules and their favorite vegetables, maybe even learning something from a PhD candidate. An exchange, not someone who was going to use her farm as a case study and leave four months later. She could sit here and let it fester, or she could do something about it.

Hot with rage, her phone's dial tone rang in her ear.

"Tellema Foundation, this is Josephine."

"Hi Josephine, this is Ellie Somers, how are you?"

"Oh Ellie!" she answered, chipper as ever. "I'm doing well. Today was the first day with Cyrus, is that right? How did it go?"

Ellie took a deep breath. *Here goes nothing.* "Well, he was only here for about ten minutes before taking off. I know this sounds a bit reactionary, but I was actually wondering about finding a replacement."

"Oh?"

"It's pretty clear he's not here to work and is only using the farm as a research station. And I mean, I want him to be able to do his work, but isn't he also being paid through you guys to be a farm hand? That was a huge perk of grant, along with the award." She finally took a breath, shaky with the weight of how important this was. The farm was everything to her. She *needed* help.

"Right, yes. Um first, let me say I'm so sorry to hear this, Ellie." Josephine started. "I'll mark down that he was a no show today, but I'll level with you, this was a late placement. So in short, no, we wouldn't be able to find you a replacement, and you don't really have the authority to fire him. That lies with the school."

"Hmm."

"And you run the risk of breaking the terms of the grant if he leaves, which could compromise your eligibility for the grant's funding." Ellie's chest sank. "However, from what I understand of Cyrus's application to our program, your farm is unique in the kind of produce you grow, and he may be out of options in order to do his research. Candidly, his advisor mentioned this would be a big change for him."

"What do I do then? Give him an empty threat?"

Josephine stuttered, "Uh, no. I wouldn't recommend threatening the student." That probably wasn't the best choice of words. "Again, if he chooses to leave the program, you may not be eligible for the award. It's all in the contract, if you'd like—"

"No, I've read it!" Ellie cut her off, frustrated, but trying to keep her chipper self steady. "Sorry, Josephine. It's been a stressful day."

"Oh, I know how that can go. Like I said, I'll mark that he was a no show, and that should reach his supervisor. Probably his advisor since he's a graduate student. Is there anything else I can help with?"

"Um, no. I'll... I guess I'll try to figure it out."

They hung up and she rubbed her face, taking a deep inhale. With no way of knowing what tomorrow would bring, she closed up the shed to continue weeding until sundown. After stuffing her face straight from the fridge with some leftover pot roast that her mom made, she showered and finally sat down for the first time since the morning.

It was 10:12 PM.

CHAPTER 3

Cyrus

"How am I supposed to do my research and work full-time at a fucking farm?" Cyrus blew up at Brad, not holding back his annoyance in how his first day had gone.

After getting his hellish schedule from the Wakuta advisor and acquainting himself with the overly strict university lab rules, he finally was back in his bare apartment. He'd found it on Craigslist. The rent was cheaper than anything he'd ever seen in his entire Manhattan upbringing. Two bedrooms, two baths, all for less than two thousand dollars a summonth. In-unit washer and dryer wasn't usually in a New Yorker's vocabulary, but here he was. Only downfall was that it was above a bar.

Brad scoffed over the phone. "Well, first of all, bud, you're not expected to work full-time, but leaving after ten minutes on day-one leaves an impression that I can't fix with an email. Second, the whole reason you're even able to do this research is because of this farm. And third—"

"No!"

"Yes! *Third,* if you back out of this, I can't get you into a research program until next spring. If you want to push off your graduation until then, be my guest."

"Fucking *fuck,*" Cyrus said under his breath, both to himself and to his empty fridge staring back at him. It was bad enough that he was in a state he'd never been to, but now he was in a town where he had nothing and knew no one. And now, he was expected to be at a farm at seven in the morning everyday. Brad chewing him out like a child was a liquor soaked cherry on top.

"You know, your dad could probably make a call," he jeered. He knew this would get Cyrus going.

"No, absolutely not. Why'd you even bring that up?"

"Because it would work. It would also bump someone from their own program, but that's my problem, not yours." *Why was he still talking?*

"Literally stop, it's not happening." He scratched the back of his head staring at the beef jerky on his counter and the container of almonds that had traveled with him in the car. He'd kill for some farm fresh eggs and some bell peppers, maybe make a burrito with some pepper jack and fresh tortillas. *If only.*

"What do I have to do to get out of 7 AM tomorrow?"

Brad chuckled, "Listen, from what I understand, this position is tied to a grant. So if you leave or get fired, the farm is out a worker and a pretty huge sum of money. Not to mention, you'd lose your research."

That wasn't an option. From what Cyrus saw of Ellie's spreadsheet, this farm was the only one that operated in line with his needs. Heirloom varieties, organic practices, and from what he could see from the driveway, a pollinator garden. It was exactly what he needed to graduate, and there was *nothing* more important to Cyrus than his research and graduating as soon as humanly possible.

"So I'm stuck."

"So you're stuck," Brad confirmed. "But your dad—"

"Okay bye, I'm not doing this."

"Good luck, dude."

Cyrus hung up and slammed the fridge door shut. In the last forty-eight hours, he'd been in the car for sixteen of them. A solution to his tightened shoulder muscles beckoned him under his feet. He probably shouldn't. It would lead to bad decisions, and probably a few regrets in the morning, but this was obviously a college town. What was the worst that could happen? No one knew him here anyway. It was his last night of freedom before sample analysis, research narratives, and trying to juggle his insane lab reservations.

Fuck it.

He grabbed his wallet, deciding right then he'd be drinking his dinner tonight. Two flights of stairs later, he sat at the downstairs bar, stunned into silence when the man behind the counter slid his gin and tonic over and asked for a whopping three dollars.

"Cash only," the bartender grunted when he presented his card, already onto the next customer. Cyrus's mouth hung open like an idiot. He hadn't carried a dollar bill in years.

"I don't have cash," he admitted.

The bartender eyed him. He couldn't have been older than twenty five, probably paying off undergrad. Cute, but not Cyrus's type. This was Wakuta after all. Even then, his curls reminded him of the wisps of hair under Ellie's sun hat, and Cyrus felt a surge of regret about the morning.

"Fine, first one's on the house since it's already poured. Second one is three dollars. Cash."

Cyrus could schmooze. "Hey, thanks man. Cyrus." He pointed at himself. "What's your name?"

"Mike," he answered, stuck in place to fill a pint glass with something on tap.

"Are you always this busy on a Monday?"

"Last week was finals week. You're here the week of move-out." He nodded towards the door, moving on. "There's an ATM over there."

The bar filled as the night went on with young, dumb kids in their early twenties or less. If wearing a McQueen T-shirt and a certified vintage Levi's jean jacket wasn't enough, his age emphasized the sense that he was completely out of his element. At 29, most of the bars he used to frequent in New York were tucked into neighborhoods or invite-only at undisclosed locations. This bar had pool tables, TVs lining the walls, dart boards in the corners, and booths for private moments.

It cost him less than ten dollars to get to a place where everyone was his friend, including a group of girls who had accosted him into a few rounds of pool. From the way they were slinging back drinks, it was obvious they were young. One girl in particular wouldn't stop touching his hip. *Shayna or... Sarah?* In a lull between games, she pulled at his belt loop with lowered eyes.

"Buy me anotheround, and lessget out of here?" she slurred, biting her lip. His phone buzzed in his pocket, but he ignored it, blissful with the ignorance of an outside world.

Another bad decision for the night, maybe he could even bum a smoke off someone outside and really add to the pile. He grabbed her hand, long acrylic nails scraping softly at his wrist, and pulled her up to the bar.

"Hey, Mike!" He looked back at the girl in his hand, smirking as if he was a regular. She stumbled into him and he took the opportunity to slink his hand around the exposed skin on the small of her back, desperate for a bit of human contact.

Mike ran over in a huff, shaking his head at the both of them. "I'm not serving you, Sophia. Come on, how did you get in? Did you get another fake?"

She looked up at Cyrus, eyes unfocused. "I dunno."

Instantly, he sobered up, feeling a ripple of nausea climbing from his stomach to his throat, not entirely from the alcohol.

"She's my cousin." Mike was shouting again. "You're gonna have to leave. I can't have you in here, Soph."

Before Cyrus could fully realize what he was doing, he pulled her out of the bar and onto the somewhat busy sidewalk, full of wandering college students in varying states of awareness. He struggled to keep her upright.

"How old are you?" Cyrus asked, grabbing her shoulders gently as she swayed back and forth.

"Erm twenny two," she mumbled. He shook his head at her answer. "Eight, hm, eighteen."

His mind raced, thinking back to his undergrad at NYU, exploring his sexuality with freedom, newly single, and running away from his name but never quite escaping it. Everyone knew he had money, knew that his dad was the largest private donor to the Department of Economics, knew that if they wanted anything from him, all they had to do was ask. Spending his parents' money became the only weapon he had against them, but their pockets were too deep for them ever to care. But every drink he bought, line he paid for, hand that took him home wasn't enough. This girl wasn't about to feel the same.

"Sophia, is it? A-are you okay to get home?"

"Mmmy friend," she started, but swallowed something down. "Drove."

With a huff, he looked down the street, cursing that a cab wasn't in sight. If this wasn't Bumbfuck, Nowhere he'd know exactly what to do. God, he missed the city.

"Do you have taxis here?"

She shrugged, handing him her unlocked phone willingly, as if she could trust him. His first instinct was to give it back, but her lost eyes looked up at him blankly. With a few screen taps, he gave her phone back and they waited, sitting on the curb side by side. At one point her head fell onto his shoulder and he stiffened with her touch. Another buzz in his pocket alerted him to check his missed call. It was Aurora, his younger sister. He didn't have time for that tonight. She could call literally anyone else.

Fuck, he wished he had a cigarette.

"Sophia!" A shrill voice screamed behind him. The gaggle of girls from the pool game spilled out onto the sidewalk and he lifted her up to stand. "What are you doing with her," she accused.

"Nothing, I promise. The bartender kicked her out. I called her a ride. Here." He took his wallet out and handed them two newly obtained twenties from the ATM. "Hopefully that covers it."

The girl who had shouted earlier pulled Sophia away from him. "Thanks."

Sophia sniffed and fell into her friend, still a bit dazed, and blinked slowly at Cyrus. "I love you."

"Okay," Cyrus said back. "I have to go. Just get home safe you guys."

Backing away, he sped up to his apartment, feeling sick to his stomach. Everything around him felt foreign, the weirdly clean public staircase, the hallway that didn't smell of weed, even his own apartment welcomed him with a strange smell of new paint and carpet cleaner. But tonight? Tonight felt the same way as an encounter with an ex feels. Intimate and invasive, bad for the long run, good for a quick fix. A dirty relapse, regretful, and ultimately familiar. He needed to get out of this place as soon as he could, and the only way out was through.

*   *   *

Way too early the next morning, he pulled into the Somers Farm driveway nursing a sports drink (who *was* he?) and a headache. Last night was the dumbest thing he'd done in a while, and he couldn't shake the feeling that his time in Minnesota was going to be cursed by it. What a way to start the summer in a new state.

He still had on his clothes from the night before, and he swallowed his pride and something else as he approached the field to find Ellie. She had on the same sun hat as yesterday, the same rosy cheeks from effort in picking weeds at the rows of sweet corn. They briefly made eye contact, but Cyrus couldn't look away, even if he did feel the heat of embarrassment brush his ears. A small comfort was the fact that Ellie didn't know about last night. She never would if he had anything to do with it.

"Hey!" he yelled out into the field, hyper aware of the electric fence a few feet from him. He took a sip from his neon blue beverage, looking for something to do with his hands. "Can you let me in?"

Ellie stood up, peeking at her watch and shaking her head. She spoke once she was within earshot.

"Thought you wouldn't be coming today," she said. Her knees were already full of dirt. "Are you ready to actually work?"

He scoffed, wanting to push her to the edge. "I'm here to collect samples."

"You're here to be a farm hand for five hours a day, that's the trade off." She had a bite, and Cyrus couldn't help but bite back. Something about her put him on edge.

He stepped closer to the fence. "You need me. You need the grant. Admit it."

"And you need this research in order to graduate," she spit. And she was right. The opportunity to sample from this type of farm came once a year, maybe a decade.

She mirrored him and took a step closer, too.

"How do you know that, though? I bet there are plenty of places like this all over rural America." Another step in. This time he could smell the faint scent of coffee wafting from her. Coffee and, hmm, *gardenias.*

"You'd lose. I spent the last six months putting together a grant application proving that there is nothing like this in the state, *in the country.* And if you'd stop insulting me, I could train you in and tell you why."

Cyrus rolled his shoulders back, fighting the urge to collapse in on himself with the one-two punch. "Fine, let's get started."

"Finally." She rolled her hazel eyes. In an expert move, her leg swung over the bottom fence line and she ducked under the top one, narrowly avoiding the electric currents. "Did you bring a change of clothes?"

He looked down at his Neil Barrett tan and black colorblock knit sweater over his white Alexander McQueen undershirt and Tom Ford light wash jeans, jogging in his Salvatore Ferragamo loafers to catch up as she marched towards the shed. "Why would I need a change of clothes?"

"You're going to get those filthy, not to mention it could get up to eighty today."

She fidgeted with some tools on the utility shelves, pulling a few items and handing them to Cyrus. A small knife, and some white rubber bands with a *Minnesota Grown* logo that matched some twist ties. What was he supposed to do with these?

"I've already done the chicken chores and I'm mostly done with harvesting. I have the cart in the field ready to pick up bins and bring them into the cooler. By that time, it'll probably be lunch, or a little after," Ellie said.

He lifted his head to speak again, but she was already on the other side of the shed, pulling a pair of boots from the closet.

"After lunch, you're welcome to take your precious samples, but I really, *really* need help with harvest and weeding today." She finally looked up at him, softening a bit. "You're also welcome to take any produce home. Perk of the job." Her barely-there smile sent a thread of tingles down his back. "Here's an extra pair of work boots. Your shoes are going to get ruined, like, actually ruined if you wear them in the field. It's too dewy."

"Um... okay," Cyrus softly answered, taking the boots from her. He pulled off his sweater and placed it near his drink and work binder, revealing his white undershirt, a little musty from the previous night. It wasn't his best look, but the boots fit well enough, and before long he was following Ellie to the field. He could've sworn her gaze lingered on his torso and traced down his right arm where his only tattoo lived. A sugar maple sprouting from his forearm, the State Tree of New York.

As they approached the electric fence, Ellie stopped.

"Alright, normally I duck through, but to turn off the gate, all you have to do is open this panel box, punch in the code, and turn off the switch." She proceeded to do just that as Cyrus watched her, fighting an eye roll. When would he ever be out here without her?

Further into the field, he saw light grey bins sprinkled about and the equivalent of a golf cart with a wooden truck bed for a back seat parked on the far end. Neat rows of seedlings lined their walk, and the smell of moist mycelium and sweet sainfoin welcomed him. The radishes caught his eye and caused his stomach to growl. He should've eaten breakfast and probably dinner the night before, but regret was a bitter son of a bitch. All he wanted to do was touch the new growth. Ellie was moving too fast to do any of that.

"If you can grab the bins and walk them to the truck, I'll continue where I was at with weeding. I have to keep up with them this time of year." If she would just stop walking for two seconds, he could've caught up to her.

"What about harvesting?" he yelled.

"We have to drop off a load in the shed first, then we'll come back," she shouted over her shoulder, leaving him alone in the middle of the spring onion patch.

With an exaggerated sigh, he tore off towards the closest bin. The soil beneath his unfamiliar boots was soft and aerated, alerting him to make a note to measure for earthworms. At every turn, this farm kept telling him it was special. Unique, singular, and meticulously cared for.

The farms he'd worked at before this were never larger than a backyard or the rooftop of a high rise. He was always impressed by the creativity of fitting hundreds of pounds of vegetables into a compact space, but here he was impressed by the sheer volume of produce even so early in the season.

By the fifth bin, his arms were giving out and his patience followed suit, not even knowing what he was carrying. He peeled open one of the lids revealing bundles of cilantro that smelled heavenly. The second bin overflowed with heads of lettuce, plump and bright green. Radishes with their leafy tops still attached stared back at him while his stomach growled on the third.

"Ellie!" he yelled, stalling to give his arms a break. "Can I eat some radishes?"

She appeared behind some bushes. By the looks of the thorny branches, raspberries. "Can't you wait until we're in the shed?"

"No!" he hollered and without waiting for her response, he took out the biggest bunch, wiping each of the bright pink bulbs on his shirt. It never stood a chance anyway. His hands were already somehow covered in dirt and it hadn't been more than an hour.

The snap of the first bite forced his eyes closed in ecstasy as the perfect balance of sweetness and spice blended on his tongue. There was nothing better than eating something picked straight from the soil. He munched through another one and jumped at the closeness of Ellie's voice and the heat of her glare.

"You really couldn't wait?"

He swallowed his bite. "These are amazing. Cherry Belle, right?"

"Yes, and they're for our CSA members."

"You said I get produce when I want it." He took another bite, fighting a smile with his correct guess. "Well, I wanted it."

"I said you could take it *home*," she rebutted, grabbing the last one in his bunch and cutting it in half with her own harvest knife. She studied the white flesh with a furrowed brow before taking a bite herself.

For a moment they shared a smirk with the mutual love of something as dumb as radishes, but the bubble burst when Ellie sped off to retrieve the last of the bins. She motioned for him to sit in the passenger's seat, and now that the midmorning sun beat down, he secretly thanked her for suggesting to ditch his sweater. Too bad that also meant his arms and face were probably going to get sunburned.

"Did you wear sunscreen? We have some in the shed if you need it. Your face is a little red," Ellie commented. *How did she do that?*

"Uh, no. But I'll wear some tomorrow." He nodded, looking past the field to see lines of small trees. "What's over there? Is that yours?"

"Yeah, we own four acres in total, one for vegetables, one has apple trees that we planted about two years ago, one is a cover crop to recover from the previous year," — that's where the sainfoin scent was coming from — "and the other is a pollinator garden. We rotate annual cover crops, pollinators, and vegetables every year."

Cyrus couldn't hold back his reaction. "Holy shit, that's really smart."

Ellie nodded as she pulled into the shed, and with only a few more words they finished unloading the truck.

The shed, as Ellie called it, was a huge building that had either been well maintained or recently built. Three times as long as it was wide, it housed a walk-in cooler on one side, a large workstation in the center, and a few sink stations on the end. Stairs led downwards, and Cyrus supposed there was a cellar of some sort below. The whole operation felt intentional and well thought out, and even had a spot for the golf cart thing to unload right next to the cooler.

Thank god, Cyrus thought. His arms hurt like hell.

The rest of the morning consisted of weeding and getting a rundown of the plantings. It was hard not to get excited about the specialty varieties, but he bit his tongue out of spite. Her determination in keeping him busy with bitch work kept his annoyance at an all time high. Weeding, transplanting, more weeding, it was all wearing him down.

He hadn't felt like this in years. Back when he was getting his master's in Food Studies at NYU, he slipped away into some of the restaurants his parents frequented growing up. One in particular was a farm-to-table bistro with a French executive chef who barely spoke a word of English. He didn't give Cyrus any special treatment in the kitchen, but he always let him pick the vegetables and herbs for the day from the community garden they operated. Working in kitchens gave him a new sense of importance he never found with money. Money couldn't buy knife skills or baking techniques and he *loved* knowing his parents would cringe at the thought of him behind the swinging doors. Never the service, always the served. That's what his family lived by.

That line of thought pushed him towards agriculture. He needed to learn where every bite came from, whether it was at the corner bodega where he once lived in East Village, or the high-end market near the Hamptons where his parents lived during the summer. All food came from somewhere, and more importantly, *someone*.

Even with all that back breaking work in restaurants with temperamental chefs, he'd never broken a sweat like this. After carrying the last of the asparagus into the cooler from the truck, he finally sat down on the workbench in the shed. Ellie bounced out of the walk-in cooler, looking just as dirt smeared and disheveled as Cyrus, but with a smile on her face instead of a grimace.

"Alright! Feels good to have that done. I think it's a good time to stop for lunch. Did you want to eat before taking your samples?" she asked, brushing off some dirt on her hips.

He sighed, "Yes, please."

"Did you bring something?" she asked.

"What do you mean?"

"Lunch? Food?" Her tone raised with her eyebrows, sarcastic and short. Why was it so hard to have literally one pleasant conversation with her?

"I didn't think I needed to bring anything for lunch. But, fuck, I guess any places to eat around here are—"

"About forty minutes away," Ellie answered for him. She took off her work boots and wiggled her freshly freed toes, covered with socks that at one point were probably grey, but now were as brown as the dirt. Her hair fell out of her sun hat when she removed it, but before it cascaded down her back like some shampoo commercial, she pulled it into a ponytail.

"You're more than welcome to join us in the house," she said. "I usually make something for me and my dad. My mom nannies a family up the road every other week, so it's just us today."

His ego outweighed any curiosity of how she could have a casual lunch with her parents. He blinked away.

"Um, no. That's alright. I'm gonna take my samples quick and get out of your hair." *What a dumb comment.*

With a curt nod, she sobered into a tight smirk. "Well, thanks for your work today. See you back tomorrow at seven?"

"If I survive the night."

CHAPTER 4

Ellie

Ellie began to feel sorry for Cyrus in the way you feel sorry when a kid trips down a hallway after telling them twice to slow down. Doesn't stop the kid from crying, but damn does it feel good to say, *I told you so.*

From the first day, it was obvious he had no idea how to work on an actual farm, but it was getting increasingly clear he also hated being told what to do. After a week in the field, however, he looked like a lost puppy, slowly realizing that Ellie wasn't out to destroy his life, but rather make it easier.

It still didn't stop him from complaining about his achy arms and shoulders, a sore back, and a very visible sunburn on his nose and cheeks. If she wasn't so annoyed by him, she would have thought it was cute or endearing.

Not to Ellie, but maybe to someone else. Someone whose type was snob-with-a-superiority-complex.

They started each day with chicken chores, which honestly were a little funny to watch Cyrus navigate.

"Have you ever worked with livestock before?" she asked their first time in the coop, but the glare he gave her after screaming when the rooster flew up at him was all the answer she needed. Ellie had to fight the urge to lose it when he started using the chicken feed lid as a shield against the angry brawler.

"What the *fuck* is wrong with that thing?"

She shrugged, which in retrospect, may not have been the most helpful response.

He usually spent lunch alone in the shed, eating vegetables from the farm and working on his laptop. They'd sometimes cross paths in the afternoon, but for the most part he kept to himself, harvesting samples of soil and new growth. Sometimes she caught him with a tape measure and a weird looking tool that she googled and later learned was a caliper. Everything seemed to be going fine. That was, until Friday when they were working in the shed together. They'd just finished bundling stalks of rhubarb before lunch.

"So, your parents are always here then? Or do you live somewhere else?"

"Nope, I live with them." Ellie knew where this was going. She'd been answering this question for years.

"Oh," he said, lowering his shoulders. "So are you in school, or...?"

She shook her head. "I didn't go to college after high school. I stayed back to help on the farm. Some stuff happened when I graduated, so I took some nannying jobs around the neighborhood, but now I do this full-time."

Cyrus furrowed his eyebrows, almost in disgust. "How old are you?"

"Out of all the questions to ask," she sighed under her breath. What kind of a question was that? "I'm twenty-seven, and I've been working on this farm, not just living off it."

Cyrus back pedaled, "But haven't you ever thought of leaving? I mean, Minnesota? Don't you want to see what the world—"

"Where else would I go? The farm is here." Her temper was rising.

He stared at her blankly. "You could go anywhere? I mean, it must suck to have to live on a farm with your parents when you're almost thirty."

She threw her soiled gloves on the counter with force. "I'm not being held here against my will. And I don't appreciate the comments about my age and living situation," she snapped before tearing off towards the house, clenching her fists as her work boots pounded into the dirt.

Who the hell did he think he was? This was their... third? fourth? real conversation and he chose to say things like this? How was he this comfortable talking down to people when he barely knew them? Chalk it up to the shelter and curse of "Minnesota Nice," but Ellie wasn't used to people talking to her like this. And she shouldn't be. No one should be.

This was exactly what she was afraid of when she first met Cyrus. His perfectly coiffed hair and probably designer sunglasses did nothing but confirm that he didn't have a clue what it took to put in a real day's work. Now he had the condescending questions to match.

With the first work week behind them, she was thanking all the stars in the evening sky that she had the entire weekend away from him to cool off.

*   *   *

Saturday markets were always the most fun day of the week, and the first one of the year had Ellie feeling giddy. Felix arrived, talking a mile a minute about how they only had eight days of school left, and luckily he could talk and move produce at the same time. Her dad's upper lip already shined with sweat, even if Felix's lanky arms were doing most of the heavy lifting. Within an hour, the stand was looking full, ready to welcome patrons with the first harvests of the season.

"I'm going to go grab coffee from Tim," Ellie looked back at her dad. Tim owned a coffee shop in town and every Saturday, he closed up shop to sell at the market, only after Ellie convinced him to. He was a homecomer from the same graduating class and moved back after his wife got a teaching job in town. "Did you want anything?"

"Sure, I'll take a coffee with cream," Doug requested.

Felix brightened. "Me too! Iced caramel latte with an extra pump of vanilla."

She paused. "Does your mom let you have those?"

"Yeah, totally." He didn't make eye contact. "But actually I'll take a green tea."

Catching up with Tim had her feeling right back in the saddle, making the rounds to the other vendors to greet them before the start of the market. Excitement and love for this community always overwhelmed her during the first market of the season, and that enthusiasm reflected into her purchases; a jar of fermented salsa from Jason, a hand-poured candle from a local goat farm, and a bouquet of fresh cut flowers from Marisol and Andrés Hernández, the cutest couple who had planted roots in Meriden a few years ago. Coming back to the stand with an overflowing tote bag and a carrier of hot beverages, her dad grabbed the coffees and soon the market bell rang out.

"Here we go!" she cheered, watching a few regulars approach the stand as Felix bagged up their hauls, marking the start of the summer and reconnecting with her neighbors once more.

"Miss Ellie," a familiar voice grabbed her attention. It was Loretta, a close family friend and adopted grandmother. Loretta grew up with her only living grandmother, who passed away when Ellie was in high school. "How are you my sweet little farmer?"

Loretta's terms of endearment always made Ellie chuckle. "Loretta, it's so good to see you. Are you here for some rhubarb?"

She walked around the front of the stand and Loretta's arms wrapped around Ellie gently in a careful hug. Years of love in one simple touch. Everything felt right again. No Cyrus to fight with. No weeds brushing at her ankles, taunting her. Just love from the place she called home.

"I sure am. These knees are getting a bit too tired for my bushes this year. Luckily I have you," she winked. An ache shot through Ellie's chest, full of motivation and determination. "Say, how are your strawberries looking?"

"They're green! The patch is looking great, we just need to clear out last year's dead foliage." She scrunched her nose. "It's on the to-do list."

"Ellie?" Another voice called her name, this time much less familiar than Loretta. A quick turn of her head and there was

Cyrus in a navy blue button down over a white shirt and dark wash jeans, looking hot and hair-swoopy as ever.

"Oh god."

"And who's this?" Loretta asked, so innocent, so unaware.

"I'm Cyrus, hi," he said, keeping his eyes on Ellie, but averting at the last second to hold out his hand to Loretta. As if Loretta shook hands.

"Oh, a boy?" Loretta preened, reaching out to hug him. "Oh my, do you ever smell nice. Ellie, who do we have here?"

"This is Cyrus," was all she got out.

Loretta chuckled with a twinkle in her eye that Cyrus dared to share with her. "Yes, that's what he said, sweetheart."

"I'm a researcher that works on the farm. Just started this week." He had some sort of charm to him that he hadn't carried before. He also kept glancing at Ellie and she wanted to shrink under his gaze.

"What are you doing here?" Ellie asked, maybe a little too pointedly. At least, Loretta's glare said so.

"Uh, I think there's a farmer's market." The joke didn't land with Ellie, but Loretta gave a garish laugh as he continued. "I try to exclusively get my produce from places like this. Used to live near a farmer's market as a kid. Never got sick of it." He smiled a pleasing, likable smile. Ellie hated that Loretta was there to see it.

Loretta swooned some more, "I live by the same standard. I had one taste of Ellie's sugar snap peas, and I was sold. Haven't purchased them at the grocery store since." She looked between Ellie and Cyrus, both visibly trying to look away from each other. "Well! I'll leave you to it. Better go pick out some radishes before you sell out."

With a tight smile, Ellie nodded her off and was once again left alone with Cyrus. Before she could pivot to man the stand, he gently reached out to her forearm sending a weird buzz up her arm, as if her hatred towards him was now turning physical.

"Hey, just so you know, I can't be at the farm Monday morning. My lab time got mixed up."

Great. Another let down. She sighed, "Okay."

"But I can come in the afternoon. Late afternoon. After three."

Ellie mentally ran through the to-do list. She would never get to it all alone. "If you can, after three would be really helpful."

He nodded and took in the rest of the market, looking a bit lost but smiling to himself. A shy smile. "Almost didn't recognize you out of your farm clothes. Your hair is curly."

Slightly stunned, she didn't get a chance to respond before her dad's voice boomed, "Ellie! Are we selling rhubarb in bulk?"

"I better get back," she said to Cyrus, pointing her thumb behind her.

He nodded, flustered and very obviously regretting his previous statement. "Yeah, I gotta familiarize myself with the setup. Do you know if anyone sells oyster mushrooms around here?"

"Yeah, Isabelle and Maya do. Around the corner and the second booth in, next to the coffee stand. Tell them I sent you, they'll give you a discount."

With a weak smile, she quickly returned to her post and bundled ten pounds of rhubarb for a curious Loretta.

"So Cyrus is cute, huh?"

"Oh goodness no, Loretta. He's only here until late August. I think he'll graduate and be off by September."

She hummed. "Doesn't mean you can't have a little fun. They don't make them like that in Meriden." Her wink was a little too obvious, and suddenly Ellie was feeling hot in her Wranglers.

CHAPTER 5

Ellie

When Ellie stumbled down the stairs on Monday, the tiredness of the season crept behind her eyes. Martha was already in the kitchen pouring coffee, putting a splash of cream in for Ellie's dad, a spoonful of sugar for herself, and leaving a mug black for Ellie.

"Coffee," Ellie pleaded, grabbing for the mug and holding it up to her nose dramatically. She inhaled the warm, familiar scent. "Hmm, hazelnut today?"

Martha nodded. "Your dad's already in the field. Did you hear the wind last night?" Her eyes went big and she shook her head.

"Mmm."

Ellie let her make idle chit-chat on the way to the front porch just as she did every morning. For as often as Ellie needed to wake up before the sun every day, it wasn't until her first hit of caffeine that she started to feel like herself. This meant most mornings consisted of Martha's inner monologue and a few hums and *mhmm*s from Ellie until the coffee kicked in.

"And just reminding you, I have the Kerns on Saturday, so I won't be able to help with the market." She sat back in the adirondack chair with a sigh. "Did you already ask Cyrus to help?"

Ellie's eyes shot open from where she was clinging on to a few more moments of sleep in her own adirondack chair. "Uh, I will."

"Loretta seems to think there's something going on between you two."

"Loretta likes to make things up."

Her mom chuckled and took another sip of her coffee, turning her gaze out to the shed where Doug was walking back up to the house.

"Is he a good worker?"

Ellie sighed. "Jury's still out."

"Well, give him a chance."

"Mhmm."

"Loretta said he was very kind."

"Hmm." Good for Loretta.

"And she may or may not have noticed how much he liked looking at you."

She sat up, feeling fully awake. It was probably the coffee. "He does not like *looking* at me."

"Who's this?" Doug asked, climbing the stairs and grabbing his mug with a smile to Martha.

"No one." Ellie shot up. "I have so much to do. See you for lunch."

She stomped off before she had to answer any other weird questions about the perceived, *nonexistent,* attraction between

Ellie and Cyrus. And if Loretta thought that an embarrassing and ultimately surprising interaction with Cyrus at the farmer's market was enough to tell Martha there was "something going on," she obviously had spent too much time thinking about it. Ellie didn't even have time to think about the awkward public encounter with Cyrus, let alone if there was anything presumptuous about it.

By a quarter to ten, her energy was depleted, spent on hauling fifty pound bins of produce around for two hours, followed by transplanting over a hundred seedlings one by one from the two twenty-foot garden tunnels.

She opened her notebook in the shed after lunch, skimming over the laundry list to find something that would be easier with two people.

Harvest list:
- ~~Lettuce (1st planting)~~
- ~~Cilantro~~
- ~~Radishes (1st planting)~~
- ~~Rhubarb~~
- ~~Early june strawberries~~
- ~~Asparagus~~
- ~~Spinach~~

Transplants:
- ~~Broccoli~~
- ~~Cauliflower~~
- ~~Brussel Sprouts~~
- ~~Sungold Cherry Tomatoes~~

~~Lettuce (2nd planting)~~
Seed Plant:
    ~~Fingerling Potato bulbs~~
    ~~Yukon Gold bulbs~~
    ~~Carrots (2nd planting)~~
~~Chicken Chores~~
Clean up Strawberry Patch
Need to trellis black cap raspberries & cucumbers
    (probably want to trellis <u>tomatoes</u>!!!)
Order BT for brassicas
Weed EVERYTHING! (if time)
* Marisol wants extra cilantro & spinach
* Loretta asked about eggs in her next share
* ~~Ask Cyrus about working markets??~~

She crossed out the last line. She already knew the answer. What was the point? The slam of a car door outside told her that Cyrus's white sedan rolled into the driveway and her panic settled with the thought of an extra pair of hands for the day.

He walked in under the garage door, running a hand through his hair that always seemed to fall perfectly around his face.

"So," he said, smiling with the same dumb, likable smile that he showcased for Loretta, "what's on the agenda for today? Any harvesting?"

"I finished that this morning. I honestly don't even know where to start." She sighed and he motioned to her notebook. He intently read her handwriting, and her scalp tingled, as if he was paying her the attention rather than her to-do list.

"Hm, well. I can help with trellising. Did that a bunch in the urban farm I worked at during my master's."

"Okay, yeah," Ellie exhaled. "That would actually be great."

"Did you need help at the markets?"

She took the notebook back quickly and already felt the blush in her cheeks. "Uh, no. I thought we would need someone this weekend, but I know you're busy. We'll make it work." He nodded without further questioning.

The afternoon sun beat down on them as they were erecting stakes together. Ellie would hold the post upright while Cyrus donned the heavy rubber mallet, securing it into the ground. This was how it was supposed to feel, like she was on a team with Cyrus. She found herself trying to hide her smile, but it didn't matter. Cyrus was smiling, too, even if he hadn't dressed for the occasion. Prickly branches held onto Cyrus's clothes, slowing them both down as they draped branches over the fencing. It was hard not to feel sorry for how ruined his henley was getting with the onslaught. Snags pilled at his wrists, visible from where Ellie worked on her own row.

"Your sleeves," Ellie muttered.

With an exasperated look at his arms, he smiled. "It's fine. Not the most expensive shirt I own. I already ruined that my first day in the field."

"That white t-shirt is the most expensive shirt you own?"

He smirked. "Oh, you remember?"

Shit, she thought, hoping he didn't notice her blush because his smile told her otherwise. "I just mean, you had to change because you didn't prepare for working on a farm. That's what I remember."

"Well, what do you expect? I've never been to Minnesota," he pressed. "I've never worked on like, an actual farm before. Only compact farms that—"

"What do you mean this is your first time in Minnesota? Like when you started school?"

He paused on a branch and picked at a leaf, examining it front and back, as if he needed a distraction before admitting what came next. "Born and raised in Manhattan. I've lived there almost my entire life. The last three years I've been upstate at Cornell in Ithaca."

Wheels turned, gears clicked into place. Every snap judgment Ellie made about Cyrus was somewhat validated.

"You were *born* in New York City?"

"I was born in New York City," he repeated. "Everything I've ever wanted was right outside my front door. Why would I ever come to Minnesota?"

"This again?" Ellie was afraid of where this was going, but Cyrus shrugged with an exasperated huff.

"I mean, come on. That's an objective statement. Why would anyone live here when New York exists?"

Her hands fell to her sides, surprised once again that he felt this comfortable around her to say something so insulting with such purpose. "Excuse you. I've never had a reason to go to New York, either."

"Oh, Ellie—"

"Can we just drop it?"

Cyrus somehow smiled. "Come on, there are so many things to see in New York, so much history and culture. Honestly, I don't know why anyone chooses to live in small towns."

"Look around! None of this exists in the city, either, Cyrus." She took a deep, performative inhale. "Smell that? Actual fresh air. No street piss."

"Street piss?! Don't you want to get out? I mean, the world is so much bigger than this." His voice raised to match hers, but from the looks of it, he didn't feel hot under his clothes, didn't share the sinking feeling in his chest cavity grow. "The Midwest is all the same."

He might as well have stabbed her, dismissing everything she'd worked toward.

"Maybe you're not paying attention!"

"Well, seeing as my apartment is above a college bar, I haven't had a good dumpling in three weeks, and my friends are all posting about a new tapas spot on the Upper East Side, it's kinda hard to see the beauty in a cornfield at the moment."

"We're not in a cornfield *at the moment,*" she echoed. Mocking him was childish, but she was ready to fight.

"There is literally a cornfield across the road."

"Alright, that's it. No more talking, we have a job to do." She went back to draping each branch over the trellis with her gloved hands, fighting the urge to cry for some dumb reason.

"No more talking," he repeated. "You're kidding, right?" She glared at him. "Oh-kay."

The silence remained the rest of the afternoon, only broken by mumbled commands from Ellie and clarifying questions from Cyrus. It was clear he was taking this as a joke, snickering at awkward pauses and rolling his eyes when she wouldn't respond to his questions if they weren't about the current project.

It lasted the rest of the week, and if Ellie was honest, she liked the new rhythm. It was safer, more predictable. Cyrus came in, looked at the list Ellie now prepared for him each morning, then would head out to work independently until lunch, still choosing to eat alone in the shed rather than join Ellie and her folks up in the house.

If this was what Cyrus wanted from her, it's what he was going to get. It was one thing to be somewhere new and feel out of place, but another thing to blatantly assume that all of rural America was a monolith. They'd never see eye to eye, and maybe that was a good thing. He'd be out by fall, anyway. A distant memory when the summer's over.

Cyrus

"Fuck," Cyrus sighed to himself, finally making it to the lab in the Agricultural Sciences building at the University of Minnesota, Wakuta. His clothes were filthy, his pants were smeared with mud and dirt where he wiped his hands countless times from cleaning the strawberry patch and the first harvest of spring onions for the year.

The expletive was caused by his realization that he forgot his lab coat at home, and either he'd be forced to work with contaminated clothes, or risk losing his spot on the roster if he ran back home and the Lab Manager found out he was late. Neither was an option.

His muddy feet carried him to the manager's desk, ringing the bell since no one seemed to ever be sitting at the kiosk after 5 PM.

"Hey Cyrus, you know you can't drag all of that dirt in here," Richard said, appearing from the back room. Richard was the TA who worked the evenings, full of so much shit he didn't seem to take any himself.

"I know, I didn't have time to change from the farm site."

"Don't you have Lab Seven reserved tonight?"

"I do, but I forgot my lab coat at home. Any chance you guys rent them out?"

Richard nodded his head solemnly. "There's a fee. I don't know how much it is though."

"Whatever, that's fine," he huffed out, looking down the hallway to make sure no one was peering into Lab Seven. The undergrads here were like piranhas.

"Seriously? I think it's like $200 or something dumb."

"Yeah, whatever. Do I pay here or is it added to my student account?"

"Sure, I'll take your money," Richard laughed, reaching behind him and into a closet full of bright white lab coats neatly hung.

"Hah, yeah good one."

"It's added to tuition payments." *Thank god.* "How late are you here tonight?"

"I have it reserved until midnight."

"Roger, I'm here until ten, then night shift starts. And seriously, stop dragging mud into the lab spaces. Clean up after yourself, or I'll tell the manager."

Cyrus nodded at Richard and tore off to Lab Seven, already feeling the start of a headache creep into his eyelids.

This was how it went most nights, sans forgetting his *fucking* lab coat. He'd get up at 6 AM, needed to be on the road twenty minutes later in order to get to the farm by 7 AM, work until lunch, collect samples until 5 PM, then rush to make it to the lab by 6 PM, trying to eat something in between. When he wasn't harvesting vegetables, he was testing in the lab, when he wasn't testing in the lab, he was writing narratives and outcomes of his research. Sleep was a luxury at this point, and even on the weekends, he usually had his head down in some fashion at his kitchen counter or in a lab if he could snag one.

It wouldn't have been so bad, but at this point he was running out of clothes he would deem as usable to work on the farm. Nearly his entire casual wardrobe was either shredded by raspberries, stained with dirt, or smeared with grass stains from picking weeds. Even if he took an hour off to go somewhere to buy clothes, he'd have to eat into travel time or lab time, which wasn't an option seeing as he got bumped every other week because he was late *by ten fucking minutes*.

The voice in the back of his mind (his dad's voice, presumably) told him this would never happen at NYU, or even at Cornell, if his father had anything to say about it. One flash of a student ID with his last name and everyone would bend to his wishes. But, you couldn't buy your way through lab rules when no one in the hundred mile radius knew who your dad was.

Like clockwork, Cyrus's phone lit up during one of the said rescheduled lab reservations. Speak of the devil.

"Hello?" Cyrus answered, trying to keep a casual tone after months of silence. It was always a performance for his parents.

"Hi Cyrus, this is Angela. I have your dad here, one second." Of course he had his personal assistant call him. Angela worked for him for the last three years, because obviously Dr. John Lexington couldn't be bothered to dial a fucking phone number. She was nice enough, but the poor thing did nothing more than a glorified intern. She probably made more in a year than Cyrus had made his entire life.

A clicking noise alerted him the call had been transferred. "Cyrus?"

"Hey Dad."

"Just got off the phone with the Dean at Cornell. Minnesota, huh?"

Took you long enough. He was bound to find out one way or another. His dad's accountant was way too detail-oriented not to notice purchases in another state. Cyrus usually used his own savings account that he'd been managing for years whenever he needed to make purchases under his dad's radar, but tuition didn't fall into that category.

"Uh, yeah. Moved here about three weeks ago through a research program."

His dad clicked his tongue, a noise he had been avoiding since Cyrus could have cognitive memories. "Minnesota? The hell is in Minnesota?"

"A farm." *No fucking shit.* "I mean, it's one that predominantly raises heirloom varieties, even has a few ancient grains. It's a huge opportunity to analyze their soil composition. Some of the most fertile land in the world, you know." Ellie told him that.

"Hmm, was that in the brochure?" his dad remarked, chuckling by myself. "How long?"

"End of August."

"And you like it?"

This was the fatal question. There was no right answer. Say yes, and his dad would chastise him for enjoying anything but money and the Upper East Side. Say no, and his dad would bully him into coming back to New York to do something "worthy of his time." As if being taken out to lunch by a group of cuckolds was worth even a second to Cyrus.

He tried to be chipper, but not too chipper. Mildly chipper. "It's fine. The research is great, but the owner of the farm is kind of, uh, rough around the edges shall we say. Don't quite understand how she's qualified to run a farm and it's obvious she's a bit sheltered, but nothing I can't handle." *Throw a local under the bus, he'll love that.*

"Doesn't surprise me if she's from the Midwest, and a farmer at that. Good thing you're there, probably can teach her a thing or two." That wasn't really what he meant, but it got them off the subject. "Well, your mom's in Wainscott for the summer already. We're closing up the condo for the season. Call if you need anything."

"Yep, sure."

"And it wouldn't hurt to come out for the fourth. Maren and Oliver will be here." He'd rather fall off a bridge than see Maren or Oliver. Two carbon copies of his mom and dad, somehow with all the worst qualities. "Aurora can't make it with school and everything."

Aurora was his youngest sibling and had one year under her belt at Harvard Law. She studied hard, but he was surprised to hear she was taking summer school. Which reminded him, *shit.* He still hadn't called her back.

Cyrus dramatically rolled his eyes from the safety of another state. "Oh, well. I might have to pull an Aurora. I think that'll be high time at the farm. Lots of analysis and writing."

"Well, we'll see you when you come back to civilization."

Cyrus bit his tongue at that comment, wanting to defend anything that his dad spoke ill of. Especially if it involved Ellie. He made a stinging connection to how he spoke to her earlier that week, probably not sounding too far off from his own father. She didn't deserve that.

They hung up soon after. He narrowly avoided any further interrogations or underhanded comments about the Midwest, and with his head back in his research, he focused on staying awake only to get up to do it all over again the next day.

*   *   *

The weather continued to improve, and Cyrus had to remind himself he was in fact in the Midwest and not some coastal destination with the sudden mugginess that hung in the air. The mornings still had a bite to them, enough to cozy into a warm sweatshirt, but by afternoon the sun beaded sweat on his forehead, mixing with the sting of a sunburn that hadn't yet turned into a tan. He'd come to the conclusion that he was categorically underprepared for this summer, and it was somehow Minnesota's fault.

His body ached and his brain was fried. Each day consisted of tireless work of the two, however, he hadn't felt this good in months mentally. Being away from the city distracted him from his vices, pushing him to prioritize things like the snap of a sugar pea in a salad, freshly cut grass at the farm, and watching the stars at night. Yeah, yeah, he was a city boy who had never really seen the stars. It was as cliche as it got, but one night on his walk home from the lab, he caught himself staring up so long it hurt his already aching neck the next day.

The negligence in his wardrobe somewhat came to a head one steamy afternoon in June. He had been helping Ellie install her brand new irrigation system, one that was a direct benefit from the grant money he now understood was so needed. But the installation and testing of water coverage didn't come without a few accidental sprays in the face and stomach. In any other scenario, he would've laughed it off and made jokes about her doing it on purpose, but the mood since their last conversation had permeated into the week, seeping deep into the root of their relationship. What little they had of it.

His clothes were soaked, the sun was out, and the inside of his jeans and long sleeve shirt had become somewhat of a sauna. Uncomfortable didn't even begin to cover it, the internal temperature of his boxers threatened to sterilize him. His irritation must have revealed itself in his gait, because as he walked (*read: waddled*) up to the shed after harvesting his samples for the day, Ellie greeted him with a remorseful yet cold apology.

"Sorry that you got wet. Did you happen to bring a change of clothes?"

He slowly blinked up at her, ready to attack. "What do *you* think?"

"Heh, I don't know what to tell you. This is a farm, Cyrus, you're going to need to bring a change of clothes every once in a while. There's dirt and water and bugs. This isn't some fancy office building in New York."

Oh please. "You don't think I know that?"

"You seem to know everything," she spat, obviously absorbing some of his foul mood.

"Alright, you know what I really don't need right now? This." Her head whipped up from the radishes she was cleaning, and she eyed him with a cocked eyebrow. "I don't have time to do *anything* let alone remember to pack a fucking change of clothes in my car. Hell, I haven't had time to do laundry in two weeks. Everyday I'm here at seven-fuck-in-the-morning and don't get back to my apartment until after midnight. Do you realize how asinine it is to work on a farm before going into a biology lab?"

Ellie took her hands out of the sink and wiped them on her pants, double patched at the knees and had triple the amount of pockets. Each of them were full. A harvest knife peaked out of one, the thick *Minnesota Grown* twist ties in another. A pair of gloves dangled where they hung out of her back pocket. Cyrus wished he had his own pair, but that thought fueled his already record high anger. How was he supposed to know this shit?

He continued, "I don't *have* a closet full of heavy duty work clothes like you, and I don't even know where to start. And that doesn't make me an idiot! I'm sorry I don't know what I don't know."

She was silent as he caught his breath, huffing and puffing with the release of emotions that had been building since he first pulled into the gravel driveway.

"Fine." Ellie paused, looking down at her hands. She picked at her dirty fingernails and refused to look up at him. "We can take tomorrow morning off and get you some work clothes."

"What do you mean?"

"You're right. That all makes sense, I'm sorry I haven't been a better employer. I didn't realize you had so much going on," she spoke softly and finally looked up at him. If he knew her better, he might say her eyes had welled up slightly. To him it looked like they sparkled. Yelling at her was supposed to make him feel better, but his clothes still steamed, Ellie was being Ellie, and now he felt like a dick.

"Yeah, it's been a lot." He swallowed, reeling it in.

"I'll go in and grab you a change of my dad's clothes from the house. I know it's hot. And honestly? You getting a rash this early in the season would set me back, too."

Cyrus didn't have time to process that statement before she was halfway to the house, her gloves bouncing and hitting her ass as she walked. Not that he was looking.

CHAPTER 6

Cyrus

"Joe's Farm Mart. That's the actual name, wow," Cyrus joked the next morning after an evening off and a decent night's sleep. It was sunny and calm, the kind of morning you spend all winter dreaming about.

"Don't start," Ellie warned.

He trailed behind her as she practically speed walked into the store's entrance. She was wearing something in between her farm clothes and the outfit she donned at the farmer's market over a week ago. The Carhartt pocket tee she always wore in varying colors (lavender today), but she had on the same faded vintage Wranglers from before. High waisted, black, form-fitting in the hips and tapered at the hem. New York would kill for a pair of them.

She had coffee waiting for him in the car when he arrived at the farm, a peace offering if he ever saw one. He thanked her by taking it and chose not to say anything. It smelled like her in the morning, and he drank nearly half before fighting with the mental white flag.

As they entered the store, a stale mechanical odor hit him square in the face. The building smelled like the inside of a tractor; soil, rubber, plastic, and something else he couldn't quite pinpoint. He was agitated at this point, but it wasn't entirely unpleasant.

"Ahh, I've always wanted to buy clothes where I get my tires," he pestered, pointing at the display held high on the back wall.

"Cyrus."

"It's just so convenient if you think about it, El." The shorthand name came out of nowhere. It was the coffee, it had to be.

She stopped him near the candy aisle. *Why was there a candy aisle in a farm supply store?*

"That's it. No more talking. Three minutes." Her smile contradicted her tone. The call back made him laugh harder than he had in recent memory, high off the energy of being somewhere other than weeding in a strawberry patch or analyzing the potassium content of a radish.

They passed more candy, an outdoor lawn ornament display, and a wall of shoes before landing at the men's workwear, with name brands that Cyrus only knew of in vintage shops. Levi's, Wrangler, Dickies, Carhartt. Ellie motioned him to follow her to an oversized rack of overalls.

"Bib overalls? God no," he pleaded. She glared at him. "Oh, sorry, has it been three minutes yet?"

And then she laughed, and Cyrus had the brain to realize that it was the first time he'd heard her laugh, really laugh, since he'd met her.

"You should get a pair, they're really nice on cooler days. Plus, they keep your shirt clean, then you only need a change of pants instead of a full outfit."

"Ughh," he duressed, searching for a size that fit him. By the time he came up for air from the barrage of tan and denim, Ellie was gone. "Ellie? Hello?"

She rounded the corner with a pile of shirts and sweatshirts. "These are really great in the field. I'm always in need of a pocket, so having one on your shirt or hoodie is great. Layering is important, too. Even if it's cold out, when you start moving around, it gets hot."

Grabbing the pile from her, he set it on the nearest display, unfolding each garment carefully to look at the stitching. He didn't care about fashion as much as he used to, but he really cared about the durability of his clothes. From what he could see, these might be up to his standard.

"Can I try them on?"

With a nod, she led him to the changing rooms, pointing out a few of the double paneled work pants along the way, telling him how they protect your knees in dry, clumpy dirt. He grabbed a pair for good measure.

He stepped out of the dressing room wearing tan overalls and an olive green shirt. His socked feet shuffled to the nearest full length mirror and Ellie grinned at him, as if to say, *I told you so*, but he didn't know what for.

"Well," she started. "You look positively midwestern, don't you."

He eyed her with a smile, feeling more masculine than he normally did. The main highlight of the ensemble was not having to wear a belt or have a button digging into his stomach when he knelt down. It rode up funny in the crotch, however.

"It looks like the straps are a bit tight," Ellie said, entering his personal bubble to adjust the buckles, smelling of coffee and gardenias again.

He hadn't seen her smile this idly before, and he realized that in a strange turn of events, Ellie had become the only person who knew anything about him in Minnesota. Even if they didn't always communicate effectively, he hadn't had a real conversation with anyone else in months. His father's voice weaseled into his mind, and guilt from how he spoke about her overcame him. The phrase *only friend* felt too real and precious, especially since less than 24 hours ago, he was yelling at her. Full blown yelling.

"Thank you for taking me shopping," he mumbled. "I'm sorry for what I said about the Midwest being all the same. And for yelling at you yesterday. It was out of line." He didn't have to speak above a whisper for her to hear him with how close she was.

"I know it was a tough day. When you said it was your first time in Minnesota, I didn't realize you moved here to work on the farm." Cyrus nodded as she transitioned to the other side. "Do you know anyone else around here? Like family or friends?"

He watched her in the mirror, gently pulling the straps to give more slack. A familiar but unwelcome feeling in his stomach sank. Why the hell was he getting turned on right now?

"No, I came out here for the research. That's all I know." He tried his hand at a joke to ease the tension. "I don't think I've hugged anyone in almost a month, heh."

Immediately, Ellie stopped what she was doing, searching his face in the mirror. All she whispered as a warning was, *"Cyrus,"* before she engulfed him in a hug around his neck, pressing her entire weight onto his.

His mind froze while his body melted into her. "Um, it's. It's okay."

"It's not." Her hands scratched his back. It was the kind of hug that made you breathe deeper. "I've been—"

"Are you two finding everything alright?"

A lightning bolt sprung them apart. That lightning bolt looked like she was in her early seventies, named Gertrude per her name tag, and had a bright orange and blue polo on.

"Yes! Yes, hi, sorry," Ellie answered for them both. "We're just finishing up, thanks."

Gertrude left with nothing more than a generic customer service smile, seemingly unfazed by their public display of amends. Wanting to be anywhere but here, Cyrus motioned back to the dressing room, but Ellie reached out to stop him.

"You should come to the Community Night on Thursday. I can introduce you to the rest of the neighborhood." She smiled genuinely at him in the mirror. "You've already met Loretta."

"Is that who I met at the market?"

She nodded shyly. There may have been more to the story on Loretta, but today wasn't the day to ask. Her reflection perked up, changing the subject.

"How do you like these? Do they feel good?" Each of her index fingers hooked under the straps, tugging them and unintentionally tightening the fabric at his groin.

"Yeah, uh," he cleared his throat, trying to focus. "I think these will work."

"Great, I might suggest getting two pairs, in case you get junk on these." What an unfortunate choice of words.

"Sure! Wanna grab me another pair? Thirty two waist, thirty four long." His voice was way higher than he meant it to be.

She nodded and he ducked back into the changing room to calm down and move on from the surprise hug. He took a deep breath now that he was alone.

For a moment when Ellie wrapped her arms around him, he felt normal. Comfortable. For the first time in weeks. Their bickering soothed him in the way that having an inside joke with an old friend is comforting, even after a fight. That's what Ellie was starting to feel like, though. The comfort after a battle. A warm, dry place to lick your wounds. Not that he needed that. He'd done plenty of healing. It's why he hadn't seen his parents in almost two years.

"These are kind of expensive. Wanna go fifty-fifty? I could write it off," Ellie said, startling him as he left the confines of the dressing room, arms full of clothes.

"Actually, we'll both write it off. This one is on my dad."

"You sure?"

Might as well help Ellie out, and his dad already knew he was in Minnesota. What was another couple hundred dollars? "Positive. You know where the boots are? I should probably get a pair of those, too. And gloves!"

He didn't really know why he winked, but Ellie smiled and they were off.

The mid morning sun illuminated every square inch of the farm when they arrived back later that morning. The silver maple tree in the front yard welcomed them like it always did, but this time Cyrus took in the gifts it gave to the entire lawn. Ample shade, a swing hanging from a branch, a centerpiece for the eye to rest on. Art. It was art.

Glancing down at the tattoo on his forearm, he smiled at the similarities of the two. The differences only revealed themselves to those who looked. One with rough, shaggy bark, the other smooth and supple. Both majestic and beautiful in their own right.

"I was serious about the Community Night, you know," Ellie said, circling her hand around the steering wheel while she parked her dark green truck next to the shed. She softly smiled at him and got out without his response.

"What time?" He chased her to the driver's side. He was always trying to keep up with her at this point. Why did she walk so fast?

"It starts at seven, and we usually go until nine or whenever. Felix's dad, Lance, brings his keyboard and Jason brings his guitar," she said, as if Cyrus was supposed to know who any of these people were. "Everyone brings food, and we just kind of," her voice got quiet and her eyes trailed around the shed, "I don't know, be together. Maybe you could stay after you're done with harvesting samples?"

He mentally ran through his schedule on Thursday, reminding himself to email the Lab Manager to cancel his evening reservation. "That should work, cool."

He garnered another smile from her.

They both agreed that Cyrus should keep his work clothes at the farm, heaven knows he would never remember to bring them back and forth. Right before Cyrus was about to take off for the day to catch up on some writing, a man walked through the shed door. He looked familiar, maybe from the market or something.

"Dad, hey, have you met Cyrus?"

Oh shit.

Cyrus wiped his hand on his pants, unsure if that was even necessary, and extended it to shake.

"Doug," the man offered his own with a bone-crushing grip. "So you're the infamous Cyrus." It wasn't a question.

"I am, yes. Hi, it's nice to meet you." Cyrus put on his most award-winning smile he could offer.

"I took him shopping today, so he finally has some good work clothes," Ellie began. "Did you need something?"

"Nope, just seeing if you were going to the field or not."

Ellie sighed at the computer. "I think I'll check on the transplant tunnel, but we're looking good for today. I might take the afternoon off so I can be available for CSA pick-ups."

Doug nodded with a smile to Cyrus. He flinched back into the present conversation. "Well good thing you have some clothes of your own, mine were probably too big for you yesterday. If you need a hat, though, there are plenty in the closet." Doug rolled his eyes. "Take the Twins one, they're playing like garbage this season."

With a glance that lingered a bit, he nodded at Cyrus, winking before leaving him and Ellie alone in the shed again. Why was everyone winking all of a sudden?

*　　*　　*

It might have been the cinched waist of her denim jumpsuit, bouncy curly hair, or the soft pink lipstick she had on, but Community Night was so much more than Ellie described it would be. A full-blown party, dance floor and all, including a potluck with courses ranging from foods that Cyrus had grown to love in New York (the laab from a family up the road), and foods he had never had in his life (some sort of tater tot thing made by Ellie's mom). With a plate of both, he sat next to Ellie and a young kid who had to be in his early teens, talking Ellie's ear off.

"And it's not so bad, really, standing all day. But on my first day I crushed a carton of eggs and now my boss tells me constantly, 'watch out for eggs,' but I haven't done it since! So it's going fine I guess."

Ellie chuckled, moving her plate to let Cyrus in. "Felix, this is Cyrus. He helps on the farm in the mornings."

"Hi Cyrus!" Felix waved confidently, breaking stereotypes of young kids always being weird and shy around new people. "I didn't know you were hiring for the farm, Ellie, could I do that one day?"

"Hopefully," she said, smiling at Cyrus. "He's also in school, so he does a lot of research, too."

Felix was back on him. "Do you like working on the farm?"

The question threw him off. Ellie was *right there*. "Uh, yeah. Yeah, I think so. I love food, so..." he trailed off.

"Did you try the laab?" Felix pointed at his plate. "My dad made it. He's Hmong, but he grew up eating a lot of Thai and Laos food. My mom's Vietnamese, though. Have you ever had bitter melon soup? It's pretty good. I only ever eat it at home. The people at school are always weird about what I eat. But it's good! Have you tried it?" He finally took a breath.

Cyrus was still chewing the bite of food he'd taken the second Felix started talking, causing Ellie to turn up her eyebrows. She shared a knowing glance with him, and there it was again. An inside joke, but Cyrus didn't quite know if he was the punchline this time.

"I have not, but I definitely would," he said with a full mouth. "And this laab is fantastic. Honestly, first time eating something out here that's not smothered in cheese."

Ellie scoffed. "Well there's cream of mushroom soup in the tater tot hotdish."

"Is that what this is?" He pointed at the creamy conglomerate of vegetables on his plate, topped with golden brown tater tots.

"You've never had tater tot hotdish?!" Felix gasped as Ellie watched him curiously.

Suddenly the center of attention, he quickly took a bite, chewing it and swallowing with a devilish smirk. "I have now." It wasn't too bad, almost like a midwestern version of shepherd's pie.

Felix laughed, and it boosted Cyrus's confidence. He couldn't remember the last time he interacted with anyone under the age of eighteen, but Felix seemed easy to talk to, made easier by the continuous laughter. Unfortunately, Felix had other friends at the party, in particular another teenage kid that made him laugh harder than Cyrus did.

Ellie left soon after, tending to her hosting duties, where she was glowing and making her rounds to guests. He knew she had others to talk to rather than sit and keep Cyrus from feeling completely out of place the entire night, but he felt drawn to her now, surrounded by unfamiliar faces that all treated each other like family. Recipes were shared like secrets, ending up on note cards and phones with loud displays of celebration confirming just the right amount of seasoning. Soon music overtook the sounds of chatter and rustling leaves. A trio of men showcased their talents and invited — *no, demanded* — others to join in dancing to the widely known songs.

Eventually Doug found Cyrus sitting alone observing the crowd and pretending to nurse a beer. It was easier than answering a bunch of questions about why he wasn't drinking.

"Hey there, Cyrus," he said, sitting down with a thud on the plastic folding table. "You liking the pilsner?"

"Huh?" startled Cyrus. He had no reason to be intimidated by Doug, but his booming voice and old farmer presence intrinsically took up space. "Oh yeah, it's great," he tried to effuse, lifting his tall boy to greet him.

"It's from a brewery in Wakuta. They also have another pretty good one. I forget what the name is, but it's something called a 'sour'. You heard of those?"

This Cyrus could handle. "Sure have. My friend in New York ran a bit of a home operation making sours out of unripe apples from up state."

Doug nodded and took a swig of his own beer. "New York, huh. That's what Ellie said. You liking it here in Minnesota?"

Like a moth to a porch light, Cyrus's gaze found Ellie's. They exchanged a shy smile and Cyrus' stomach fell. He'd worry about that later. "I think I am. To be honest, I wasn't at first."

"No one could tell," Doug laughed and Cyrus followed out of nervousness, but Doug's hand reached around to gently pat his shoulder and he suddenly relaxed.

"What? Was it that obvious?"

"Oh, buddy." They both laughed some more. "But I knew you had it in you. And hey, don't be too hard on Ellie, okay?"

Cyrus' smile faded, and he felt a buzz in his pocket, snapping him out of his realization that he was staring at Ellie again.

Doug continued, "We've never had a hired hand or anything. It's pretty new, but she really cares, you know? She felt terrible about the work clothes thing. All that to say, we appreciate you being here. Hope you know that."

"Yeah, I do know that. Thanks," Cyrus said as Doug rose and nodded him off. Alone again, he pulled out his phone and sighed with the notification that he'd fucked up. Twice.

He never emailed the Lab Manager about canceling his reservation tonight, booting him for the evening, and causing his spot to be pushed to the next morning. On top of it, a text from his father told him the accountant had reconciled the books and saw his splurge earlier in the week.

7:12 PM Dad Work Cell: Joe's Farm Mart? Call me.

As if he didn't have enough to deal with at the moment. He reluctantly made the decision to head back, if only to get some time alone in the car before explaining to his dad how the hell he spent $650 at a farm supply store. Independence came with a price, and this time it was looking like he'd have to pay in a phone call to his parents to share all about his summer thus far.

He tried finding Ellie through the crowd to tell her he couldn't come in tomorrow, but all he saw in the glow of the twinkling lights around the maple tree were strangers laughing and dancing.

A brush of a hand on his shoulder stopped him from walking two more steps.

"Cyrus?" Loretta from the market had found him. "Well, look who it is! Oh, look at your outfit. You look so sharp."

"Uh, thank you," he turned to face her, smiling with his teeth. "I'm trying to find Ellie. I have to get going."

"Leaving so soon? You must be busy, busy." She said it in a way that somehow wasn't condescending, but rather soothing and validating.

"Yeah, I have a lot of work to do yet tonight. If you see Ellie, can you tell her I can't come in tomorrow? But I'll be back on Monday. It's just some stuff with my school." He tried to get it out in one breath, knowing that the vortex of Loretta would pull him back in if she tried. "I really have to go, though. Great to see you!"

And with that, he was gone without another goodbye.

Ellie

Ellie dried off the last of the dishes, excited to go back outside. If she was honest with herself, she didn't know if inviting Cyrus tonight had been a good idea, but he seemed to get along with everyone great. Hopefully it wasn't a front. She couldn't handle another off-handed remark about rural America, or some huge political debate about why no one should live in small towns.

After wiping down the counters, she walked past the mud room and stepped back onto the lawn with bare feet, squeezing the grass between her toes as she searched the crowd.

It was such a great turnout. The Khangs pulled out all the stops, Tracy with her laab, Felix with his 15-year-old-boy energy, and Lance with his keyboard. Jason brought his guitar along with fermented salsa that paired beautifully with Andrés' hand drums and Marisol's barbacoa, respectively. Jason's girlfriend, Caroline, was around here somewhere, probably chatting with Isabelle and Maya about their mushrooms. Even the Ortegas showed up, three kids and all. Noah at age fifteen, who was joined at the hip with

Felix. A twelve-year-old Brielle, trailing behind like their shadow, while Grace stayed close to her mom's side at the vulnerable age of eight. Every so often, Cyrus caught her eye, but she couldn't find him at the moment. Not before Loretta was barreling over to her.

"Hello, my precious pickle. Cyrus just left. Sounds like he's busy with some schoolwork. Oh! And he wanted me to tell you he won't be in tomorrow."

Oh. Ellie tried to hide her disappointment, but Loretta must've noticed.

"Is he someone new in your life?"

"Oh goodness, no. He's our farm hand. He's only here for the summer."

Loretta placed a comforting hand on her back, drawing her into a side hug as they watched the trio of men finish a song. "Well, you'll find that someone soon," she suggested, resting her head on Ellie's shoulder.

She'd heard that before. After the last ten years of watching everyone around her grow up and away from Meriden, that sentiment had become an empty promise. Hell, even her own sister moved to Seattle the second she graduated from college.

Those changes came with partners, weddings, kids, the whole works. Time moved on and so did people. Yet here Ellie was, still living on the same acre she was raised, with her parents no less, nearly ten years after high school and eight years after her last relationship. So secretly, yes, she wanted to believe that she would find someone soon, but with how this summer was turning out, it wasn't happening anytime in the near future.

She smiled at Loretta and tried not to think about it.

What was "it"?

Cyrus. Every thought led back to Cyrus.

CHAPTER 7

Ellie

It was lonely without Cyrus in the field, but Ellie would never admit that to anyone, let alone Cyrus. He wasn't at the Farmer's Market the next day either, but Ellie didn't notice or anything. In fact, she convinced herself that thinking about him every hour of every day over the weekend didn't actually mean anything. It was just something that happened. A simple observation, nothing more.

So when she came back from getting an early start in the field Monday morning, she definitely didn't stare at him as he walked out of the shed restroom, turning off the light and greeting her with a smile that might as well have blown every fuse in the county.

The hug was also something that just happened. No reason behind it, she simply felt the need to hug a coworker when she saw him, standing there in his new tan overalls, a light grey pocket shirt and her dad's faded Minnesota Twins baseball cap. The way his eyes lit up when she approached him? Insignificant. No really, none of this meant a thing. She was doing him a favor. He needed hugs, everyone needed a hug every once in a while.

"Well, happy Monday!" he cheered as they pulled apart. "Wow, two hugs in a week. My quota is starting to balance out, El."

"Sorry, I don't really know why I did that," she blurted, unable to think straight with the use of his new nickname for her. No one had ever called her El, why did it make her brain cells melt. *Change the subject, Ellie.* "Did you have fun at Community Night? You left before I could say goodbye."

"I did have fun." He adjusted his hat, releasing his dark strawberry blonde swoop for just a moment until he swept it back and replaced his cap. "And yeah, sorry about that. I kinda fucked up and forgot to switch my lab, so I got bumped to Friday morning." He paused, looking sincere as his fingertips brushed Ellie's shoulder earnestly, sending what felt like a radioactive wave to her chest. "I'm really sorry I couldn't be here on Friday. I meant to come to the Farmer's Market to explain, but some test results got botched and it took up the whole weekend to redo the analysis. This whole week has been a shit show."

"That's okay, I—"

"It's not okay, though. I know I haven't been super reliable. Still getting the hang of everything."

Ellie took a deep breath before answering, trying to think clearly. "It's not that you haven't been reliable. Maybe I had unrealistic expectations, you know? A PhD candidate from Wakuta, a predominately ag-focused school," she motioned in quotation marks. "It paints a picture of someone who could tell me all about best practices, or the chemical makeup of my soil. I'm still so new to this." She spoke the last sentence quietly, as if she didn't want him to hear it, but he smiled at her in return.

"I can tell you about your soil if you want that. I might not know much about combines, but I am getting a degree in the physiology of fruits and vegetables," he spoke while moving to the closet to grab his new work boots. "Here, follow me."

And so she did, smothering the desire for him to pull her hand while they made it to the field, because that would have been weird and super unprofessional.

He had his three-ring binder with him, as if he was about to lecture a group of plant enthusiasts. His knees sunk into the soil near the first planting of carrots.

"See how the ground is so fluffy? It's almost bouncy. From the samples I've gathered, there are parts of your soil that have up to thirty earthworms per square foot."

"That's good, right?" Ellie asked, feeling the excitement of a grade schooler.

"For your operation, yes. But here's the interesting part. Earthworms aren't native to Minnesota, let alone North America. They came from Europe and probably Asia by some way in the early 1600s; but now that they're here, they provide some good, some bad."

Ellie shook her head. "I thought the more worms, the better."

"Yeah, they kind of raise the temperature of the soil, so climate change and all of that."

She shot up. "So my soil is causing global warming? Oh, god!"

He reached out his hand, making contact with hers and pulling her back down to his level. Her stomach definitely didn't swoop. "No, no, no. Stop. You can't think about it like that. Think of the offset of growing food and feeding people within the fifty mile radius, that's doing plenty of good for the environment."

Ellie took a breath, still enthralled with his knowledge. He stood up, motioning towards his binder. He hadn't stopped smiling since they entered the field.

"Additionally, I've been testing the makeup of your soil, and you have fairly high iron and magnesium. So adding phosphorus can help with balancing that out. Too much magnesium and the plants have a harder time absorbing potassium. But," he said, leading them further into the neat rows, "I've been doing analysis on your radishes, and they seem to be at standard levels of potassium, so it isn't affecting your crop. I can't wait to test the carrots. Also, calcium."

He silently walked them over to the tomatoes, and in some strange turn of events, Ellie was the one trying to keep up. "Your calcium levels are really balanced in the tomatoes, and based on your documentation of the calcium magnesium supplements you added this winter, it's helping a lot. That sainfoin over there is a great nitrogen fixer, too. It looks like it's the main seed in your cover crop blend." His eyes finally met hers. "You either do a lot of research, or you get really good advice from your farmer friends."

"A little bit of both maybe," Ellie admitted. "This is all really fascinating."

"Glad to hear. Usually about now is when my friends in New York tell me to shut up and chop the onions or something."

They exchanged a sweet smile that rivaled the smell of strawberries in the air. Her teeth were going to hurt if Cyrus kept up this level of syrupy kindness.

The rest of the morning, Cyrus was absolutely in the forefront of Ellie's mind, no questions asked. As if she wasn't already developing a competency kink, she couldn't stop revisiting the way his knuckles looked covered in dirt, or the way his cheekbones were highlighted in the morning sun. His eyes? Don't get her started. Woodsy amber, fiery and wide as he spoke about the things that obviously kept him up at night like earthworms and soil composition.

It wasn't until they made it back to the shed, unloaded all the bins into the cooler, and fed the chickens when Ellie asked if he wanted to join her for lunch with her folks. After a hesitant glance at his computer lying closed on the workbench, Cyrus finally said yes.

At that moment, Ellie realized he'd never been inside the house.

Luckily, when she kicked off her boots and entered, the house was quiet since her mom was at the neighbors nannying Nick Kern's two little boys. She thanked the skies above that the kitchen was somewhat clean from making breakfast that morning.

"I was going to fry up some asparagus and maybe make a salad. That sound alright?" she asked the last part to Cyrus, who stood in the entryway taking in the scene around him. "What now?"

"It's um, really midwestern in here."

"Hey!" She hit his arm just to touch him, but like a switch, Ellie felt her defenses rising yet again. Sure, her mom had a few too many signs that read *Home* or *Farmstead* but at least there wasn't any *Live, Laugh, Love* artwork on display.

"What do you mean?" She eyed him, pulling out an old beat up wooden cutting board, knowing he probably would comment on it. She couldn't get rid of it, it was made from a black walnut tree in the backyard after a lightning storm.

"I mean, like, it's homey. Lots of cherry stained wood."

"They remodeled in 2006, peak cherry stain era," Ellie answered right as her dad walked back into the kitchen from the mudroom. "Can you cut asparagus?" she asked Cyrus.

"Uh, yeah, I think I can handle that," he smiled. *Why was he so cute when he smiled?*

Doug's voice caught them both off guard. "Ellie convinced you to join us for lunch, now?"

"Yeah! Beats eating a granola bar in my car or stealing snap peas from the cooler."

Ellie countered, "We've been over this. You know it's not stealing. I've offered them."

Cyrus raised and lowered his eyebrows in response.

She got to work, chopping onions and washing lettuce in the sink while her dad and Cyrus chatted away. They spoke over the drone of WCCO, a once farm centered talk radio station that had kept them company Ellie's entire life. It was hard to tell if Doug was humoring Cyrus, or if he was genuinely interested in what he was saying. Either way, she wanted to hear it all.

"So what got you into all this science about plants and whatnot?" Doug asked. He stole a cherry tomato from Ellie's bowl and leaned on the counter next to her.

Cyrus stopped chopping to think. "Well, that's a long answer."

"Not going anywhere," Doug chuckled.

With a deep breath, Cyrus began, "I went to undergrad for social sciences, which was the furthest degree away from economics that my dad would let me apply for. My dad's a pretty big finance guy. He's an adjunct professor at NYU and teaches a class about investment management, but has no qualifications other than 'born rich.' Anyway," he huffed, going back to his knife to do something with his hands. Ellie thought back to buying his work clothes and connected the dots. "In an anthropology class, I learned about how food influences culture and vice versa and got really interested in cuisine and stuff. I started going to all the upscale restaurants my family frequented, just to meet their kitchen staff and hear their stories. I made friends with a lot of chefs that had been feeding me for years. So for my master's, I broke dad's heart and went into gastronomy." He grabbed the salt pig from where it sat next to Ellie, and he had the audacity to brush his chest against her shoulder.

"And gastronomy is…?" Doug asked, now opening a bag of coffee grounds.

"Fancy word for food studies. And from there, I got super into the biology of everything. So I also got a master's in botany."

"Jesus Christ," Ellie said under her breath, unintentionally.

"I know, lots of school. But, it gets my dad off my case. If I'm in school, he isn't asking about my career, because the second he realizes I don't actually know what I want to do with my life, he would drag me into some investment firm and I'd never see the sun again. Anyway, that's when I started working in kitchens, mainly farm to table type things that got really popular in New York around that time. Everyone suddenly wanted to know where their basil came from and the name of the cow whose milk they were drinking. It was a wild time."

Doug laughed, watching the coffee drip into the pot. "And if they lived around here, they could milk the cows themselves!"

"That's true! Didn't think of that," Cyrus laughed with him.

Ellie's insides churned a bit, internally noting all of the differences between her and Cyrus's past, yet somehow they both ended up in her kitchen. It all felt a bit unfair. Guilt draped over the thorny vines in her stomach for thinking it.

"After that, my dad had so many questions that eventually telling him I wanted a PhD seemed to be the only way to shut him up. Selfishly, I wanted to learn more. So, all that's left now is one more round of research. And here I am," he said with a flourish of his hand.

At this point he was at the stove, expertly sauteing the asparagus, as if he'd been in this exact kitchen more than once. A chameleon, that's what he was. Shifting to whatever his surroundings were and somehow looking comfortable along the way.

Ellie plated up the salad, tossed in a milk dressing, and began topping it with freshly cracked pepper. "And what exactly are you studying for your doctorate?" she asked, led by her curiosity.

He settled into an elevator pitch. "I'm trying to prove the correlation of heirloom seeds, ancestral and indigenous farming practices, and the health and nutrients of our food. It just means testing the nutrient levels of the soil and the crop. There's lots more to it, of course," he scratched his neck, "but that's the gist. Um, I've been talking a lot, sorry. Is there something I can put the asparagus on? It should be done."

Ellie jumped into gear, holding a plate out for him to dish out his perfectly cooked spears cut at an angle, because of course it was. She brought it to the table as Doug shot up.

"Coffee's ready. Can I pour you a cup, Cyrus?" Doug asked, already grabbing three mugs from the cupboard.

"Uh, sure! That sounds great."

He barely touched his coffee, but Doug and Cyrus continued their conversation as Ellie listened along, munching on the perfectly seasoned asparagus and crisp salad, washing it down with fresh hot coffee. The perfect meal for a day like today. Sunny and muggy, the chance of rain looming in the West.

"So what about you, Mr. Somers? When did you start working on the farm?" Ever the charmer. Ellie fought an eye roll, but kind of wanted to stare at him indefinitely.

"Oh please, call me Doug," her dad responded.

Ellie chewed quietly as Doug laid out the timeline, starting with his work as a fourteen year old, helping his father bail hay and pick rocks every summer. From there, he dove into the hay days of farming in the seventies when he had a full community of farmers around him getting married and starting families. That all came to a halt when the Somers narrowly avoided foreclosure during the farming crisis of the 80s. Fast forward to 2008 when a windstorm took out their entire crop that didn't qualify for insurance, followed by a year of declining prices, a line of credit that was swept under them, and a high school senior with aspirations of going to college. They ended up selling 90% of their land to stay above water, and a four year degree was something no longer in Ellie's purview.

She shifted silently in her seat. She'd heard this story countless times, and had shared it a few herself, usually on some grant application to benefit the farm. For some reason with Cyrus next to her, she felt hot with embarrassment that twisted into resentment. He got degrees for fun, when her lack of education was a sob story that national nonprofits sopped up.

Doug couldn't hold back. "I'll get too worked up if I tell you how much Ellie has changed things for us, but we're more than grateful that she's turned this farm around. Probably wouldn't be living on it if it wasn't for her," he muttered, clearing his throat into his napkin before tossing it on the empty plate in front of him. Ellie stood up, grabbing the dirty dishes.

"Well, it's because I love this place. Having the freshest vegetables in the world's most fertile soil isn't something I take for granted," she said, flashing a proud yet slanted smile towards her dad.

"Starting to realize that more and more," Cyrus joined, both in conversation and helping with the dishes.

While Ellie wanted to believe him, it was hard to trust his motives now that everything was out in the open. *Rich Manhattan boy goes to a small town to work on a struggling vegetable farm.* The Hallmark movie practically wrote itself. She wasn't about to be swept off her feet because he had kind eyes and straight teeth and perfect hair. And yet the fight was mostly with herself, because all she wanted to do was hear him talk more about the things that lit him up. He was always one sentence away from full luminosity.

She motioned to the clock on the stove. "I have some work to do in the shed this afternoon, are you planning on heading back to the field?" she asked at the sink as Cyrus dried the dishes she had just washed.

"Yeah, yes. Lots of samples to collect. Your ever-bearing strawberries are coming in nicely."

Doug animated, still sitting at the dining table. "Oh they're delicious! We should've brought some up for lunch."

"There's always tomorrow," she half-promised. Her palms were a bit sweaty. She had to stop thinking they would be anything more than co-workers.

The moisture hung in the air as they walked back to the field. Cyrus practically bounced behind her, driving her crazy.

"Your dad is great," he started. Ellie nodded back at him. "Both your parents seem really supportive."

"Yours do too," she blurted out sarcastically, unable to stop herself. It always seemed so difficult to be sincere around him. "It must be nice that they have deep pockets."

Cyrus's eyebrows shot up and he scoffed. "Oh, that's what you got from all that? Cool. Well, must be nice to have parents who are actually proud of you."

She veered off towards the shed, keeping her performative smile. "Alright, bye!"

"Ellie!"

"I have work to do," she yelled back, watching him stand there looking dumb.

He dropped his shoulders and furrowed his brow before turning and heading to his car. So what if he left. Ellie had gotten what she needed from him for the day.

Cyrus

Cyrus rummaged through his backseat, grabbing his equipment, and tried awkwardly carrying his sample bin, a scale, and his research binder to the field in one trip. He looked ridiculous, and felt it too, but he was too mad to do anything but stumble angrily towards the field.

So this is how Ellie was going to act towards him, now that she knew his parents were loaded? This was exactly why he ran away from New York City. Hell, this is why he left NYU. When people found out who he was, they either wanted to use him or dismissed him completely. Usually the latter were the people he wanted to be around the most.

He would dismiss himself if he could. He wasn't hiding behind the privilege, it was real. Palpable, and destructive. It bulldozed every relationship he ever tried to have by revealing intentions at one point or another. His dad was an ass, his mom hadn't had a freeformed thought in decades, and even his siblings acted as moles instead of confidants. Honestly, what good was family if all they did was exploit you?

The strawberry patch finally came into view, healthy and green with pops of bright red berries the size of gumballs bursting against their leaves. It calmed him, being here. He managed to take a deep breath and smelled rain in the air.

Maybe to spite Ellie, maybe not, he popped a ripe red berry into his mouth and exhaled with satisfaction. Everything that grew here tasted better than anything he had back home. The sweetness reminded him of the designer berries he once spent fifty dollars on to impress his old coworkers, but nothing compared to something picked seconds prior. With a taste test complete, he started weighing out the crop, picking only the brightest of the bunch. He grabbed a few unripe samples just to see what would come up on the DRIS analysis.

His bin was almost full, but his optimism in beating the rain met with the reality of him losing track of time. Soon the sprinkles that tickled his shoulders turned into fat drops smacking the back of his neck. He'd managed to get his scale back into the case and his three ring binder tucked under his arm, but the bin full of ripe and unripe strawberries, once separated neatly now jumbled together as he ran back to the shed.

One problem: the electric fence was closed shut.

It took him several moments of wet pelts to assess his next move. There was absolutely not one ounce of an option that he was getting electrocuted, *in the rain* no less. And there was no way he was agile or small enough to copy Ellie's gymnastics of swinging a leg over the lower line and ducking under the top. Nope. He only had one thing left to do.

"ELLIE!" he shouted, whining like a fucking baby. Water gathered in his sample bin as rain poured around him, soaking his entire ensemble from head to toe. His overalls hung with the new weight of water, and he fought some weird instinct to start crying. "Ellie! I'm locked in! *Damnit,*" he cursed to himself in a whisper, sinking to sit in the dirt and give his tired arms a rest. "Hello?! Anyone!"

After the weekend he'd had, of course this was how Monday was going to go. It had started off so well, Ellie greeting him with an unexpected hug, getting to smell coffee and gardenias up close, a new favorite scent of his. Showing her the beauty in her own field, touching her hand, learning about her father and the selflessness she showed in staying to help on the farm. The build up, the hope that maybe something could happen where they would be friends, or more. It all came crashing down as the skies and his past ripped themselves open. This is why he kept trying to run away from his upbringing. It always pissed off the people he cared about most.

"Ellie, please!" he screamed, not even knowing if the wetness on his face was from his own eyes or the weather, when finally he saw a figure come out of the shed. *"Ellie!"*

"Stop yelling!" she answered back, her voice a beacon in the downpour.

He stood up frantically. "I'm locked in! It's fucking pouring out, and I don't want to get electrocuted!"

She jogged down the hill, shaking her head under the hood of a rain jacket but very obviously hiding a smile. "You're not locked in, Cyrus. And the electric fence isn't on." With an annoyed huff, she opened the gate with one hand, letting him out.

The heat of embarrassment pooled in his stomach as he grabbed the bin of waterlogged strawberries and tried juggling it to pick up his binder. His efforts were futile.

"Here," Ellie said, calming his panic and carrying his binder and scale for him. It might as well have been his first day on the job. He felt like an idiot all over again.

When they made it back to the dry, warm shed, Cyrus all but threw the sample bin down, causing a few rogue berries to jump out and roll across the workbench.

"That was the dumbest ten minutes of my life," he snapped, trying to catch his breath.

"Ten minutes? You were screaming for thirty seconds, calm down. I saw you out the window when I heard the rain but I had to grab my jacket," Ellie bit back. She peeled said jacket off, revealing a completely dry shirt. "It's just rain."

"I can never fucking win with you, huh?"

Her head whipped towards him, searching for an explanation. "Excuse me?"

"Why do you constantly try to make me feel like an idiot?" That's right, he wanted to push.

"I didn't do anything!" she sputtered. "You shut the gate behind you, and I didn't turn on the fence. Why would I turn on the electric fence if I knew you were in the field?"

"This isn't about the electric fence! Why did you blow me off after lunch?"

The question took her back. Her mouth hung open. "I didn't blow you off after lunch—"

"Yes you did! We were having such a good day and out of nowhere you made that remark about my parents, as if I don't already know how privileged I am."

"Well," she started, cutting short with clenched fists over her eyes. "You act like a good person but then I come to find out that you've been handed everything your entire life."

Cyrus laughed out of spite. He'd heard this line of thought before. "And those two things are mutually exclusive, aren't they."

She searched him silently.

"Do you want a run down of all the shit I've done to try and offset what my family does? How about access to my own, secret bank account that I've been using since undergrad so my parents don't ask questions? Or that when I do use their money, it's usually for anyone but myself, and I still have to pay them back in details about my life when all I want is to disown them?"

With her arms crossed, Ellie looked around the room. Her eyes flooded.

"Yeah, it's not all sunshine and fucking roses," he said, trying to soften his voice after the outburst.

Her head lowered. "I'm sorry, I didn't know."

With a frustrated sigh, he leaned over the workbench, cradling his head in his palms and pressing them to his eyes. The rain pelted heavy drops against the window and the wind gusted every few minutes. They were like oil and water, shaken up every once in a while and forming the best kind of emulsion, only to separate the second the dust settled. He couldn't do anything right.

"You can go home, you know," she whispered and sniffled.

"I hate driving. I'm not driving in this weather."

A beat. "Did you not drive in New York?"

"Never," he muttered. "But don't hate me because I own a car. It was my dad's and I've had it since high school."

"I don't hate you."

"Hmm. Could have fooled me."

"It's just, I have this idea of who you are and it keeps changing. Sometimes I don't know why you're here, why you chose this farm."

"Well first, let's be clear, I didn't choose this farm." The joke didn't land. Not even a smirk. "Listen, at every turn, the idea I had in my head about this place is being proven wrong, too. But in the best way possible. You are *really* good at what you do, El."

"You are, too." She blinked up at him, finally softening. There was a change in her body language. The cold tension of their frustration shifted to something else as she revealed a subdued smile. "After this morning, I feel like you know my farm better than I do." She hoisted herself up on the counter where her laptop sat open.

He struggled not to smile. Emotions clashed in his head. Annoyance, frustration, exhaustion, curiosity, and... hope? He didn't want to fight with her all summer. Finally it seemed they were at a place where that would be possible. In a moment of surrender, he grabbed the reddest berry he could find in his bin, already a lost cause for his research.

"Do you want a strawberry?"

Ellie's gaze lifted, and her eyes landed on the berry in his hand as he walked towards her.

As if the clouds cleared outside, her smile illuminated the shed. Her laugh filled the room like music, undeniable and never ending. Without hesitation, Cyrus joined in, knowing the tension had been broken by something as ridiculous as a strawberry.

She took the peace offering from him and smiled as her teeth bit around the plump fruit, juice pooling at the corner of her mouth. Her hand flung up to wipe it quickly, and Cyrus couldn't look away. This was worse than trying on the overalls, worse than her fingers running up his back.

"The first ones of the season are always amazing. Mmm," she moaned with delight. Suddenly Cyrus realized he wasn't laughing anymore and had been staring at her mouth for the last ten seconds.

"Um, you, uh... you don't need to stay out here. I can wait until the storm passes," he said, snapping out of it. The tension was right back, only this time it felt hot instead of cold.

She shook her head. The rest of the strawberry was still clenched between her thumb and pointer finger, and as she studied it, she answered a different question.

"I know it's not mutually exclusive. Your upbringing and you being a good person. I, um, googled you while you were in the field."

His stomach dropped. "And what did you find?"

"That your dad manages a shitload of money, and about ten years ago he became the Head of the Economics Department at NYU. It looks like he's donated an insane amount of money to the school and, back in the nineties, to a certain political party that I don't agree with."

"Right, but that was before—"

"*And* that you have siblings. Maren, Oliver, and Aurora?"

"You were thorough." A pause. *Was that it?* "Anything else?"

"Your headshot at Cornell." She smiled, finally meeting his eyes. "You used to have darker hair." He matched her smile and met her on the counter, heaving himself up to sit next to her.

"I sure did. A nose piercing, too. I was a little edgy back in the day. Or at least, I thought I was," he nudged her shoulder with his.

"You look healthier now."

He took a breath, knowing what she meant and curious why she made a point to comment on it. "I feel healthier. That was about four years ago, when I first started my PhD. I moved upstate because things kind of..." he trailed off, knowing that when he lived in the city that never slept, he didn't either. Cigarettes replaced meals and well, some other stuff replaced sleep. He hadn't touched that shit in half a decade, though. "Listen, I'm an open book. But, I can't help who my parents are."

"I know."

"I really do like working here."

"I like you working here."

Warmth ran through him, even if he was dripping wet from being caught in the downpour. "Then can you at least try to give me a chance, El?"

Instead of a yes or a nod, she got up from the counter to rummage through his sample bin, only to return with a bright red specimen. "Do you want a strawberry?"

They both laughed, but he reached out to steady her hand. His dirty fingernails pinched over her matching ones and the pads of his fingers rested on her knuckles. He maintained eye contact while he bit into the fruit, only to see if it riled her up as much as he wanted it to.

It did.

"Cyrus!"

"What?" he asked with a full mouth and smile.

"It was a truce strawberry. I'm not feeding it to you!"

He popped the rest of the berry in his mouth, green leaves and all. "Is that still a yes?"

"I've always given you a chance. I care about this, and if we hire a full-time employee soon, this is almost like a trial run. I need it to work." Her eyes pleaded with him.

"Then stop taking me so seriously," he clutched her arms from where he sat on the counter. She rolled her eyes playfully. "I know you care about this place. And everything you've shown me so far makes me care about it, too. But I am not my parents."

"I'm sorry."

"Same," he returned. Out of the corner of his eye, the actual sun broke through the clouds and set the shed ablaze. It gave him a dumb idea to bookend the day. "Hug?"

"You're soaking wet."

"I know, I just want to make you even a percentage as uncomfortable as I am right now."

He jumped off the counter and she sped around the workbench, putting a barrier between them and laughing at his antics. This was the Ellie he wanted to see more of, he knew she was in there somewhere. With a fake to the left, she ran to his right and he caught her in a bear hug on the end of the table.

"Cyrus, no!"

"It's just rain, El. Calm down!"

She laughed at the words thrown back at her. He peeled himself off like the rain jacket, only this time she stepped back with a damp spot on her front where he pressed his soaked torso into her.

With a playful push to his chest, Cyrus finally exhaled with relief. They both cared about this farm. They both cared about each other. Well, that's what he was telling himself as he drove home, smiling as his mind drifted back to the shed and all the mornings and afternoons ahead of them.

CHAPTER 8

Cyrus

There was a sunbeam over the farm that next week, and Cyrus couldn't help but wake up each morning excited for the day. Ellie had finally let herself be in proximity to him without having to hold up the wall she'd been building since they first met. Or maybe Cyrus was the one holding it up too, shielding himself. Either way, something had changed and every time they met eyes, smiles were easy. An invisible string kept them ten feet apart or less, pulling them together with bright cheers as they discovered new fruit bearing on the plants, or a sweet crunch of a freshly picked spring planting. June did that to Cyrus.

That string tugged a bit when he couldn't make it to Community Night on Thursday. It was written all over Ellie's face. Disappointment crept inside of Cyrus's chest, too, but his doctoral review committee was firm on the timing of his update hearing.

The review went off without a hitch, and afterwards Brad gave him a call to congratulate him.

"Sounds like they're keeping you busy over there. That's a lot of data," he complimented, keeping the casual tone. "And I don't know if I've seen you smile that much in a while. Minnesota seems to be treating you well."

Cyrus didn't want to admit it, but a few times he caught himself in his own video conference square and his advisor was right, he didn't remember the last time he smiled this much talking about, well, anything. He was less than two months out from the final presentation, and maybe this time he would actually find excitement in the thing.

On Saturday he decided to head to the farmer's market. Not because he missed Ellie, but because he needed some mushrooms. And celery. He could probably get that from Ellie. He was also looking for a fresh chicken, and he was sure to find it somewhere around here. Ellie probably knew where.

The amount of people bustling about still surprised Cyrus. For a small town farmer's market, it felt undeniably active. Isabelle and Maya greeted him happily, somehow remembering him.

"You coming this Thursday?" One of them asked. He never met them individually. His confusion about their names must've translated to confusion about what was happening on Thursday, which was also true. "For Community Night!"

Oh right. "Ah, yes. I'll try to make it. I had some stuff for school this past week."

"Ellie says you're getting your doctorate, is that right?" The other asked. "I have a master's in biology, I studied mushroom cultivation if you can believe it." She motioned to the array of fungi in front of her.

"I do believe it. You're an expert at what you do." He pulled his bottom lip. "Wait, I know you're Isabelle and Maya, but which of you is which?"

They looked at each other to laugh, which made sense. The two looked nothing alike.

"I'm Maya." She was the shorter of the two, and had hair that matched with one side tucked behind her ears in a short bob with tight curls. Her umber skin shined under the morning sun and her smile was luminous.

"And I'm Isabelle, or some people call me Izzy," the longer haired woman said, and placed a hand on her chest. She had an oversized oxford on, unbuttoned enough to show a tattoo on her collar bone of some flower that looked to be a violet. "And I have a bachelor's in Gender Studies, if you can believe it." They laughed again and Cyrus felt in on the joke now.

"Thank you, it's good to meet you for the third time. Your mushrooms are fantastic, honestly."

"Well thanks, we put a lot of work into them. Which, you know all about as a fellow farmer," Maya smiled, but Cyrus felt like an imposter. He couldn't really consider himself a farmer. He was simply coat tailing off Ellie at this point.

He waved goodbye with a full tote and not two steps later ran head first into a plume of coffee and gardenias. Ellie's hazel eyes brightened in the morning sun and her smile felt like it was for him, as if she was actually happy to see him. He straightened his back and ran his hands through his hair, two things he would have done on the walk over to her farmstand if he'd been prepared for this moment.

"Cyrus!" Ellie effused.

"El, hey! You found me before I found you. I was just about to head your way."

"You'd have missed me. I need coffee. Can I get you one?" She kept walking as she talked, seemingly always on the move. He jogged to keep up with her pace.

"Actually," he whispered, bowing down to her level. "Don't tell anyone, but I don't drink coffee."

"You *what?*" Her sudden change of voice jolted him. "How is that possible?"

"Keep your voice down, everyone will hear you," he joked, eyeing the crowd around them with a smile. "Coffee makes me crave cigarettes. And I'm a recovering New Yorker."

Ellie softened with his admission and reached to stroke his bicep as they stood in line. Another card shown, another kind reaction.

"You're nicer than you claim to be," she said. Cyrus furrowed his brow. "You took coffee when my dad offered you some. I noticed you didn't drink it."

So she was *noticing* him. *Hmm.*

She still ordered him something, and proceeded to tell the barista all about her stand and the offerings this time of year. Cyrus internalized a chuckle, thinking that it was Ellie being Ellie, telling everyone who would listen about her produce. It wasn't until they had gotten their drinks that she ended her monologue with, "Come by and grab what you need, and I'm not taking your money."

Cyrus realized she never actually paid.

"Did you need cash? I have some," he offered.

"Nope, we work on barter. Tim gets produce, I get coffee. *You* get a Lavender Fog. Have you ever had one?" She handed him a hot to-go cup, steaming through a sip hole. "They get the lavender from us."

Cyrus took a whiff and involuntarily sighed. "Holy shit that smells good."

"Tastes even better."

She was right. In an unspoken agreement, he continued following her around the market, recognizing a few folks along the way. The guy playing drums from Community Night was at a stand with his wife selling flowers. Marisol and Andrés was how Ellie introduced them, whispering something in Marisol's ear that garnered a shy giggle. She also stopped at the guitarist, Jason, a guy that was probably Cyrus's age, selling fermented salsa. He couldn't stop eating it at Community Night and ended up buying the biggest jar he sold.

When he asked Ellie about finding a chicken, she led the way, taking him to a farmer outside Wakuta who gave him the deal of a lifetime since Ellie was in tow. The farmer nearly refused the extra twenty he tossed onto the table, but he snuck in a dozen eggs at the last second and Cyrus wasn't going to fight him on it. He hadn't had farm fresh eggs in months and they would go great with the newly purchased salsa.

On the way back to Ellie's stand, her shoulder nudged his full arms. "If you want fresh eggs, you should take them from the farm. You do chicken chores, for goodness sake."

"But I only feed them. I always make you reach in for the prize."

She laughed, and it sounded like music again. "Our roles were established early on. Plus, our rooster *hates* you."

"Can't argue with you there."

They leisurely found their way back to the stand. Cyrus greeted a tired Doug and hyper Felix, bagging customers' purchases with a smile. The crates looked more bountiful than the last time he was here with spring onions presented in bundles splashed bright green against pints of strawberries that caught his eye and brought the memory of Ellie's lips front of mind. Even the radishes seemed to glow bright pinkish red, the rhubarb and lavender fragrant as ever.

He set a bundle aside and decided then and there he'd be making a strawberry-lavender-rhubarb-something later that weekend, intent on taking advantage of the season's blessings.

Felix rang him up. "Eighteen dollars."

"Oh, Felix, we won't charge him. It's Cyrus," Ellie interrupted.

"Hah, no. I'm paying for this."

"Absolutely not. You helped harvest half of what's here," she fought with him.

"And you've done all the work to keep them alive all summer."

"You have, too!"

Felix stood in the middle looking between the two bickering. Cyrus winked at him, and continued the charade. "Alright, I'll just give Felix a twenty, and he can do whatever he wants with it."

Doug heard what was happening and joined in with a chuckle.

"No," Ellie sang, pushing Cyrus's hand away. He wanted to grab it and do something reckless.

"I'll take the twenty!" he cheered. Felix broke into a giggle as the two stared each other down.

"See, problem solved. You're not going to let Felix miss out on an opportunity to make twenty bucks, right?"

"Cyrus."

"Ellie."

There it was. Buttons. Pushed.

He slid the twenty on the table towards Felix as Ellie watched, shaking her head with a smile and an eye roll.

"Pleasure doing business."

He carried on the bit with a mob boss nod, pocketing the twenty and glancing around the market before collapsing into laughter. From that day on, he knew he had a friend in Felix.

*   *   *

The meal Cyrus made that night, alone in his apartment, was one of the best meals he'd had since moving to Minnesota. Fresh chicken, locally grown mushrooms, spring onions and herbs from Ellie. And even though his stomach was hungry and his mind refreshed after finally having a day off from the labs, he couldn't help but wish that he had someone to share it with. He hated eating alone, it made his mind wander to places he didn't always want it to reach.

So he phoned a friend. Matteo this time. Matteo was an anomaly. They'd gotten close on the tail end of Cyrus's undergrad and kept up after all these years. He managed half a dozen urban gardens hidden on rooftops or tucked into greenhouses the size of alleyways and supplied local produce for multiple eateries in Manhattan, specifically two of his friends' restaurants. Ray at Du Soleil and Rosie at Pintxos. They each held their own in the kitchen, but Matteo was someone who held his own in Cyrus's life. He brought light into every room he entered.

"Cyrus!" He picked up on the first ring. "Oh my god, babe, it's been so busy. I've been meaning to call you."

"Oh, yeah? Great minds. I was just sitting down to eat. How've you been?"

"So good. So good, Cyrus. I actually have some news."

"Oh?" This could have meant anything from *there's a sale at Saks on Fifth* to *I won the lottery and I'm moving to Boracay.* It was usually somewhere in the middle.

"Well you can't get mad, because it was a really small thing, and it's not even Instagram official yet. You know how it is when you don't want your family involved, and someone canceled last minute at the MoMA, and—"

"Teo!" Cyrus yelled in between a bite.

"Arie and I got married last weekend."

"Damn."

His fork hit the plate with a loud *clink*. It wasn't like this was out of the question. Arie and Matteo had been engaged for over a year, together for six. But rather than hearing about it over a phone call *that he initiated,* it would've been nice for Cyrus to at least get an invite.

"Oh, right. I mean, congratulations! That's what I'm supposed to say, huh?"

"Babe, it's been such a whirlwind."

He paused, and Cyrus didn't know if there was anything else he could say other than, "Why didn't you tell me, man?"

"Well, I knew you were in Minnesota, and the space at the MoMA opened up on *Thursday,* and since Arie works there, he swept in with a really great discount since the deposit was already paid. And I knew if you flew out, you would have to use your dad's money, and it was, like, thirty people, Cyrus. Most of them were Arie's family since I don't talk to mine. It's shit."

"Yeah, no, I get it." Cyrus was in Minnesota. Matteo could've stopped there. In no way could he have made all of that work without using his dad's credit card or letting Ellie down in some way. "Was Rosie there? Ray?"

"Ray catered."

Of course. "Right."

"And Rosie couldn't get off work since he got promoted to Executive Chef at Pintxos like two weeks ago."

"Executive Chef?!"

"Oh shit, did you not know that?"

Suddenly he wasn't hungry anymore. The three friends he considered closer than family all had lives, which he was learning by the second continued on even if he wasn't in New York. Because of course they did. It wasn't like time was going to pause just because he was out of the state. Not only that, but he had to admit it had been a while since he'd reached out.

"I didn't, no. Damn. Sounds like he's doing well. Life continues, huh?"

"Yeah," Matteo said, sounding like he was smiling. "We miss you, you know. Ray has completely settled into the condo. It looks amazing."

He hummed. It was all he could offer.

"You're pissed, aren't you."

"I'm not pissed." Sad, maybe. Lonely, too. But he didn't have the energy to be pissed.

"You have to believe me when I say I wish you were here. And I get why you're not. But New York isn't the same without you, babe. When are you coming back?"

"My research is done in August. If all goes well, I'll be back in September."

"We're making plans before you land. I want to be the first person you see off the plane."

Cyrus let out a chuckle. "Deal. It'll be a great time for fall menu changes at Du Soleil. Maybe we can sneak in a tasting."

"I'll withhold the catering payment to Ray until he says yes." They laughed together, knowing that Matteo would never have the gall and Ray would never let him get away with it alive.

"Hey, I miss you, too. Give Rosie and Ray a kiss on the cheek from me."

"They'd kill me first."

Cyrus huffed, "That's why I said it. And tell Arie congratulations from me, too."

"I will, babe. Any cute guys in Minnesota?"

"Uh, not exactly." He couldn't fight his smile and his mind from traveling elsewhere. Hazel eyes and sunkissed skin. The weight of a hug, the smell of a farm supply store.

"Any cute girls?"

"Well…"

"Cyrus! Tell me everything. How did you meet?"

He sucked in some air through his teeth, not wanting to admit even to himself where his head was at all day. "She owns a farm."

"Of course she does."

"The farm I'm working on."

"You're joking."

"I'm not," Cyrus started. "It's just in my head. She's way too good for me. You know how I get."

"I sure do, honey. I sure do," Matteo sighed and the conversation slowed. After a few more attempts to conceal any more FOMO on Cyrus's end, they finally hung up.

A shadow of guilt blurred his thoughts as he fell asleep. His mind wandered back to the market, winding its way through a memory as a childhood in Manhattan and comparing the two. Normally his daydreams about New York landed in some dark bar with bright lights and loud music, the bass thumping through his chest. But today, all he could think about was the way Ellie's apron cinched her waist and the pebble of her nipples in a tight shirt that revealed everything. He focused on the latter. Especially as he laid in bed working himself up with visions of curly brown hair, juicy strawberries, and the smell of coffee and gardenias.

Yeah, he was in deep.

CHAPTER 9

Ellie

"Cyrus coming tonight?" Doug asked Ellie. They were in the kitchen with her mom, gathering materials to take out to the tables set up outside for Community Night. Plates, utensils, and paper towels overflowed in Ellie's tote bag.

"Yeah, I think so." She tried to remain cool and casual even though when Cyrus told her he'd be coming back later that night, her chest swelled with excitement.

Simply put, this week had been the most fun she'd had on the farm since she took it over. She laughed more in the past five days than she had in the last five years, partially due to the incessant bickering that now felt flirty and thrilling rather than grating. Everything was brand new again, and with the end of June approaching, there was even more to look forward to. Especially tonight. Because tonight she was going to dance in a sundress under twinkling lights with Cyrus. She felt it in her bones.

"Have you asked him if he's available to work the market on Saturday? It would be a lot of help," Martha asked, snapping Ellie out of her daydream. Doug was asked by a local farmer to drive tractor for a late planting on a neighboring farm, causing him to miss the Farmer's Market.

"I'll ask him tonight," Ellie answered, and she left with a smile on her face, anticipating spending more time with him in any fashion.

Neighbors trickled in, and it wasn't long before Jason and Andrés were on the makeshift stage, setting up before the Khangs arrived with Lance and his keyboard. An oddly familiar voice caught her attention while fiddling with an extension cord, pulling her from the task.

"Where can I put the keg?"

No way. No *fucking* way. In the flesh, a ghost from her past, stood Tyler Kavanaugh.

There were few people from Ellie's upbringing that rattled her like Tyler Kavanaugh. When she decided to stay in Meriden after high school, running into her 8th grade science teacher in the grocery store was bound to be a common occurrence. But an ex from high school who continuously tried to rekindle the flame? A whole other kind of hell.

Tyler grew up in the neighborhood, which meant seeing him at every 4-H meeting, every church potluck and barbeque, they even went to daycare together. And while a fifteen year old Ellie loved a man in bootleg pants and a cowboy hat, as she grew up, it was clear that proximity was a powerful potion. Two years of handsy prom dates and back row movie make out sessions later, he prided himself on taking her virginity their first year out of high school. It took her years to get to a place where she decided that didn't matter. Virginity was a construct, and she'd only realized it with the help of her sister.

They broke up when Tyler went off to study Agronomy at Wakuta, but dropped out to work at the manufacturing plant in town that had since closed. After that, whenever he was around, she was convenient enough for him to call, knowing she was alone and single, working herself to death on the farm. She'd taken the bait twice, *she was human after all*, but each time left her feeling worse than the last. Now Ellie was pretty sure he traveled to work on oil pipelines across the state, set up in man camps to destroy the planet and Minnesota's aquifers. She hadn't seen him in two years, at least.

From an outsider's perspective, the community seemed to love the two together, but inside, Ellie felt like he was a disease that she couldn't shake. Tonight was bound to be a flare up.

"Tyler, what are you doing here?"

"Bringing the party! I hear you're still hosting community nights. Kinda cute, Liz." She *hated* being called Liz.

"It's Ellie, and you know that, I haven't gone by Liz since grade school. Also, we already have beer," she said, pointing to the old feed bin, full of ice and local pilsners from a brewery in Wakuta. "And this isn't a rager or whatever. Families come to this."

Tyler set down the keg with a dramatic, *oof,* and placed his hands on his hips, sticking his pelvis out in some disgusting power stance. "Chill out, babe, I thought you'd be excited to see me. It's just some Coors. I knew you'd be pissed if I came empty handed. I'm only in town today and tomorrow, got some time off."

"Well, I'm hosting, so I can't really sit and chat."

"We don't have to chat if you don't want to. Come on, back of my car like old times?" A wild heat full of rage and embarrassment engulfed her body. Thank god Felix and the Ortegas hadn't shown up yet to hear this.

"Stop. I'm serious. I have to help set up." She managed to peel away from him to run back to the kitchen where her mom was finishing the last touches on a veggie tray.

"Mom, Tyler is here."

"Oh, for Christ sake," Martha exhaled. "Did he bring any of his cronies?"

"I don't think so." Ellie couldn't stop the tears from forming as the vision of the night slowly faded in her mind. "I don't want him here."

Her mom rounded the counter to place a comforting touch on both her shoulders. She knew exactly how he could be, and maybe was the only person in Meriden who didn't want them to end up together. "Do you want me to ask him to leave?"

"He'll make such a scene. It's fine," she gathered herself. "It's fine. It'll have to be."

For the most part it was. When Ellie came back out to the yard, she found Cyrus already in conversation with Felix and Trang, setting a tray of bánh mì down on the table, and instantly felt better. He looked undeniable tonight. Tight black jeans with a pine green T-shirt. The sleeves rolled up a few inches so his shoulder muscles peeked through. His hair was still damp, telling Ellie that he was freshly showered and probably smelled of detergent and cotton. She wasn't even fighting it anymore, the feelings she had for him swarmed in her mind with ease.

She grabbed her own plate once most of the crew had a chance to eat. The Khangs happily chatted with Isabelle and Maya, Cyrus sitting in and listening to every word. *They must be talking about mushrooms,* Ellie thought. Jason and Caroline were laughing at something Andrés said while Marisol looked on, eyes sparkling in love. The Ortegas weren't in attendance, and Ellie was grateful for it. Felix probably missed having Noah to chase, but Brielle and Grace were a bit young for the antics of a drunk Tyler, and by the looks of it, he was already halfway there, pumping what had to be his third or fourth beer by now.

A voice brought her out of her spiral. Loretta, thank god. "Ellie! Come join us!"

Ellie did so, pulling up a seat next to Nick Kern, a father of two boys under the age of three, the same boys her mom nannied every other week.

"Hey Loretta, hi Nick," she tried, putting on her best smile to push down her discomfort in Tyler's presence. "No kids this week?"

"Nah, they're with their mom. Miss them already," he said. Nick and his ex-wife Danielle split six months ago. He handled the separation with the kind of levity and grace that impressed nearly everyone. They had been together over fifteen years, but just four years into marriage and six months after their second child, separated on amicable terms. Ellie didn't know how they did it, but when Loretta was your grandmother, good role models were well within reach.

"And you, my little muskmelon," Loretta started again with her precious pet names. "Must have your hands full with Tyler and Cyrus here tonight."

"Yeah, I'm not sure why Tyler is here."

As if to summon him, a loud clunk on the table tore her from Loretta. "You talking about me?" Tyler asked, proud of himself. The glass of beer he'd poured not two seconds prior was already half gone.

"Where did you even get a glass?" Ellie blurted, noticing the drinkware sticking out against the cans and bottles of local brews. Nick shifted in his seat, obviously uncomfortable with how intoxicated Tyler already appeared to be.

"Ah well, I know where the cups are. I've only been here a couple hundred times, Liz."

"It's Ellie."

"Tyler! Now, tell me, what are your parents up to these days? Are they loving Florida?" Loretta saved the day, bringing the group back to center. Ellie took the moment of relief to see where Cyrus was, and by both a miracle and curse, he was already watching her. He smiled softly and her insides loosened. She'd give *anything* to be sitting next to him instead of here. Hopefully he knew that.

As Tyler went on about some racist reason why his parents hated their neighborhood, she snuck up from the table and Cyrus did the same at his. Their eyes held on to each other as the distance between them shortened. Why was she so excited to see him? It hadn't been more than two hours since he left, but the anticipation of the last few steps had her giggling with excitement when they finally embraced. Cyrus's arms found Ellie's waist, lifting her up slightly and laughing in her ear. A shiver went down her spine.

"Cyrus!" she squealed.

"Hey, El." He put her down, cool as a cucumber. "You look great. Never seen you in a dress before."

Suddenly she was very aware of her body. "Right, yes. It's a warmer night, figured I'd break one out. I'm so glad you came!"

"Well, this time I actually emailed the Lab Manager." His eyes roamed her face. "I wouldn't miss it."

There was a moment of uncertainty. Time stopped as the breeze blew through Ellie's hair and the warm glow of the sunset illuminated Cyrus's dark amber eyes. The golden hour. A strum of a guitar snapped them from their moment, simultaneously realizing they were holding hands. Cyrus coughed out a laugh and turned towards the stage. All Ellie could do was watch him.

"I heard about your friend." Cyrus nodded to Tyler, since his hands were in his pocket now. Ellie's brow must have furrowed in confusion, because he continued, "Isabelle told me."

"Ah," she finally reacted. So they *weren't* talking about mushrooms. "Isabelle graduated with my older sister. She knows the whole story."

"She sure does," he chuckled. "And you have siblings, too!"

"One, just Hannah."

"*Just* Hannah?"

"No, she's great, she's in Seattle. Has been for—"

"Uh, watch out," Cyrus interrupted her. Something caught his attention behind Ellie.

"Hey babe," — *goddamnit* — "you ready to call it a night?" Tyler already had an arm around Ellie's shoulder and let out a belch in the same ear that Cyrus's laughter had tickled moments earlier.

"I'm hosting, Tyler. I said that already." She removed his hand and glanced up at Cyrus. "Excuse me, sorry."

Fighting tears, she made rounds to all the tables, clearing any trash and taking a bit longer to avoid talking to anyone else. Tonight had the potential to go so differently in her head. She didn't intend to leave Cyrus' side, introducing him to everyone now that their friendship had been solidified this week, the shy proposition of asking him to dance, the gentle touches and giggles they'd share under the spring of lights on the maple tree. It all made sense. Luckily, she'd be seeing him again tomorrow, and hopefully Saturday.

Saturday.

Damnit, she still needed to ask him about Saturday.

Whatever song the trio was playing came to an end, and all but one cheered and clapped appropriately. Tyler was whooping and hollering, requesting "Freebird" by Lynyrd Skynyrd. A few chuckled and looked to Ellie to do something, but she resented their stares. She wasn't his handler anymore, she never should have been in the first place. This was always what it was like with Tyler, babysitting a toddler who couldn't handle his liquor and having to play mom the entire evening. High school parties were one thing, but they were in their late twenties, why the hell did anyone let him keep acting like this?

He stumbled back to the keg, but this time two sets of eyes were on him. Cyrus kept him in his sights, and Ellie watched on from the table of food, pretending to focus on wiping down the plastic lined tablecloth. Her shoulders fell with disappointment.

The house was her only safe haven as she took a bathroom break and some deep breaths in the mirror, but when she exited, the scene around her divulged into chaos. Tyler was trying to get up on the stage, with Jason on mic calmly suggesting he take a breather. Cyrus was closely following Tyler, who kept screaming something like, "Come on, let me sing, I know the words!" but his slur was heavy and thick with inebriation.

Ellie tried running to see if she could talk some sense into him, but she wasn't quick enough. In a wild motion, he missed the second step up completely. His entire body lunged forward and crashed to the ground, drink and all, causing the crowd to gasp and sigh while watching the scene unfold. Broken glass sprinkled the stage.

"Tyler, *please*," Ellie yelled, but before she could reach out to him, Cyrus was there pulling him up by the arm.

"Come on, buddy."

"My knee. *Damnit,*" Tyler moaned. Cyrus half carried him, before Doug joined, grabbing him under the other arm.

"Yeah, let's get you home. You're alright. It's all good," Cyrus comforted. He made eyes at Ellie, as if to say *sorry* and *I got this*, with one look.

She stood stunned, unable to process how quickly things had escalated. Tears streamed down to her chin as she watched Cyrus help Tyler into his car, a trickle of blood appearing on his knee where his light wash jeans must have caught on a piece of glass on the stage. Something poked at her ego. Here Cyrus was seeing a side of her, a side of Meriden, she wished she could put away.

A soft hand on Ellie's back caught her off guard.

"Honey, are you alright?" Her mom was here, rescuing her. The stage had no less than five people on it, picking up shards of glass, wiping down the floor, and drying off extension cords covered in beer. "Ellie," Martha said again.

All she could do was cry into her mom's shoulder. Years of anger and regret spilled out of her, just like beer on the stage floor.

CHAPTER 10

Ellie

The morning after the incident, Cyrus was right on time, rolling in at 6:58 AM. Ellie was still emotional from the night before, even after crying around the campfire that her mom put together for those that chose to stay after the chaos. A campfire was supposed to be the perfect spot to cuddle with someone after dancing with them earlier that evening, but alas. She woke up exhausted, emotionally spent, and counting the seconds until she'd see Cyrus.

He walked through the garage door with a somber smile, reaching out to initiate their morning hug that had turned into a habit at this point.

"Morning El, you doing alright?" His voice vibrated as her head rested on his chest. She wanted to stay in his arms to cry, get it all out before stepping back, but she knew she had to face it.

"I'm okay." She wiped her cheeks. "I don't know why, but I can't stop crying."

Cyrus' smile warmed. "Kind of tough to see a friend like that. Even if he doesn't feel like a friend right now."

That was probably the sweetest thing she didn't even know she needed to hear.

"I'm so sorry if he did anything or said anything offensive on the ride home."

"Ah, he was fine. He's going through it." His smile fell. "I've seen it all before. Don't know if this is his rock bottom, but the poor guy needs some help and it's absolutely not your job to fix him." Her mom had spoken the same words to her countless times, but from Cyrus it felt like she could actually believe him.

"I've always felt guilty for some reason." The tears kept coming, and she kept wiping them away. It was all involuntary at this point. "I've known him my whole life. It's like I wish I could have done something before to help him."

Cyrus approached her, wrapping his arms around her neck in another embrace. "Well, from what he shared last night in the car, it sounds like you've helped him more than you know."

A few moments passed and Ellie got her wish, breathing in Cyrus as if he could read her mind. She nuzzled her face into the soft turtleneck sweater that once symbolized an annoying lack of understanding and now served as the most comforting touch she'd experienced in months. Cyrus was the best thing that could have happened to her this summer.

She finally calmed down enough to speak again. "Are you free tomorrow morning? We need help at the market."

Cyrus jumped back, pushing Ellie out in front of him. "Really? I'd love to!"

Cyrus

Cyrus was a lot less excited now that it was 5 AM at the farm. He willingly helped carry bins of produce from the cooler to the trailer, however, Ellie's chipper early bird demeanor was doing nothing to help him cling on to the sleep he didn't get the night before.

"Felix will meet us there, and then we'll set up! I'm so excited to show you everything. Hopefully it's a busy morning," she finally finished, starting the car and driving off with her mom and the trailer.

He followed her in his old Benz, his mind traveling back to Thursday night when he took Tyler back to his hotel, sending a rush of sadness and hope that something would come from the business card Cyrus left in his back pocket. Tyler's words still echoed in his head.

She was the best thing that ever happened to me... I fucking hate my life... She wouldn't stop looking at you... Do you love her back?

It was all in a drunken stupor. Cyrus knew that.

He'd been in the exact place that Tyler was in before, crying for help in the most boisterous way possible, yet no one would listen. He hated his life in New York, though from the outside he had everything. All the friends money could buy, and no one who actually cared enough to notice how in the depths of it he was. That's why it was near devastating to see Ellie upset the morning after, knowing that if anyone at Community Night saw Tyler hurting, it was her.

It didn't stop him from cycling through each of his words over and over and over. He couldn't get past it anymore. In only two months, he'd gone from never expecting to step foot in

Minnesota to developing feelings for someone he knew would never leave.

He pulled up to the Farmer's Market parking lot, and found the strength to smile when he found Ellie, her mom, and Felix. They immediately got to work. Chives, cilantro, basil, parsley, and lavender. Sage, dill, thyme, and rosemary, and that was just the herbs. The abundance of produce was overwhelming. It was all gorgeous, and all smelled delicious. Within minutes he felt grounded again.

Felix had the same morning energy as Ellie, Cyrus soon found out.

"So what do you do outside of the farm? Do you work somewhere?" he asked, handing Cyrus a beet so round it looked fake.

"I'm in school. Getting my PhD."

"Does that mean you'll be a doctor? Did you know my mom's a doctor? But like, for girls. Like moms and stuff, too."

Ellie chuckled in between writing out prices on their chalkboard.

"Uh, well. You could call me Dr. Lexington, but that's not really my vibe. It's more like I'm doing a bunch of research to prove a theory. Technically I'm not getting my doctorate, but outside the field sometimes people confuse the two. Or they use it as an umbrella term."

Felix made a face that meant everything he just said went directly over his head, but he nodded and stopped asking questions, so Cyrus counted it as a win.

The stand was set up in no time. Once Ellie had triple checked everything, she let out a deep sigh and announced she was getting coffee, offering to get drinks for everyone. Felix followed her and nearly bounced as he ran, leaving Martha alone with

Cyrus. Within seconds, he stiffened. He hadn't had a single conversation of any substance with her, and it would have been funny, but her opinion had a tight grip on him. He smiled to hide his discomfort.

"So, uh, Mrs. Somers, you're retired, right?" His hands stuffed in his pockets without anything to do.

"I sure am." She smiled, but got serious immediately after, and something told him it was a precursor for what was next. "Oh, and Cyrus, thanks for taking care of Tyler the other night. Ever since he graduated high school the poor boy has been so lost."

"Oh, yeah. I can tell he's struggling with something."

"He's been like that ever since Ellie broke up with him." *Ah, there it was.* Cyrus could connect the dots on his own, but Martha confirmed it. "I'm glad that you were there on Thursday," she said, looking off and shaking her head. Her sightline followed a couple holding hands. This felt like a tough conversation for her.

"Ellie said you were very kind to her yesterday. I could tell it was a tough morning for her." Another pang of guilt stung in his throat. Ellie always seemed to say the nicest things about him to her parents. Martha smiled at him, breaking him from his thoughts.

"Is there something happening with you two?"

The question sidelined him. He might as well have been the one falling off the stage, trying to find his footing with only six words instead of beers knocking him over.

"Um, I... don't quite know. Friends? Ellie is so fucking great. I mean, shit! I didn't mean to swear. Sorry, um—"

Martha cackled, *cackled* a laugh, pleased with her results. "Oh Cyrus, it's just me."

"No, I'm sorry, honestly, Mrs. Somers—"

"Martha, please."

"Martha. Ellie is one of the best humans I've ever met, truly. I'm just glad to be able to learn from her at this point." He cleared his throat into his fist, hoping to buy him some time. How long did it take to get coffee?

"Honey, I asked in case there was news. She's been talking about you a lot, so I wondered. Didn't mean for it to be a pop quiz."

The pit in his stomach lifted, but filled with butterflies as Ellie rounded the corner. Her smile made it seem like she knew what they were talking about. First Tyler's drunken confession, now Ellie's *mom?* The first one he could write off, but Martha felt like a reliable source.

Ellie handed the hot drink to Cyrus with a brush of her fingertips on his, and it was all he could take not to jump out of his skin, unsure of how he was supposed to act. The lavender in his drink calmed him nicely, and he managed to take a couple of deep breaths before the market opened and a rush of customers enveloped the stand.

Time moved differently at the market. Between greeting customers, replenishing produce, and making jokes with Ellie, it felt like everything sped by before he could fully enjoy it. Everyone seemed so happy to see the stand, it made Cyrus happy to be there. Kids, adults, couples, elders, they all loved Ellie's vegetables, and they all loved Ellie.

Half way through, he was restocking some cabbages, and a woman approached him with a gnarly midwestern accent. "Well, hello there. Who do we have here this morning? I haven't seen you around." She had yellow-ish blonde hair, bulbous cheeks, and painted on red lipstick with blue eyeshadow, perfect for eight o'clock in the morning.

"Oh, hi Helen. This is Cyrus. He's working part-time on the farm while getting his PhD." Ellie came to save him. He might have been staring.

"PhD! Wow, that's quite the path. Lots of time to do that. Sure hope you can pay off all of those loans."

Damn that was a strong Minnesotan accent.

"Er, heh, yeah."

Ellie chimed in again, "What can I get you today, Helen?"

"Well, I was hoping for some tomatoes."

"Yeah, those won't be coming in for a few weeks. The cherry tomatoes will be turning soon, though!" How Ellie still had a smile on her face was beside him.

"Hmm. How about sweet corn?"

Cyrus stifled a laugh.

"Yep, still three weeks on the corn," Ellie responded coolly.

"Well, I guess I'll get a cabbage," she started, eyeing the radishes. "When were the radishes picked?"

"Yesterday morning," Cyrus responded, glad to know an answer. Ellie nodded along.

"Hmm, not very pink, but I'll take a few I s'pose." Her passive aggression astounded Cyrus. He had never seen anything like it. She grabbed a few more items, allowing Felix to ring her up without another assault. "Well, it was lovely to meet you Cyrus. Don't work him too hard now, Ellie. Hi, Martha!"

Martha paused where she was helping a customer and gave Helen a cheerful smile long enough for Helen to walk away from the booth. The entire mood shifted once she was gone.

"You survived your first Helen encounter," Ellie giggled, shielding her voice from Felix and her mom.

Cyrus blinked back into reality, matching her whisper. "What the *fuck* was that? Your radishes are the pinkest I've ever seen."

"Cyrus, don't worry, that's just Helen." She reached out, placing a calming hand on his forearm and shuffling into his space, still chuckling.

"And corn! It's only the last week in June! Does she even know how corn grows?"

"Probably not to be honest." Ellie continued to laugh, and it continued to sound like music. It was quickly becoming his favorite song.

*   *   *

The rest of the weekend, Cyrus had to fight the urge to randomly show up at the farm, but he really didn't have a reason to. Ellie sent him home with so much produce, it barely fit in his fridge.

Sunday was a day for catching up on writing, but from the looks of it, he was in a really good place with his research, especially after notes from his committee review came back with flying colors. Things had been going well for a couple of weeks, and either he had gotten used to the insane schedule, or he'd grown to enjoy it. Either way, when each morning came around that week, Cyrus got up before his alarm. Like clockwork, Ellie ran to hug him in the morning, energized and caffeinated, smelling of coffee and gardenias. It's all he could think about. *Coffee and gardenias.*

"Felix is coming today! He wanted to draw before Community Night tonight," she said, pulling away, but keeping both of her hands on his forearms. "He loves you. He thinks you're '*so cool*.'" She put the final words in quotations.

"Ah, what can I say, he's a smart kid."

"Or misinformed," Ellie punched back without missing a beat.

They took care of the chicken chores together, chatting mindlessly about the few hours they spent apart the previous evening. These days it felt like Cyrus wanted to know it all, even if all she did was sit in an empty house because her parents went to a card club.

Lunch had become something to look forward to every day. Getting to know Ellie through Martha and Doug's stories of her childhood gave him a peek into a life he never knew he missed; neighbors that felt like family, potlucks with pork burgers and potato salad, embarrassing stories of runaway calves at 4-H livestock shows. Things he never knew existed.

It took at least a week for Doug to stop asking if Cyrus wanted coffee with lunch. The final time, Martha pulled out an old pickle jar filled to the brim with loose leaf spearmint tea that was so alarmingly refreshing it cleared the fog of his pollen filled sinuses. The local honey from down the road added sweetness he couldn't deny.

"Did she get this at the farmer's market?" he asked Ellie in a hushed voice, chopping spring onions for the salad they were sharing.

"No, that's from our mint patch. She googled how to dry spearmint for tea."

It took a second for him to process that. "She what?"

"I told her about the coffee thing." She smiled for a moment before going back to washing the lettuce in the sink, as if what she had just told him wasn't the sweetest thing anyone has ever done for him. The more he thought about it, the more his throat tightened.

When lunch was finished, Ellie followed him to the field, but veered off to check the transplant tunnel, leaving him alone with the pepper plants to track their growth and pollination. Less than an hour later, he heard rustling near the gate and looked up to see Felix trotting into the field with a sketchbook held close to his chest.

"Cyrus! Look at what I found!" He stumbled into a jog. "There are monarchs in the pasture."

He turned his sketchpad to reveal an intricate drawing of a monarch caterpillar climbing up the stalk of a milkweed plant. The realism was astounding, almost unbelievable that a fifteen-year-old had drawn this with just a pencil.

"Felix, what the hell? This is insane." The boy's smile brightened. "Show me where the caterpillars are, I wanna see them."

They ran towards the pasture, wading through wildflowers and milkweed that hit past their knees, full of moths, grasshoppers, and butterflies.

"Watch out for bees! Noah got stung last year!" Felix called out behind him. They reached their destination, a clearing that Felix made near a few milkweed pants, his pencil case and erasers placed about. He must have been out here for hours.

Cyrus crept down on his knees, finding at least three caterpillars munching away at the leaves. "These must be hatchlings from the migration, they're not super big yet."

"They're my favorite butterfly. My dad and I used to raise them. We used to bike all around the neighborhood to try and find as many as we could. They're so cool. I want to find a chrysalis one day, I've never seen one in the wild."

"Yeah, they're hard to come by. They mostly pupate in branches or trees, something sturdier than milkweed. Maybe we can keep an eye on these this summer!"

Felix nodded happily. He sat back down and sketched an outline of another caterpillar before looking up at Cyrus, about to leave to go back to the field.

"Do you have a girlfriend?"

He froze. Was this some kind of prank? Had Ellie set the people up in her life to ask him these questions when he least expected it?

"Uh, no. I don't. Why?"

"Um," Felix looked away, and for the first time since he'd introduced himself confidently to Cyrus, he looked shy. Scared, even. "I kind of have a crush on someone and I was wondering something."

Cyrus sat back down among the flora. It was suddenly a conversation to stay for. "Wondering what?"

He took a deep breath and without looking up said, "So my mom knows this. And I think my dad does, too at this point. But, I kind of have a crush on my best friend."

Cyrus paused, waiting for the ever-talking Felix Khang to continue. But nothing came. He just stared at his drawing, delicately tracing over his lines.

"Yeah, that's happened to me. Does she go to your school?"

Felix's eyes shut momentarily. "It's *not* a girl."

Cyrus's eyebrows shot up and before he could stop it, a smile bloomed across his face. *Fuck yes,* he thought. He knew he liked Felix from day one.

"Neither was my best friend," Cyrus answered as Felix stopped drawing. "Felix, did you know I'm bi?"

With a laugh, he placed his sketchbook aside and leaned toward Cyrus. "No way!"

"Mhmm."

"What did you do? About your best friend?"

"I dated him for five years," Cyrus answered honestly. Ian Fluharty, his first love. "Have you told your 'friend' how you feel?"

"It's Noah."

"I figured it was Noah." They both chuckled.

"Not yet. I can't. I don't even know if he likes me like that. Or any boys like that." Felix got nervous again, shaking out his hands. "It makes me sweaty just thinking about it."

He'd felt the exact same for the last month. He probably needed to tell Ellie if he was going to give the same advice to Felix. So he didn't.

"It's okay to take your time. There's no rush. Do you think he feels the same way?"

"I don't know. I mean, we spend *so* much time together. During school, we always sat next to each other at lunch. And he came to my soccer games in the fall, so I went to his tennis games in the spring. Our dads are really close and we go over to their house a lot, but his younger sisters always want to play, so I don't really get any alone time with him, you know?"

Cyrus nodded and took a breath to answer, but Felix plowed through. "No one makes me laugh like he does, and he never judges my family for the food we eat. And it's dumb but I think his hair is nice. Plus, he's really smart in math. I hate math. Whenever he helps me with my homework, he's always like, 'Don't just copy the answers, you'll never learn!' but then he helps me get the answer anyway. He's a good person. My mom says so, too."

"So your mom knows?"

"Yeah, I came out to my parents last year. And Ellie knows. But no one at school," he paused, smiling up at Cyrus, "*yet.*"

"I'm glad your parents know. That's sometimes the hardest part." Cyrus remembered when he told his mom about Ian. She wasn't upset, but her words still lived in his brain. *Don't tell your dad, yet. I'll tell him.*

"Does Ellie know you're bi?" Felix asked.

More questions to throw him off balance. "Uh, no. Why should she know?"

"Oh, I was just wondering. She's really great with that stuff. You know her sister is gay? Her name is Hannah. She's awesome. Isabelle grew up with her! I always wondered if they dated in high school, but Ellie always denies it."

"I did not know that."

"Yeah, Ellie actually knew before my parents. I spent a lot of time here last year. I don't know, it's always felt like a place I could come when I need to think."

A warmth washed over him, as if he could admire Ellie more than he already did. Cyrus thought back to the day that Ian sat him down, asking him if he had ever thought about dating boys. He wished he had someone like Ellie to talk to back then, or even *one* adult figure in his life that wasn't an ultra-rich conservative or an employee of his dad.

Cyrus stood up again, brushing off pollen and foliage from where he sat. "She's pretty great, huh?"

"Ellie?" Felix questioned, smiling at Cyrus. "She's the best. Are you guys secretly together? You'd tell me, right?"

"Felix!" Cyrus laughed out of surprise.

"Sorry," he mumbled, smiling back at his drawing and refusing to make eye contact. "Mom always says I'm too nosey."

By the time Cyrus made it back to the field, documented the peppers, and started on the tomatoes, Ellie was walking back to the shed, finished with whatever tasks she was working on. If Cyrus had more self discipline, he would've stayed in the tomatoes to pick a few samples and measure their progress from last week, but the invisible string was back, pulling him toward the shed to follow her.

This had to stop. Right? He mentally calculated the days left in Minnesota, landing on the number fifty-eight if everything went to plan. But what was supposed to happen after those fifty-eight days? Move back to New York? To Ithaca? Buy a house upstate and be away from his friends in the city? And the worst scenario, move back to Manhattan and mooch off his parents while trying to make it work somewhere? What about Ellie? None of those options made sense or lit a fire inside of him the way that following Ellie to the shed did.

If she felt even a fraction of the feelings he was developing, he'd drop everything to figure out how to make it work. They could have a farm in New York, they could move even further upstate. Hell, he would even consider the idea of staying right where they were, as long as—

He cut himself off.

CHAPTER 11

Cyrus

"Hey!" Ellie cheered when Cyrus walked through the garage door, arms full of equipment. "Let me help you with that!"

She took the scale and caliper from him so he could set the bin and binder down. He still hadn't had time to pick any samples or measure a thing. He'd have to try again tomorrow.

"What are you working on?" Cyrus asked, hoping to fill in the silence.

"Updating my tracker. I just finished spraying the brassicas with BT. The worms were eating them up."

BT was short for *bacillus thuringiensis*, something that he studied a bit one semester during his master's program. He fought the urge to tell her that.

Still feeling rattled and giddy after his conversation with Felix, he took a deep breath before breaching the subject. "So Felix and I were in the pollinator pasture earlier. He was telling me about Noah. Noah is William's kid, right?"

"William Ortega, yeah." Ellie smiled and scrunched her nose. "Oh Felix, he's so cute. Literally has been in love with Noah for the last two years."

"Think Noah feels the same way?"

"That's the question on everyone's mind. Noah's parents are in full support, so I hope so." She smiled down at her hands and picked at her dirty fingernails, something he noticed she did when she was a little anxious.

"Okay, so," Cyrus started, curious about how these people all fit together, "it's the Ortegas, the Khangs, and then there's the guy who makes salsa. Then Isabelle and Maya." He paused, eyeing Ellie. "Are they together?"

"The Myers? Yes, they're married. For the last six years."

Damn. "Are they like, out?"

"For the most part. To people they trust."

He nodded with the thoughts of what he'd always considered to be true in flyover states. It was wild that she had created such an open and inclusive space in such a rural community. But then again, this was Ellie after all.

"Does everyone who comes to Community Night actually live around here?"

"Within Meriden township, yes. Here, I'll show you," she said, grabbing her notepad and sketching out a few roads that connected to a main street. Little boxes lined the routes, clustered at first, then becoming more sporadic on the outskirts of the page. They were side by side now, leaning over the workbench, and Cyrus's gaze followed Ellie's pencil carefully. She started with a house that was on the bottom right hand corner.

"This is us. Here's the field, and that's the woods behind the house." The trees she drew looked like arrows and the field vaguely resembled a rectangle.

"Maybe you should get Felix to draw this," Cyrus prodded, and Ellie playfully smacked his ribcage.

"Directly to the west here is Loretta. Her husband died a few years ago, his name was Gary. Gary Cottrell." She smiled with a hint of sadness. "He was a farmer and helped my dad a lot growing up. Their daughter Gwen got married to Wayne Kern and they had Nicholas, or Nick. He lives on the same farm, but there are two houses. He's the one with the two boys that my mom nannies." Cyrus remembered that detail. "Wayne and Gwen live in Wakuta, and Loretta would nanny them, but she has a hard time with two toddlers at seventy eight."

"She's *seventy-eight?* She doesn't look a day over sixty."

"Make sure to tell her that," Ellie quipped. "And then if we go back to the main road, up a little further is the Hernández farm, Andrés and Marisol. They have about two acres for their cut flowers. They haven't announced yet, but Marisol is expecting."

"Oh, damn!" Cyrus felt the sincerity of her excitement.

"I know, they've been trying for months. Then, on the other side of them are Isabelle and Maya."

"Isabelle and Maya are that close? We can see their house from here!"

"I know, it's the best," Ellie cheered with him, energized by the telling of her neighborhood's story. "Okay, and then further up, we get into town. If you can consider a few houses and the town hall a town. So here are the Ortegas, it's Keather, William, Noah, Brielle, and Grace."

"Noahhh," Cyrus smiled.

"Keather is Isabelle's older sister. Their family has been in Meriden forever. Two doors down are the Khangs. You know them."

"That's Felix, Trang, and... Lance?"

"Exactly," Ellie praised. "And then here's Jason. He's the one with the fermented salsa. He has a huge garden, and everything he grows is for it. The best tomatoes, even better peppers. He's got a good sense of humor, too. One time he invited me over and dared me to try a pepper that was so spicy it made me cry for like twenty minutes." She laughed at herself. "And his girlfriend, Caroline, does family photography and lives in Wakuta. Everyone thinks they're going to get engaged soon. She spends so much time out here. Hmm, that's pretty much everyone."

"There's still one more house left."

"Oh," she started, lowering her shoulders. "And here's where Tyler used to live. His parents sold the house about a year ago. The new neighbors work for the clinic in Rochester. They're never really in town. The Robrans I think."

"How far away is Rochester?" Cyrus asked, curious as to why anyone wouldn't want to be a part of the Meriden community.

"It's about forty-five minutes, but in the opposite direction of Wakuta. Lots more to do over there, so it makes sense." Ellie flipped back the notebook to the list of chores she had crossed out. "Anyway, that's Meriden."

He put his hand out towards the notepad. "Wait, can I? I feel like at some point there *could* be a test."

Ellie tucked a loose strand of hair behind her ear and smiled as she ripped the drawing from the book. "You can take it if you want it."

"I do. Thanks for sharing all of this."

"Thanks for listening. It feels special to share it with someone."

In a moment of weakness, Cyrus reached out to her hand, rubbed a thumb over her knuckle and squeezed it. He guided it around his waist to pull her into a hug to chase the scent of her. His fingers ran through her hair and he cradled the back of her head to press her forehead against his lips. Before he could do anything else dumb and risk his research, or worse, *their friendship*, he took a step back.

He couldn't do this.

Her wide eyes mirrored his shock, stunned into silence. Maybe he was imagining it, but something in her body language contradicted her expression. Shoulders relaxed where her brow furrowed with tension.

"Well then!" He cleared his burning throat. "I'll see you tomorrow, El!"

Fuck.

Ellie

Ellie's mind floated elsewhere the next morning. Hollow, empty, full of incomplete thoughts. They all centered around Cyrus and the hug that lasted just a little too long to be considered normal between coworkers.

Community night was supposed to go off without a hitch, but rain clouded her judgment. Cyrus didn't show, which was for the best. Everyone had left before the pork patties even hit the grill.

She plodded down the steps, meeting a chipper Martha Somers in the kitchen pouring coffee. "Well, there she is."

"Morning," Ellie croaked. The coffee was good today. Hot and strong.

"Didn't see Cyrus at Community Night yesterday."

This again. "Mmm."

"I thought you were inviting him now," her mom began, pouring cream into a mug for Doug. "You know, he really is pretty sweet. Felix couldn't stop talking about him for the ten minutes the Khangs were here last night."

"Huh."

"And he seems to think very highly of you, Ellie." She finally met her mom's eyes. "You know you can tell me if something's going on."

"There's nothing going on. I don't even know what that means. I'm like, his boss sort of."

Her mom gave Ellie a sly smile, one that was usually reserved for late night ice cream binges or after a particularly hysterical interaction with Helen. "Ellie, you know I'm not one to condone a power imbalance in the workplace, but he doesn't quite come off as someone who follows all of the rules."

"*Mom.*"

"Alright, I'll drop it. I'm just saying."

Holding on to a bit of her angst and uncertainty, she pointed at the cup of creamy coffee on the counter. Her dad was nowhere to be seen. "Why do you make Dad's coffee when he's not here? Isn't he helping spray at Bruce's?"

Martha looked down at the untouched mug. "He'll be back."

"But he could just make his own cup when he gets here."

"I like making it for him," she lectured. Ellie shrunk under her pointed look. "And what else am I going to do now that I'm retired? Are you this ornery with Cyrus when he tries to do something nice for you?"

"I thought you were dropping it."

With pursed lips, Martha shook her head and left Ellie alone with her bad mood in the kitchen. They didn't even make it to the porch today.

Not one cohesive thought entered Ellie's brain on the walk to the shed. Her mind kept drawing her back to the previous afternoon and the hug that tingled her skin when she thought of it. His arm had wrapped around Ellie's ribcage so far that his hand roamed up her left side. The other hand caught on her neck, then tangled in her hair. His breath was hot against her scalp, and if she would have hung on to him instead of freezing and letting go, they might have. Well. They were leading up to something, if only she wouldn't have been so paralyzed.

Despite her mom's words, this couldn't happen. None of these feelings could go anywhere. He had what, two months left? What was Ellie supposed to do, be his little summer fling? Something that was convenient in Minnesota, but out of the question once he was back in New York?

One thing was certain. She would have to face him and act like nothing happened. Yesterday's hug was just a hug. They hugged almost every morning. Today would be no different.

Except, the morning hug didn't happen. In the haze of Cyrus swirling around in her head, Ellie forgot her sun hat in the house, and during the ten minutes it took for her to find it, he had already arrived, changed, and started chicken chores. She met him in the pasture, building up the courage to go into the coup to fetch the eggs.

"Did you need me to do that?" she asked.

He jumped with the sound of her voice and bursted into a laugh. "I'm so sorry! It's ridiculous. They're just so unpredictable."

The poor thing had his work gloves on and everything. She laughed with him. "It's okay. I can do it. Did you already feed them?"

He nodded, watching her enter to retrieve the eggs. With the warmer weather and cool nights, they had been laying like crazy. Twenty eight today alone.

"So, it's going to rain today. I say we work on lettuce, a fresh picking of spring onions, herbs, and call it a day. What do you think?"

Cyrus adjusted his hat, the same Minnesota Twins hat her dad lent him. He didn't have on the overalls today, but she kind of wished he did. Instead he opted for the double knee utility pants. Slate grey, just like hers.

"Uh, well. I didn't finish my measurements for the tomatoes yesterday. If I fall off the wagon now, it'll be a bitch to get back on. So if you're okay with a shorter day, I am too."

"Can I help with the measurements at all?"

Cyrus blinked into a smile. "Yeah, actually. If you have time."

She nodded, thankful that things between them seemed normal and good, her angsty mood far behind her.

They finished the harvest list quickly, working on different parts of the field to speed up the process. Every time a bin was full, they'd carry it to the cart together, sharing comments like, *"The cilantro smells amazing,"* or, *"The zucchini is starting to fruit."* It was finally starting to feel like they were an actual team.

They took an early lunch that consisted of leftover pork patties from Community Night that went uneaten because of the rain. A line of clouds teased them in the west, and less than twenty minutes later, they were back in the field, Ellie carrying Cyrus's equipment as he followed her, laughing at his own story about a chef in New York.

"We would try to get him drunk and pronounce words like Massachusetts or jewelry. He always had the upper hand, though, because half the words in cooking are French. The most I could say was, 'Ç'est mon bitte! Touche pas!' But I think it meant something other than, 'That's hot, don't touch that,' because the French guys would laugh whenever I said it." Ellie smiled back at him. "Still got him to back off a hot pan, though."

"Do you still keep in touch with him?" Ellie asked, curious about Cyrus's life in New York. They set the gear down at the row to tomatoes.

"Not so much. A year or two back, he sold the restaurant to one of my good friends. He's back in France now. A Marseille guy through and through."

Cyrus proceeded to walk her through his equipment and notes. The diameter of each fruit was recorded in his journal, then compared to a color scale that he had tucked into his folder. They had to measure every last tomato that was growing, even if they were new, and record the numbers to compare against the set from the previous week. Then, as Ellie found out, they moved to the next row to harvest samples to test back at the lab. Ellie had given him a section of plants to do so early on in his research, marking them with flags in the dirt so they wouldn't get confused.

By the ninety-sixth tomato, however, they both had descended into madness. Everything was funny, a grasshopper scaring Cyrus into a screech, or Ellie losing her balance after kneeling for an hour. Nothing was making sense anymore, only their laughter on repeat as they discovered new things to find hilarious. They finished counting the one-hundred-and-seventy-eighth tomato as thunder rolled in the distance, unbeknownst to them, because unfortunately they had gotten on the topic of Helen.

"So where did she come from? Like how do you even know her?" Cyrus asked. Ellie had to admit she kind of enjoyed how defensive he was getting.

"She lives in Wakuta. My mom used to work with her at the school. I think she's the secretary to the Superintendent, so she knows everyone's business in town, which has made her the most passive aggressive human on the planet, because if you cross her, she can make your life hell."

"I hate Helen."

"Cyrus! She's just nosey. It's easy if you're nice to her."

"Is this where that 'Minnesota nice' comes in? You secretly hate everyone but are nice to them because you have to tolerate them?"

Now he was getting it. "When you live in a small town, you can't just avoid the people you don't want to associate with. Doesn't mean you have to be their best friend though."

Cyrus paused at that, plucking a golf ball-sized green tomato and gazing at it in deep thought. Interested in what he was going to say next, Ellie stopped what she was doing to watch him.

"Here's my impression of Helen buying some sage."

She laughed, thrown off by the surprise that *this* is what he was thinking of. "Oh no."

"So she comes up to the stand and looks at our bundles, touching every single one and goes, 'Ooh, well, not very soft... not very pungent,'" his voice was shrill and heavy with a Minnesotan accent. She noticed the use of *our* immediately, and wondered if he meant that. He leaned towards her, as if to share a secret.

"Meanwhile, our entire setup smells like sage. And then she asks you to lower the price down to a buck a bundle, and she says it like that, 'How about a buck a bundle?'" The accent was back.

Ellie tried to stifle her amusement, but it was bubbling out of her. "And I say no—"

"And you say no, ever so politely, so she raises her eyebrows and goes, 'Well, I s'pose I'll only buy two bunches, or maybe three,' and you're all sweet with, 'Okay! Will that be all for you?' and *then* she moves on to the tomatoes."

"What does she say about the tomatoes?"

Cyrus finally laughed. A big, vibrant laugh that didn't sound like it came from his body, loud and uninhibited, escaping from him so fully that he put a hand on his chest, as if to contain it. "Well first, this is set in August. Because June tomatoes in Minnesota don't fucking exist, Helen!" Ellie laughed at his hysterics. "At the tomatoes she goes, 'Not very red.'"

Ellie plucked a green tomato on the bush in front of her and picked up the exaggerated accent. "Not very ri-yup."

Another laugh, this one causing him to lean into her, dropping to his knees completely where he was crouching. A bolt of lightning illuminated the darkened sky, pulling both of them out of their own little world built around Helen. Ellie nearly forgot why they were out here in the first place.

"Shit, we should probably get inside before it starts raining," Ellie said, as if to cue the skies opening as thunder rang. Within seconds, rain sprinkled on and around them, gaining vigor with every drop.

"No! Not again! Come on," Cyrus yelled, grabbing Ellie's hand and pulling her up to run towards the gate. It was pouring now.

"Wait, your equipment!"

"Fuck!" Cyrus screamed, causing both of them to laugh, soaked and out of breath. "Go, go, go! Save yourself!" he offered.

She didn't want to let go of his hand. "I'll help!" Another crack of thunder boomed around them. Cyrus pulled her close, a valiant but useless attempt to shelter her from the downpour. They tucked Cyrus's instruments under their shirts, shielding them from getting waterlogged and finally made it back to the shed in one piece.

The sound mixed with the residual heat of the day created an environment of full security. Safety from the elements raging outside. From the looks of it, the rain wasn't letting up anytime soon.

"Holy fucking shit, that came on fast," Cyrus said, wringing his shirt out, showing a slight happy trail that made Ellie's stomach swoop. Wet fingers ran through his hair, dry underneath her dad's soaked baseball cap. He placed his bin and binder down, wiping the wetness from the plastic cover.

"It really did." Ellie jumped up on the workbench, her feet dangling off as the rain pelted the metal roof.

"My shirt is soaked!" Cyrus whined dramatically. "My clothes are in the car." He threw his head back, but still had a bright smile on his face.

"You're fine, it's just rain."

"Oh, you're the worst."

"Do I need to tell you to calm down?" she said, a heat rushing over her body that had nothing to do with the temperature in the shed. Was she blushing? She hoped she wasn't blushing.

"I stand by my last statement." He slipped his shirt over his head, as Ellie tried to avert her gaze from the softness of his chest. The barely there hint of abs held her attention just long enough for Cyrus to notice. He smirked as his hair fell perfectly to frame his face like it always did out of the confines of his hat. "Lucky my pants didn't get as wet."

Ellie swallowed, and the air in the room stilled. She couldn't look away from his dark eyes, following her with reciprocating curiosity. His torso was so bare, revealing sparse light brown chest hair cascading down his pecs. Yes, *pecs*.

He stepped closer to her, crowding into her space. She said nothing, did nothing, but their eyes didn't waiver. She wasn't going to shy away from him this time.

His smirk only deepened.

"Oh, now you don't have anything to say?" he asked.

"I... um," she started, looking down at her dirt-soiled fingernails placed on her knees. His eyes followed her gaze, and he placed his hands on hers, pulling them apart and taking her legs with them until she was straddling him as he stood.

He was so close, now. So close she could feel the warmth of his bare waist pressing into her inner thighs, igniting something wild in her.

"El?"

Their eyes met again, but the moment his attention lowered to her lips, her instincts took over. Grabbing his jaw, she brought him close, finally pressing a damp kiss onto his lips.

A switch flipped. He sealed the gap between their bodies, pressing her lower back as she arched into him. Heat, friction, desire, all of it met at the intersection of their hips grinding into one another. Cyrus's wandering hands furthered up under her shirt, and she lost the fight to push him away.

He *worked* for her for goodness sake. This schoolgirl crush that had developed into something scary and whole was destined for a dead end. This wasn't like her. In less than two months,

Cyrus would be leaving Meriden and moving back to New York to live the rest of his life as intended. What was the end goal here?

They finally broke apart for air, and Cyrus shifted back on his heels, revealing a very obvious strain in the crotch of his pants.

"That was so dumb," she blurted, snapping out of it.

His face went slack.

"What a shitty thing to say to someone you just kissed."

"No, I didn't mean— Cyrus!"

She'd already shattered the moment. He grabbed his shirt off the floor in a violent motion and marched towards the door. The moment it burst open, thunder cracked and the intense noise from the downpour entered the shed.

"And for the record, that's what happened here," he shouted, motioning between the two of them while his shirt flopped about erratically. *"You* kissed *me."*

Stunned into silence from the truth, she sat there, staring out into the rain. Her legs still open wide, missing the clench of Cyrus's curious wandering hands. Anger and loss fed into her thrust off the workbench. Maybe she was the one who initiated the actual kiss, but he broke the barrier. Coworkers didn't crowd up into each other's straddling legs they had just pried open.

"Cyrus, wait!" she yelled into the night. The rain resaturated her hair and shirt, clinging uncomfortably as she ran towards the house. His car sped by, leaving without a trace of hesitation.

The crack of thunder was constant now. The wind whipped around her, causing the rain to sting where it hit her flushed cheeks. She nearly sprinted into the garage, finally dry and cool. Her dad's booming voice broke her from the delusion of the last hour.

"What are you still doing outside? Get in, there's a tornado warning," he scolded.

Panic replaced anger. Cyrus couldn't drive in this. He barely had experience driving in clear skies and sunshine.

"Dad, Cyrus just left. He shouldn't be driving in this." She stepped into the house after removing her work boots.

"Why didn't he leave earlier? The hell is he thinking?"

"He wasn't. We kind of got into an argument," she admitted, beelining it for her bedroom to find a dry change of clothes, but freezing at the top of the stairs. "I should follow him, right? What if he goes in the ditch? Is the ball hitch on the truck? I think the trailer is still attached from the market—"

"Ellie, you're not going out there," her dad yelled up.

"But, Dad! He could get hurt. He shouldn't be out there," she cried. "What's his number? I'll call him and help calm him down. I'm sure we have it on some document." She was frantic now, foregoing the dry clothes and running down towards the office.

She started skimming her emails and found a note from the department, Cyrus's information attached.

Cyrus Lexington, PhD Candidate
Physiology & Ecology of Horticultural Crops
Research Term: May 16th - August 26th
Phone Number: 507-555-3500

Immediately she dialed and brought her ear up to the phone. After a few rings, she hung up to try again and again, refusing to let it go to voicemail. This was too urgent. She texted him, but they weren't going through:

(Undelivered) 8:49 PM Ellie Somers: This is Ellie. I'm sorry, Cyrus, but I'm worried about you driving during this storm

(Undelivered) 8:50 PM Ellie Somers: Can you call me when you get this? Or just text me back that you made it home safe?

Nearly two hours went by with no response before admitting it was no use. She couldn't quite pinpoint why she was so worried. The storm passed with relatively no damage. However, the worst case scenario meant they were down a worker for the rest of the season, a worker that Ellie cared about deeper than she wanted to admit. The guilt of breaking a boundary with Cyrus set up residence in her stomach. Whichever way you spun it, Cyrus probably wouldn't be at the Saturday market the next morning, and Ellie had no one to blame but herself.

That's why the tears showed up, and they didn't leave until she fell asleep, still without a single word back from Cyrus.

CHAPTER 12

Cyrus

Rain tickled his face. The droplets transitioned from cool to warm, trickling down his cheek with a calming heat that lingered on his chest and pooled in his pelvis. Leaves or grass of some kind brushed up behind his ears. *Wildflowers? Milkweed?* No, tomato bushes cradled his head like a soft pillow given by mother nature herself. The sweet, sharp taste of fresh strawberries filled his palette, making his mouth water and feel slippery. The rhythmic patter of the droplets surrounded him and a weight in his lungs pressed, pleasing and heavy.

Someone was kissing him; his neck, his jaw, his cheekbones, his eyebrows. Curly locks tickled his temples where they fell loosely around his head. He took a breath in, *coffee and gardenias,* and exhaled into a smile as gentle as the afternoon sun.

Motivated hands moved from his neck to his chest to his stomach to his —

BEEP, BEEP, BEEP.

The ring of his 6 AM alarm not only startled him up out of bed, but interrupted the best dream he'd had in weeks, maybe months. Reluctantly, he got up and focused on his determination to face Ellie today.

Luckily the rain had eased within the first ten miles back to Wakuta. That didn't stop him from spending fifteen minutes in the driveway, trying to make sense of what had happened the previous night.

Ellie kissed him. *Kissed him.*

More than a kiss, too. There was hunger, an unspoken willingness to escalate to who knows what. He felt that from her body, from the way her teeth scraped his bottom lip. And the only thing she could vocalize was how dumb it had been.

That kiss meant everything to Cyrus. The emotional weight of this week, a kid coming out to him, falling in love with the neighborhood, and the realization of his feelings for Ellie all pointed to maybe, just maybe, the potential of finding a place he could call home. Ellie washed all of that away with four simple words. *That was so dumb.*

He wasn't letting it go without a fight. With a bit more grit than he felt, he held his head up as he approached the Somer's Farm booth a little after nine o'clock. It was already hard to take his eyes off Ellie on Saturdays, but today her eyes were dark. Her body moved slower, as if it mourned being awake.

"Good morning," he said, causing her head to whip up at him from where she was finishing up with a customer to hand off to Felix. "Hey there, Felix."

"Morning, Cyrus!" he greeted back before turning his attention to the customer. Ellie searched him.

"What are you doing here?" she mumbled, eyes wide.

Before he could answer, Doug greeted him, too. "Good mornin', Cyrus. So you made it back safely last night?"

"I did, yeah. It was a little rough at first, but it cleared up in the end."

Ellie glared at him as she replenished green peppers out of a bin, placing them on a display delicately. His facade cracked. Why was *she* the one that got to be angry? If anything, Cyrus's hurt was righteous. He turned his attention to the bundles of sage on the stand, perfectly fragrant.

"Sage is smelling nice," he said, poking the beast.

She rolled her eyes, but not before catching a glance at this chest. His insides churned. She was holding herself back and he knew it. He leaned over the stand, crowding into her space.

"What are you on about this morning? I'm trying to be normal," he whispered.

"I'm tired. Move," she motioned him away, but with a glance around Cyrus saw there was a lull. He wasn't letting her treat him like this without a conversation.

"Hey Ellie, do you mind showing me where I could get some honey? I know there are a few spots, but I'm sure you have a favorite," he nearly shouted, ensuring Doug and Felix could hear if she blew him off.

"Right around the corner. A few booths down from the Myers."

"Could you show me?"

Doug chimed in, "We're good here, Ellie. Go ahead."

"Great! Anyone want coffee?"

Ellie shook her head. "No we're not—"

"That would be wonderful," Doug cheered, replenishing bundles of fresh basil next to sage. "Little bit of cream, Ellie."

"I'll have a tea," Felix declared.

She reluctantly moved them away from the stand. "Stop, Cyrus."

He practically shout-whispered once they were out of range, "What the *fuck*, Ellie?"

"No, *you* what the fuck?"

A voice broke their dumb charade. "Good morning Ellie!" It was Helen, because of course it was.

"Morning Helen!" she performed, plastering on a fake smile. Her voice lowered back at Cyrus, "I'm not having this conversation in the open like this."

"Fine. I still need to finish measuring the tomatoes. Can I meet you at the farm after the market?"

"Cyrus."

"*Please.*" He was begging, but he didn't care.

She gave in with a sigh, and the two of them walked towards the coffee stand, Ellie huffing and glancing at him every two seconds.

"I can do this alone."

"You can't carry three drinks in one hand. And I want a Lavender thing, er—"

"Fog. Lavender *Fog.*"

"*Okay,*" he seethed, fighting every ounce of himself not to roll his eyes. However, when the person ahead of them ordered, he froze.

"Hi! I'll take a caramel latte with oat milk, thanks." He recognized her voice instantly, the waist-length, pin straight, dark brown hair. The long nails unzipping her wallet. It was surprising that he hadn't run into her sooner.

"And I'll do a medium cold brew," the guy next to her said. Mike the bartender. It had to be.

All the feelings of regret and panic caught up to him. Before he could explain, his feet were shuffling him back.

"Actually, I don't need anything. I'll meet you at the farm. I'm sorry, El," he mumbled, not staying long enough to know if she heard. The last thing he saw were her eyes, searching for some kind of explanation. An explanation she deserved.

*   *   *

A few hours later, he could finally relax his shoulders as he rolled into the driveway and found her forest green truck. The silver maple tree acted as a beacon, guiding him safely into the driveway. Nose diving into research provided a distraction after the market, but it didn't quite help after coming face to face with the consequences of his vices. Luckily Ellie was there, and the white trailer attached to her truck was already nearly empty.

"Need any help with that?"

"Oh, Cyrus!" Doug hollered with a wave. "You here for lunch? Martha made chicken pot pie."

As much as he wanted to say yes, he was determined to speak to Ellie and finish up the tomatoes. "I have a few things to finish up in the field, otherwise I would," he said, now within earshot. Ellie refused to acknowledge him. Cyrus asked again, "Did you need help unpacking?"

"Nope."

Doug eyed his daughter. "Just finished. Most of the produce that doesn't sell goes to the food shelf. Not too much this week, we sold almost everything." He glanced back at Ellie, still ignoring the two of them. "Anyway, well. I'm headed inside. Starving. See you in there, Ellie?"

"Yeah, thanks for your help today, Dad." She smiled quietly at him before closing the trailer up. Cyrus had to read her mind to follow her into the shed, since she closed the garage door without a word.

He stomped inside. "Why are *you* the one who gets to be angry right now?" he asked, realizing how stupid he sounded as the words left his mouth.

"What, is there a fixed amount of anger in the world?"

He fought an eye roll. "Forget it. I'm going to the field."

"You know how to open the gate."

She was being impossible.

"Cool. I'll just go fuck off then. Have a great rest of your day," he said, dripping with sarcasm.

Whether it was the lack of sleep or the events of the last twenty four hours, her sharpness was reaching a breaking point for Cyrus. He grabbed his equipment awkwardly and set off for the field, not caring about Ellie's reaction or if she was following him. Her shouting voice told him she was.

"You're only here for another two months. And you didn't let me explain last night, even after I said sorry!"

"You never apologized."

"I did, too!"

He approached the gate, fumbling with the access code several times before Ellie caught up with him to turn it off herself with a huff. If Cyrus wasn't so pissed, he would have laughed at the whole charade. Instead, he kept walking and opened the door with his foot, effectively brushing her off. This was ridiculous.

"What am I supposed to do?" She was still yelling. Ellie was here to fight and so was he. "Am I just supposed to let you *use* me until you can go back to—"

"I'm not going to use you, Ellie."

"—fucking your usual standards in New York?"

Breaking point reached.

"Are you *kidding me?*" He dropped his gear at the base of the tomato plants, hot with anger and the complete misunderstanding in who he was as a person. His motives had nothing to do with standards or status, or anything for that matter. Did he have to lay it out for her? "No more talking. It's your turn," he spit out as he approached her, stepping close enough to feel her irate breath.

"You don't get to—"

"No!" He grabbed her jaw, steadying her, and immediately she softened into his touch. "No more talking until you listen to me, okay? Stop trying to tell me what my intentions are, because you keep getting it wrong." Her eyes welled up instantly, tears threatening to escape. Cyrus couldn't control his own emotions while seeing her in this state. His voice wavered.

"The truth is your laugh is my favorite sound. In the morning you're my favorite smell, my favorite way to start the day. I literally can't stop thinking about you, El. *Please.* I don't know what this means or what's going to happen after my research, okay? But today? Today you are driving me fucking crazy."

Her breath calmed ever so slightly, but her grasp on his waist tightened. She studied his face but remained silent.

"Tell me to stop, El. Tell me you don't feel the same way, and I'll leave. I'll never bring it up again." She swallowed, and huffed out an exhale before pushing her face against his hands, as if to kiss him again. He pushed back. "No. Tell me to stop."

"I-I don't want you to stop," she whispered. *Finally*.

Their lips collided as his body engulfed hers. His entire nervous system awakened, fingertips tingled where they intertwined in Ellie's hair. Her palms pressed firmly against his back, forcing his chest closer. She tasted like coffee, smelled like Ellie, like everything he'd fallen for this summer. He chased it as she pulled away.

"Shed?" she whispered.

He nodded after realizing he was already following her. He'd follow her anywhere if he could get his lips back on hers. They grabbed the discarded equipment with secret smiles and the kind of urgency that felt heated and exciting. Before Cyrus got both feet inside the shed, Ellie was back on him.

"El, wait," he huffed out between kisses, but all that did was direct her teeth to his neck. A rush of hunger lowered in his stomach. "Wait, please."

He grabbed her arms to push her away, losing the fight with his smile when he saw her face. She was beyond fucked out, drunk on the anticipation that led them to his moment. God, he wanted to hoist her up on the workbench, make every hair on her body stand up, grab every bare inch and bite it, but the knowledge that her parents were less than a hundred yards away stopped him.

And there was so much more he needed to say.

"Let me take you home—"

"Okay," she started, reaching for his neck to kiss him again.

"No, not like that. Come on, this is too important. Let me cook you dinner, let's talk okay?"

Ellie closed her eyes and took a long, deep breath, pressing her forehead to his shoulder. "I don't want to talk. If you make me talk, I'll have to think, and I don't want to overthink this."

"Then I'll do the talking. Please, just hear me out. Come home with me." For the second time he used the word *home*, and meant it. Home was beginning to look more and more abstract every day.

Finally, Ellie nodded against his chest, letting him lead her to his car. The second they got on the highway, his earlier tension melted away. Sure, he was out of practice, but the thought that he'd have Ellie in his space uninterrupted was exciting. Thrilling, even. He focused on his breath, on the tingle of his lips where Ellie kissed him, the sunlight hitting the dashboard of his '09 Mercedes SL550. He felt marginally high once they got out of the car. That was, until they stepped through the door.

Ellie froze in the entryway. "It's so empty."

"Uh, yeah, I haven't put a lot of thought into furniture."

"You don't even have a couch."

"Well, true. When I drove here from New York, all I packed were my kitchen essentials and clothes. It's kind of all I care about."

He hadn't thought about the optics of her seeing him like this. He just wanted some privacy and this felt like the best option.

"You hung up my drawing of Meriden?"

Shit.

"Uh, yeah. Didn't you say there'd be a test?"

She gave him a playful glare. "You academics are weird."

"Hey, I like studying things I'm interested in," he said, drying off his hands on the tea towel near the sink.

She continued to look around until she was satisfied before turning her attention to Cyrus and what he was doing in the kitchen, but now that Ellie was in his space, he had no idea what to do with her.

"You like mushrooms?" he asked.

She nodded and sat on a stool at the kitchen island. He had that, at least.

"I love mushrooms."

"Phew, okay good. I marinated some to preserve them, and then chopped them up in a lazy tapenade. You are hungry, right?" His brain was moving a mile a minute. "I also made bread this morning. We could have little crostini," he tried to be as lighthearted as possible, but Ellie only matched his nerves.

"That sounds good." She was fidgeting with her fingernails again.

"Do you want a glass of wine?"

"Not really."

"Thank god, I don't actually have any wine," he said under his breath, but she must have heard because she chuckled, shaking her head. "Um, do you want some tea?"

"Only if you're having some," she answered.

This was bordering comedic.

He reached in the cupboard for his assortment of herbal teas right when the toaster popped up. At one point in his life he was working in kitchens of the busiest restaurants in New York, and now closing a cupboard and making toast frazzled him beyond reason.

"Can I help?" she asked, standing up before he could answer. "Where are your plates?"

"Upper cabinet above the dishwasher."

They moved around each other with ease, soft touches on lower backs, fingertips brushing when passing the salt, smiles at the drizzle of the olive oil. Cyrus plated everything up with a flourish, knowing that if he could impress Ellie with anything, it was his plating skills.

But instead, she giggled.

"What?"

"You're putting so much effort into it. It's just me, Cyrus," she muttered.

He was leaning over the island after wiping the plate and lifted his gaze to meet hers. "This might sound cheesy, but you're worth putting effort into, El."

"That was really cheesy."

With a nod, he stood up, walking around the counter. "I know."

"Like, *so* cheesy—"

He cut her off with a kiss, grabbing both sides of her face with force. "Is this how it's going to be? You roasting me every time I try to do something nice?"

The sun rose in his apartment. She was smiling again. "I'm sorry, but yes."

"Ah, great." Another kiss for good measure.

After the first few bites, it finally felt like Cyrus could relax. The dishes were still dirty in the sink, the tea cold on the counter. But with their plates empty, Cyrus grabbed Ellie's hand and led her to the bedroom.

She followed him onto the bed, sitting cross legged while their hands rested on his lap. With a slight pause, she took a breath, speaking and surprising Cyrus right out the gate. "I haven't dated anyone since Tyler. Eight years. I have no idea what I'm doing."

"Well, it's been four years for me," Cyrus admitted.

"I live with my parents. What's your excuse?"

"Rehab."

Her eyes darkened briefly before she caught herself. Yeah, they were going there. "For what?"

He thought for a second, debating how far he wanted to take this. Might as well rip the bandaid off.

"Coke. Alcohol, too. But that was never my main problem." Ellie swallowed and kept staring at him. "At Tim's coffee stand this morning, the girl in front of us, she was— I had a bit of a relapse my first night here. I almost did something really dumb. That week was so terrible." He took a deep breath. "I haven't really dated since rehab. Fucks with your worth, you know. It was self-admitted. I stopped before it got that bad. I promise."

A gentle hand reached up to his face. Ellie's thumb swiped over his cheekbone, and his breath lost its pace. Everyone he ever admitted this to knew exactly how it happened. With unlimited money, came unlimited vices. His dad did it socially, his mom popped benzos like Tic Tacs, and his older sister was a high functioning alcoholic. Years of suppressing actual human emotions led to this. Yet, here he was, breaking himself open to Ellie. He wondered if she'd ever seen cocaine in her life.

"I'm sorry, Cyrus."

"Sorry for what, El?" He gave her a kiss on the inside of her palm before leaning back on the bed. She chased him and soon they were lying side by side, hands on each other and ankles interlocking.

"For everything. For kissing you and saying it was dumb. For yelling at you in the field today. For all the times I judged you, or thought I knew you. I'm just," her eyes flooded again, "I've been so confused. I don't want to get hurt."

"I don't either." The words sat for a moment in the empty room. Only a bed, a dresser, and a clothing rack kept them company. He reached out to run his fingers through her hair, hoping to comfort her.

"But you're only here for the summer."

He remembered what she said, and how she didn't want to talk about it. He wasn't going to push. "I know, but I meant what I said. I just want to spend as much time with you as possible until then. And I kind of can't stop thinking about kissing you."

She gave him a teary smile. "Me either. Not since last night."

"Not so dumb after all," Cyrus joked, but lifted himself up to envelop her, letting his tongue gently greet her lips before his. He put everything into the kiss, his joy, his hope, his nerves, even his uncertainty. She ignited underneath him, brought to life by the finality of their charade all summer. They *liked* each other, and what was more evident, they both were immensely eager to touch, taste, and tease any exposed patch of skin.

Running her hands under Cyrus' shirt, she peeled it up and off, latching back onto his lips as he reached under and around to unclasp her bra. With the release of the garment, he cupped her breasts under the fabric and his breath caught with the new sensation of her nipples on his palms. She met him with focus and his ever growing desire that jerked under the pressure of her own wandering hand. This wasn't where he intended things to go this evening, but he was laying himself bare for her, grinding his erection into anything that would give him the friction he had been craving.

And just like everything else that was presented to him this summer, he was unprepared.

"Fuck, *fuck*, El," he whispered, detaching himself from her with a huff. "I don't have anything. We can't do this. I didn't expect this tonight." He rolled over and plopped down beside her trying to regulate his breathing. By the sounds of it, she was just as worked up as him.

"I feel like a teenager," she laughed, and he joined in. Something about the way they were lying next to each other, Cyrus shirtless and Ellie's bra undone underneath her t-shirt caused the bubble to burst.

Giggles peppered the silence every time he caught her eye. He couldn't stop smiling, high off spending so much time with the person who made him feel normal these past few months.

"What were you like in high school?"

Ellie snorted. "A high strung goody two shoes who rarely had any fun." Her head lolled to the side to look at him. "You?"

"Oh, the biggest prick. You would have hated me. Give me a rule, I would find a way to break it."

It was true, his dad was on a first name basis with the principal, simply because they called so much. He hated living in his sister's shadow.

"Of *course* you were."

He nodded against his pillow, glad that the topic of their pasts sparked curiosity rather than fear. "If you would have gone to college, what would you have gone for?"

Her eyes wandered in thought, and he took the opportunity to grab her hand to kiss and it brought her attention back to him.

"I was enrolled at the University of Minnesota in their Family Social Services program before I pulled out. But I couldn't justify going into thousands of dollars of debt when that's exactly what got my family into the mess we were in."

"Would you ever go back? Get a degree?"

"No. Not now." Silence settled around them, and Cyrus could tell the lack of explanation meant there was more, but not today. She clicked back into Ellie. "What do you miss the most about New York?"

"Mm. The food."

"Really?"

"Absolutely. Although, Trang makes a mean bánh mì."

The sun was setting outside his window, signaling that it was getting late. He looked over at Ellie, peaceful and content with her eyes closed.

"El?"

"Sorry," she whispered. "I'm so tired. I didn't sleep for more than two hours last night."

Cyrus rolled over, pressing his body against her side. It felt safe to be in her space again. "Why's that?"

"Because *someone* stormed out of the shed while there was a tornado warning," she said against his temple. "You never answered my calls or texts."

Cyrus lifted his head. "I didn't get a call or text from you."

Ellie wriggled to reach into her pocket. She pulled out her phone and showed him the one-sided text conversation. "There. I told you I apologized."

"That's the school's number, El."

"Oh god." She smacked her hand up on her forehead, laughing again.

"Huh. So you acted all mad at me this morning, when in reality you were worried sick."

"Cyrus."

"Enough to text a random number. Didn't it send you to a generic voicemail?"

"Listen. I was frantic! I didn't even let it ring that long."

"Aww, Ellie," he pushed, fishing for the compliment. "Were you worried about me?"

"Cyrus."

"Do you *care* about me, El?"

She sat up on the bed. "Alright, that's enough of that."

Cyrus laughed in response, grabbing around her waist and pulling her back to bed, amused that this already felt so easy and fun. A squeal rang out as she fought with him, but slowly the roughhousing progressed into more kisses. Kisses on collarbones and forearms, stomachs and inner thighs. He wanted to reach every corner.

They settled further against one another. Ellie's shirt had since been thrown on the floor, Cyrus in nothing but his stretched out boxer briefs. Both tangled up in the blankets like two high schoolers after a night of homework and a heavy makeout session. They could have done more than touch and feel and lick above the waist, in fact, all Cyrus wanted was to rip her clothes off and have his way with her, but with each kiss came a conversation.

If you could live anywhere, where would it be?

"Around lots of trees," answered Cyrus as her finger traced over his tattoo.

"On the farm," said Ellie.

What's your favorite smell?

Ellie closed her eyes and inhaled, as if it was in the room. "The dew on a summer morning."

"Coffee and gardenias."

What are you most afraid of?

A beat before he responded, "Letting people down."

"Me too."

The last one took it out of Cyrus. A wet sniffle gave him away. And as Ellie had proven time and time again with this kind of information, all she did was comfort him, holding his hand under the covers, bringing it to her chest. Skin to skin.

Their breaths deepened, and it wasn't until Ellie spoke again that Cyrus realized she had been watching him sleep. It gave him goosebumps.

"Cyrus?"

"Mhmm."

"Of course I care about you."

He smiled against her shoulder, kissing the soft skin there.

"I know, El. I won't tell anyone."

CHAPTER 13

Ellie

It may have been the best sleep she'd had in months, but that didn't stop Ellie from freaking the *hell* out when she woke up next to Cyrus the next morning in nothing but her underwear. Yesterday felt like a fantasy, a peek into someone else's life.

This wasn't something she did.

This was Ellie.

Hardworking, focused, straight-laced *Ellie Somers*.

She slid out from under the covers as quickly as possible, needing to use the bathroom more than she needed air at the moment. Bundling her pile of clothes in her arms, she crept into the stark white bathroom and stared at herself in the mirror only to find a mark on her neck matching the ones that lined her sternum. Hickies. A trail of hickies. He had to be kidding.

A few moments of relief later, she tiptoed out of the bathroom fully clothed and ready to give him hell. Jumping on the bed where Cyrus slept on his stomach, she straddled his back and hissed into his ear.

"Hickies, Cyrus? Really?"

He moaned into a smile. "Well, good morning to you, too."

"There's one on my neck. I have to face my parents today."

A chuckle was stifled into his pillow. "We could stay here."

"We really can't. I was supposed to prune the bitter melon yesterday."

Cyrus rolled around, pushing her off in a swift move and getting up from the bed. She looked away with the state of his boxer briefs. It was morning, after all.

"I should probably finish taking samples of the tomatoes. For the third time." He adjusted himself before disappearing into the bathroom without closing the door. Ellie froze. How was he this comfortable this quickly?

"Can you close the door?"

A flush.

Cyrus poked his head out. "This is *my* apartment."

"Cyrus!"

He laughed and she could hear him loud and clear. Because his door. *Was still open.* She flopped back on the bed and within minutes, the shower was running. She imagined him behind the glass, wet and warm, steamy from the heat of the water. Suddenly she didn't feel the need to leave. Getting up from the bed, she approached the bathroom, leaning up against the wall his room shared.

"What are you doing?"

"Uh, taking a shower?" Right. *Duh.* "Open invitation."

She rolled her eyes. "You gonna give me another hickey?"

"No promises."

"What am I supposed to tell my mom and dad?"

"You could tell them you're a grown ass woman." Her body tingled with him describing her like that, and she was glad he couldn't see her blush. "Or you could borrow one of my turtlenecks."

"Yes of course, wearing your clothes after spending the night at your place. That'll go over really well." He didn't answer her. A few moments passed and her fuse was almost up. "Are you almost done? I need to get back."

Cyrus popped his head out again, his hair dripped beads of water down his jaw. She didn't even realize the shower had stopped. "El, do you need coffee?"

"That, and I need to brush my teeth."

"I wasn't gonna say anything."

"Hey!" She pushed his arm to throw him back into the bathroom and tried to close the door. He was too quick.

"Kidding! I'm kidding. But I am about to come out of this bathroom to change. And I am not wearing clothes."

She grunted, but it was a tactic. Like a child, she put the palms of her hands over her eyes and waited. His footsteps went from the bathroom to the clothing rack, then the squeak of his closet door opening. A few more moments of silence, and she felt his warm damp hands on hers.

"Ellie?" She peeled them back with the help of his fingers. "You ready to go?" He was fully dressed. A navy blue pocket shirt and some faded jeans that literally hugged his thighs. Hugged them for dear life.

With a nod and a glance at his ass, they were off, returning to his parked car outside.

"I can't believe you live above Buck's. It's the grossest bar in Wakuta."

"Yes, went there once and that was enough," Cyrus laughed as he backed out of his parking spot.

Ellie couldn't stop looking at him. He radiated freshness, smelling of body wash, toothpaste, and a bright, woodsy cologne. Meanwhile Ellie hadn't brushed her teeth since yesterday morning and was in clothes she wore to the market, now covered with a turtleneck sweater that probably smelled of her BO. A shower with him would've been ideal, but for some reason she didn't share the same comfortability that Cyrus did.

He rested his hand on her thigh, seemingly needing to touch Ellie at any chance. And while she felt grounded with the squeeze of his fingertips, she couldn't help but worry about what her parents would say when they pulled in.

Her dad saw them first. He waved at them with raised eyebrows from inside the garage.

"Remember, grown woman," Cyrus said, smiling back at Doug through the windshield. "Do you want to tell them?"

"Tell them what? That we made out and you got to second base?" The pit in her stomach had returned from where it took up residence after their first kiss. "No, we're not telling them."

Cyrus turned the ignition off and they both exited the vehicle.

"Hey, Dad—"

"Doug! Good morning!" Cyrus exclaimed, cutting her off.

"Morning, Cyrus!" he answered, as if this was normal. "Hey Ellie, your mom's got coffee on in the kitchen. You headed to the field later?" She nodded and led Cyrus into the house, not entirely sure why he was following her.

Martha seemed as unfazed as Doug. "Oh, good morning you two. Coffee's fresh. Would you like some tea, Cyrus?"

"Sure that sounds great!" he said, pulling a mug from the cabinet.

What the hell was going on?

"Alright, um. I have to shower, so," she started, not knowing who she was talking to, her mom or Cyrus, "I'll be back in a bit."

They both nodded at her blankly.

What kind of alternate reality did she step into? Normally, if she was away for a weekend or a night, she would have to give the entire rundown of where she was and who she was with. It came with the territory of living with her folks. Sure, she hated it, but the trade offs made sense. And if she was honest, she didn't get out too much. In fact, she couldn't remember the last time she slept anywhere else except for some farming conference or a family vacation to Seattle to visit Hannah.

The water pelted down on her, cleansing the last two days from her body. Her mind traveled to what the future could look like with Cyrus. She could never live in the moment with guys, always thinking about next month, next year. With Cyrus, it was clear that he had no idea what his next step would be. Which could be a good thing. Maybe she needed a little reminding every once in a while that life didn't always have to go to plan. This summer sure didn't.

When she made it downstairs, laughter rang in the kitchen.

"Yes, I understand that already," Cyrus's voice trumpeted. Her mom laughed again.

Ellie cut them off, "Ready to head to the field?" She grabbed a thermos and poured herself some coffee.

"Yeah, let's do it." Cyrus turned to her mom. "Nice to see you, Martha."

"You too, Cyrus. We'll see you tomorrow for lunch? I don't have the Kerns until Wednesday."

And there was that million watt smile again. "Absolutely."

On the walk to the shed, Cyrus kept pace with Ellie, and didn't say anything until they were out of earshot of her dad and only steps in front of the shed door.

"So they know."

With a gust of emotion, pushed him aside to enter. "You told them?!"

"They might have seen us kiss in the field yesterday," he said, now in the confines of the shed. Her thermos landed on the counter with a *thunk*. "And your mom kind of mentioned how excited she was to see you dating again."

Of course she was. Her mom's intentions were sweet and almost sincere, but this was Martha Somers. When Hannah had the kids, all she talked about was how far away they were, and how it pained her everyday to only see photos rather than the real thing. Not to mention, when Hannah got married, there were two mothers of the bride, so she split duties with Florence's mom, putting pressure on Ellie's future. *Why was she even thinking about weddings?* Were they even dating? It had been less than 48 hours since their first kiss. A kiss, not to mention, that caused World War III.

"Um, we're not going to talk about that right now," Ellie responded. She looked up, and Cyrus was in her space again.

"We don't have to. Plus, I don't really want to talk right now," he said against her lips, pressing his entire body up against hers. Before she knew what was happening, his hands hooked under her ass and lifted her up to the workbench, mirroring the night of the storm with the same urgent energy. From the sounds of it, he had been waiting to do this all morning.

Her arms instinctually wrapped around his neck, holding him right where she wanted him. He broke away, only to latch on to the back of her ear, breathlessly whispering. "God, you smell like heaven. I can't help myself."

The words sent a spark straight to her groin. If she said she *hadn't* thought about how hot it would be to get railed by Cyrus in the shed, she would be lying. But not like this, not when her parents were home.

A few more minutes of over the clothes grinding and just the right amount of friction later, she stopped herself and pushed him away. He looked how she felt, completely and utterly intoxicated. Somewhere in those eight years since Tyler, she had forgotten how much fun making out could be.

"Pruning," she breathed.

"Sampling." He removed his thumb from where it was undeniably pressing into her crotch. His eyes followed his fingers tracing over the inner seam of her faded black overalls. "Pack a bag and come home with me tonight?"

"Cyrus."

"Sorry, that's fast. Sorry." He seemed to be fighting with himself. "I know you spent the night last night. I'm sorry, I just," he exhaled, "kind of want to be around you all the time."

She gave him a final, drawn out kiss in response and let go of his face so they could finally get to work. Butterflies danced in her belly with every stolen glance across the field, and again when they held hands on the way back to the shed, and one last time when he kissed her goodbye.

While she didn't want to get her hopes up, something about the fact that he was going to be here tomorrow, the next day, and the next, was all she needed to be convinced that perhaps this was exactly what she needed. *Living in the moment,* or whatever. Because maybe the current moment was all she would ever have with him.

*   *   *

Thursday's Community Night rolled around and this time Ellie was determined everything would be perfect. Except, Jason had texted her that he and Caroline were out of town, meaning no guitarist or lead vocals, so no music. No music meant no dancing, causing everyone to kind of stand around chatting and catching up on events of the last week, killing her vision of a moonlit sonata with Cyrus yet again.

One thing was going right; he wouldn't leave her side.

He had helped in the kitchen after work, asking if he could shower upstairs, to which Martha said, "Of course! Ellie can lend you a towel from the closet." (She had never been like this with Tyler.)

He set up tables and chairs outside, joking with Doug about the hot days approaching while Doug gave him crap for how he was going to survive them in the field. He even helped with greeting guests, making eyes with Ellie as Felix and Noah ran to hug each other when the Khangs arrived. It felt natural. It felt good.

Once most folks had settled in, Cyrus and Ellie grabbed plates of food, filled with a beet salad and a beef stew that smelled of lemongrass and garlic. Someone brought a fresh strawberry pie and Ellie caught Cyrus taking seconds, more whipped cream than pie. They pulled up seats next to Marisol and Andrés, who welcomed them warmly.

"Cyrus, good to see you again," Andrés greeted him with a pat on the back. "And you got some beet salad, always a favorite. Those are your beets, Ellie."

"What is the name of it in Spanish?" Ellie asked. Marisol only started learning English two years prior, so any time she could speak in Spanish, she lit up.

"Ensalada de betabel y naranja. In Mexico, we have sour orange. But, I add limes. Is that right? Limes? ¿Limas o limones?" She looked to Andrés.

He nodded with a loving smile. "Limas, si. Yep! Tastes phenomenal, her mom used to make it all the time back in Mexico City. Usually for Christmas."

"Ensalada de navideña de betabel dulce," Marisol added. "Different a little."

"Well, it's delicious," Cyrus moaned into a bite.

The night continued on, filled with the smell of a humid, cool summer's evening and the sounds of laughter, chirping crickets, and the occasional sizzle of a cicada. Loretta shared the recipe of the strawberry pie to Cyrus and Cyrus alone, only when he wouldn't stop talking about it to Martha. The fireflies were out in full force, rivaling the twinkling lights that hung over William, Noah's dad, who was seen in conversation with Lance, smiling and laughing about something. Isabelle and Maya Myers stood at the food table with Andrés, pointing at the beet salad, while Nick Kern kept busy with his two toddlers. They occupied Brielle and Grace long enough for Felix and Noah to sneak off somewhere in the yard. And then there was Ellie, at the center of it all watching on from the comfort of a lawn chair. Marisol and Trang sat beside her, gabbing away about the body changes and hormones from the newest addition to the Hernández family, starting to reveal itself in her belly.

Even with the amount of people she loved surrounding her, Ellie felt a gravitational pull towards Cyrus, unable to focus on much of anything except his movements and where he ended up throughout the night. It felt right to be next to him, as if she was his partner through all of this. That was true enough, he no longer felt like a hired hand, he was a partner.

As the sky darkened, folks dropped off. The Khangs left with a moody Felix, begging to invite Noah over for a sleepover, but unable to get his wish. The Ortegas gathered their belongings and bid their farewells, and Marisol announced her exhaustion to Andrés. He led her to their car with kisses on her hand, and the Myers followed close behind. Soon all that was left were dirty dishes, tables to be put away, and speakers to take into the house. Cyrus helped with all of it.

"Did you two want to have a fire? Everything is set up on the back patio," Martha said, keeping an eye on Cyrus.

"Sure, are you guys going to join?"

Doug winked. "Not tonight. You two have fun."

They shuffled into the garage with the tables and extra chairs and nearly seconds after Doug and Martha went inside, Cyrus's hands were on Ellie's waist.

"What do you think?" he asked.

"A fire sounds nice."

He smiled into a kiss on her cheek, and within minutes Cyrus was trying and failing with the fire pit. On the third attempt, Ellie couldn't contain her laughter as the small flame reduced down to a glow, then to a wisp of smoke that caught in Cyrus's throat, throwing him into a coughing fit. A valiant effort on his part, but this is what Ellie was made for. She grabbed kindling from the woods and immediately the main log caught on the first try.

"That's just embarrassing," Cyrus chuckled to himself as Ellie approached him on the lawn chair. His arms were out in a grabby motion, inviting her into his lap to watch the flames rise. The smell alone calmed Ellie into a sleepy trance. She'd been up since 5 AM.

Cyrus' scratchy voice tickled her ear. "You can say no if this is too much, but I was wondering if I could work the market with you on Saturday."

She turned to face him, kissing him gently on the lips because, well, because she could. "Why would that be too much?"

"I don't know. If I'm bothering you or anything. I know you see me every day."

With her forehead pressed into his neck, she settled deeper into his lap. "I like seeing you every day. Maybe after market we could go back to your place and...?" She hoped he knew what she meant. The swallow she felt in his throat signaled he did.

"I'll make sure to stop at the drugstore beforehand." And with that, they chuckled into another kiss as the fire crackled in front of them.

CHAPTER 14

Cyrus

It was happening again. He could feel it. The hyperfixation, the constant thoughts, the habits already forming. This happened in almost every relationship Cyrus had started. He would obsess over someone, give in to their every whim and shower them with gifts and time and attention. It was an addiction.

There was this girl at NYU. During undergrad. Clara. She was an English major in his Anthropology class. He and Ian had been separated for six months and he didn't know what to do with himself, so he drank. He partied. But Clara was studious and poetic, like some sort of flower. He gave her everything, bought her meals with his school account and took her to the best restaurants he could get into. Even helped with rent during months that got tight for her. And while she seemed happy to be wined and dined, her priorities were non-negotiable. The more he offered, the more she stepped back, always focused on school work or an internship. She broke up with him after just five months.

So he drank. He partied. He forgot.

Relationships became one night stands, one night stands became transactions. Intimacy by way of liquor, weed, whatever. It all was easily accessible and well within his means. Was it fulfilling? No. Satisfying? Some days. But after rehab, he vowed to take a step back from the dating pool. Four years later he met Ellie.

Ellie started off as someone he dismissed. A know-it-all who was too tightly wound to really enjoy the world around her, but in many ways Ellie created the world that Cyrus enjoyed so much. The vegetables she grew, the community she built, even the way she pushed against pleasure or rest. Her undying need to take up as little space as possible to make others around her feel comfortable was a trait Cyrus wasn't familiar with. Not in New York, and definitely not in the transactions of his past.

He saw it in her commitment to the farm, to the earth, and especially to the people. Even if those people were Helen at eight on a Saturday morning.

"Hello Ellie! Oh, and there's that Cyrus again. How could I forget you?" It sounded like an insult. He stepped towards the bin to replenish the zucchini.

Ellie, pure and poised, smiled calmly. "Good morning, Helen. What can we get you this morning? The basil is smelling gorgeous."

"Tastes great, too," Cyrus chimed in, determined to be included.

"Hmm." Helen scrunched her nose and Cyrus wondered if he could punch it without causing a scene. "No, not if you don't have tomatoes."

"Ah, right. Just a week or so! We should have a few next Saturday," Ellie promised.

Helen nodded solemnly then, like clockwork, proceeded to take a head of lettuce, some cucumbers, and a bundle of radishes. Felix rang her up with a smile, but Doug chuckled next to Cyrus, obviously amused with the interaction.

The touch of Ellie's hand comforted his lower back and suddenly it was fine. Her fingernails scratched up his spine and he lost track of what he was doing. Zucchini. He was going to get more zucchini.

"Felix!" A voice rang out. It was Noah and his dad, arms full with a jar of honey, a small bouquet of flowers, and what looked to be five pounds of ground beef. Noah was dressed like he just came from some sort of sporting practice, a bit sweaty and red from the sun. He grabbed the flowers from his dad and very obviously ignored Cyrus, Ellie, and Doug as he walked up to the stand. "I got these for you. They're from Marisol and Andrés. Marisol said they were called delphiniums. Right, Dad?"

William nodded, but stood back to let them have their moment. The market seemed to stop for them. Except Ellie. She jumped in at the perfect time, right after Felix thanked Noah with a shy, blushing smile.

"We have a few empty jars with water in them from the cilantro. Wanna stick them in there? We can put them out during the rest of the market, then you can take the whole jar home, Felix."

Finally Noah and Felix broke eye contact, and he agreed to give them to Ellie.

"Thanks, Ellie," Noah offered, now greeting the rest of the group. "Good morning Mr. Somers. Hi, Cyrus."

William exchanged a look with Ellie, and instantly Cyrus knew there was something he was missing. Some update or gossip that only existed between the adults in the room.

"Noah, did you want to buy anything?" William asked. He placed a grounding hand on Noah's broad shoulder, bringing him back to center.

"Um, I don't know, did mom want anything besides lettuce and onion?"

"I don't think so. But if anything else looks good, we can get it."

Felix, ever the upseller, spoke up. "Cyrus says the basil tastes good. My mom puts it on pizza. Even frozen pizza tastes better with it."

Noah's eyebrows raised at his dad, who shrugged as if to say, *it's up to you.*

"Okay, yeah. We'll take that." The son and father continued to share a look, having an entire conversation silently. "Oh and, um, my mom said you could come over for dinner tonight."

Felix nodded and smiled. His fists clenched against his chest. "Okay, I'll ask my mom."

Another amused look between William and Ellie. Trang must have been in on this already.

"We're having burgers and hotdogs on the grill. If that's okay," Noah muttered.

"Cool!"

"Cool, okay, um, Dad?" Noah passed it off to his father again.

William nearly chuckled. "We'll also take a head of lettuce and a red onion."

"Oh right. Thanks, dad."

Felix jumped into action to bag up the produce and handed it off with a smile, completely forgetting to ring him up. "Oh! Sorry, um. Seven dollars."

William threw a ten down and waved the crew goodbye with a bright smile and a wink.

The entire rest of the stand reanimated, no longer hanging off the conversation between the two teenagers. Ellie was the first to break the silence.

"Cyrus, can you come with me to grab some coffee?"

"I'll take a green tea!" Felix piped up, luckily unfazed by Ellie's energy.

"Little bit of cream," Doug added.

The moment they were out of their line of sight, Ellie grabbed Cyrus's arm so tightly he lost circulation. She squealed, hiding her face in his bicep.

"Oh my god!"

"What?"

"I'm on a group chat with Keather and Trang. Felix and Noah kissed on Thursday at Community Night. I bet that was the first time they've seen each other since." Her smile was brighter than he'd seen in weeks.

"You're joking."

"I'm not. And Noah asked his parents if they could invite Felix over for dinner so that he could ask him out officially. Keather is kind of strict about dating, but I get it. Felix is Noah's first real crush. And he's the oldest."

They moved up in the line at Tim's. Cyrus matched her smile. "I love everything about this."

"He really looks up to you, you know."

"Felix?"

Ellie nodded. "He talks about you a lot with Trang. Trang loves you."

His chest puffed out, even if he didn't realize it. He soon lost that bit of confidence with the thought that Felix was talking about him with his mom.

"Did he, uh, say anything in particular about me? Or like, why he looks up to me?"

Ellie started to answer, but they were next in line and Tim greeted her with a peppy smile. "Hey Ellie! What can I get you two? Cyrus, right?" Cyrus nodded.

She ordered the usual; a black coffee for herself, a green tea for Felix, coffee with cream for Doug, and a Lavender Fog for Cyrus. Though, his appetite wasn't quite available at the moment.

They shuffled away to wait for their drinks, and Ellie still hadn't answered him.

"El?"

Her dazed eyes met his, placing both hands on Cyrus's hips and smiling up at him. "Yeah?"

"Did Felix say anything specific about me? Did he mention what else we talked about when he told me about Noah?"

"Oh." She relaxed. "Are you nervous about him telling me you're bi?"

He let out the breath he was holding. "Kinda."

"Don't be. I was glad to know." She hugged him and he wrapped his arms around her shoulders, trying to loosen up. She stepped back, probably still feeling how stiff he was. "You know my sister is married to a woman, right?"

"Hannah?"

"Hannah."

"And your parents?"

"Were the first she told when she got engaged. Little shit, she didn't even tell me before she called them." Their drinks were ready. They each took two, but Ellie paused before she took a sip. "You don't ever have to tell my parents if you don't want to, though. It's none of their business."

Cyrus smiled down at her, wishing they didn't have so many hours between now and when he could undress her. "Hey, thank you. This might sound dumb, but I didn't realize so many queer people existed in small towns like this."

"They exist. But if you don't know of them, it's probably because none of them trust you yet. At least, that's what Hannah always said growing up. When she came out after high school, a few old classmates got in touch and came out to her, but almost all of them moved away, too." Her smile faltered. "That's why I love Izzy so much. She chose to come back. I wish she didn't feel like she had to leave first, but we got Maya out of the deal! I convinced them to move to Meriden when they were looking at houses."

They walked side by side back to the stand, their strides a bit lazier than normal. An unspoken agreement that they needed to finish this conversation before returning. Cyrus could understand why people left. He's seen products of that migration his whole life, mainly from transplants that came to New York looking for a fresh start, a new, more authentic way of living. In some ways, the story always involved villainizing their hometowns, which Cyrus loved to tack onto, even if he wasn't quite versed on what it felt like to be queer in rural America. And sure, New York had its issues, too. Ian wasn't out to his parents the first four years of their five-year relationship, and his dad worked in TV.

"What does Isabelle do now that she's back?"

"She works part-time at a family planning clinic with Trang. Maya sells her mushrooms year round, and she helps with that, too." Ellie took a sip of her coffee, unfazed by how quickly Cyrus gained respect for the Meriden community. A community that was better because of Ellie. He was sure of it.

Towards the end of the market, she started gathering up the produce into a bin while Felix counted the till. Doug hopped into the trailer to get some supplies, and Cyrus felt stuck without a job.

"Uh, what should I be doing?"

Ellie popped up from putting herbs in a bin. "The food shelf always does a sweep after the market. Take what you want, the rest will go to them."

However unbelievable it was to give so much produce away for free, he goggled at the options before him. He took a fair share of onions, the first of the season, fresh and crisp and ready for anything. And he couldn't deny the herbs, so he grabbed one with a sheepish grin from the bin Ellie was working on. She only met him with an encouraging smile.

Isabelle and Maya stopped by before they were all packed up.

"Cyrus, we have some extras today. And a prized Lion's Mane that we finally got started. Saved it for you!" Maya carefully cradled a towel and revealed a hairy mushroom the size of a softball.

"Holy shit," he began. This was too much. "For me? No. I can't take this from you. It's gorgeous!"

Maya laughed. "We know, but now that we got the hang of it, we'll be growing them like crazy."

"We've eaten a ton already, and we wanted to share before we started selling them," Isabelle said, insisting Cyrus take it.

He turned to Ellie. "I know exactly what to make with this."

*　　　*　　　*

Even if Cyrus had a hard time admitting it, he wished he could have followed her home. But alas, Ellie had to stop at the farm to drop off the trailer and grab a bag before she met him at his place. Which was fine. Because she was her own person and he couldn't follow her everywhere. Plus, she wanted to have her own vehicle at his apartment so she could be an adult and leave the next morning without having to catch a ride from Cyrus. And Cyrus was an adult and didn't need to go to the farm the next day, because well, he could be alone for a day. His research was slowing down a bit, so he really didn't have any reason for the forty minute drive other than to continue being Ellie's shadow.

In fact, he had been kind of keeping it from Ellie that his research in the lab was almost completely finished. All that he had left to do was put his findings into a narrative format for his dissertation, then defend it in just over a month. They would either push him through to officially complete the program, or he'd have to do another round of research. At this point, he knew they wouldn't let him stay on the farm if that happened, but he wasn't thinking about that. His only thought at the moment was how quickly he could get Ellie's clothes off after dinner. He had already gone to the drugstore to buy everything he needed. Condoms, a few candles, some lube. Because again, they were adults. Busy, productive, tired adults.

Her hair was still wet from a shower when he met her downstairs. The pork butt had been going for an hour before she arrived, and it filled the apartment with aromatics.

"It smells amazing. What are you making?" she asked as he came back to the kitchen from setting her bag down in his room.

"Something like carnitas. Are you hungry?"

"Starving." *Perfect.*

He hid a smile and started chopping the fixings for the meal. Onions, cilantro, lettuce, all from the farm. While Ellie took over, he retrieved the lion's mane batter that had been resting in the fridge.

"And for an appetizer, mushrooms cakes."

Ellie grimaced. "That sounds…"

"Not great, I know. It's like a crab cake, but instead of seafood, it's the lion's mane from Isabelle and Maya. Wait until you try one."

Sure, vegan crab cakes didn't really go with carnitas, but his excitement in cooking for someone else was getting to him today. He couldn't stop thinking about the chocolate torte cooling in the fridge. The "crab" cakes were done a few short minutes later, and he cut into the best looking one with his fork.

"Here, try," he floated it to her mouth. Her eyes said it all.

"Cyrus. That tastes better than real crab." Her mouth was full, but she grabbed the fork from him to take another bite. "What did you put in here?"

"Some lemon and bread crumbs. The egg, parsley, and chives are from you, and then mushrooms. Some spices, too," he shared, confident and loopy from her satisfaction.

They munched contentedly and gathered the toppings for the carnitas while Cyrus toasted the tortillas in his favorite cast iron. Not a detail left unnoticed. It was dumb how much he enjoyed making food with her, but cooking beside Ellie was no match to sharing the actual meal. She moaned with so much pleasure it was nearly sexual, gasping at the chocolate torte.

"You've been cooking all afternoon," she effused, keeping the energy in the room while chatting happily about everything from seed varieties to secret family recipes. It could have been about a wart on her foot for all Cyrus cared. He was just happy she was there.

It wasn't until halfway through sharing a piece of dessert that he understood why. He must have been deep in thought, because Ellie put her fork down to get his attention during a pause in their conversation.

"What are you thinking about over there?"

He pulled the fork out of his mouth slowly, wasting time to think about his answer. "I don't know. Just thinking about how happy I am that you're here. Um," he took a breath, gaining courage. "I've been really enjoying having lunch with you and your parents everyday. And just now, all I could think about was how good it feels to eat with someone. With you." He didn't mean for it to turn so sincere, but Ellie reached out her hand and he immediately grabbed it, like some sort of lodestone, and found the assurance to continue.

"When I moved out of the dorms at NYU, I lived alone. Lived alone for almost all of my adult life. And whenever I had to eat, I cooked for myself because — fuck, I hated eating alone in the caf. And then I got to know the staff at some of the restaurants and usually the cooks all ate together after our shifts. When I moved upstate, I just ate alone *all the time.*" He raked his free hand through his hair and rubbed his face, hoping not to take away from the mood.

Ellie pushed the plate away and moved her stool closer. Their knees interlocked.

"I'll eat with you every day if you want me to. You should start staying over for dinner."

"El, no, I didn't mean—"

"No! I've never thought about it like that. My god, I can't remember the last time I ate a meal alone." She was having a full blown existential crisis over dinner companions.

"Listen, I only bring it up because I've realized that being out here makes me feel more human. Eating with someone makes me feel more human." Ellie's brows furrowed with concern and admiration. "And can I say something cheesy?"

Her face relaxed. "I know what you're going to say. Don't do it—"

"—*you* make me feel more human, El."

"Gross!" Ellie whined, but she fell into him, hugging him awkwardly and kissing his jaw and cheek over and over.

In a sweeping move, he wrapped his arms around her waist, lifting her up. Her feet dangled in front of his legs as he brought her to the bedroom, giggling all the way.

"The dishes!" she screamed.

"Will be there in the morning!" he yelled right back, throwing her on the bed with a rousing confidence.

The hunger in Cyrus's eyes contrasted how full he was from dinner, but he crawled up to kiss her as if he hadn't had a taste in years. They tangled up into each other, hands on necks, kisses on collar bones, clothes on the floor. He managed to get her completely naked and with that confidence, spoke into the valley of skin between her tits.

"I haven't showered since the market. I will literally be five minutes. I'd ask you to join, but..." He bit the underside of her boob, leaving a mark in a more discreet location.

"I know. I showered before I got here," she breathed. "Be. Quick."

He tried, he really did. But he needed to shave, and he thought he would tidy up a bit *down there*, so he deep conditioned to multitask. His teeth probably could use a brushing, too. By the time he sprayed his cologne over his moisturized body in nothing but a condom and a towel, he opened the door to find Ellie fast asleep.

"El?"

Nothing.

She had to be kidding.

"Ellie?"

He couldn't stop the laughter from bubbling up. How were they so bad at this? It was only half past eight.

He dropped the towel and peeled off the unused rubber, crawling in next to her and relishing in the full body contact, void of any layers of separation. Sleep was pleasantly creeping over him until Ellie gasped awake beside him.

"Cyrus?"

"Hmm."

"Did I fall asleep?"

"Mhmm."

"Damnit. I've been up since five."

He chuckled, too tired to do anything about it.

"Morning?" she asked.

"Absolutely."

She sighed, accepting his answer, and wiggled around to be the little spoon.

*   *   *

When the sunbeams shined through his bedroom window, Cyrus was hard and ready. It didn't take much when there was a gorgeous, incredible woman lying next to him in bed, fully nude. He started off as gentle as possible, kissing her shoulder where it relaxed on his chest. She was laying on her stomach, a knee propped in between Cyrus's legs. He ran a soothing hand from her neck down to her ass, grasping the fullness of it in his palm.

"Mmmm," she stirred. She was awake, *thank god.*

"Good morning, El," he whispered into her ear, grinding up into her thigh and hoping she would get the memo. The miniscule amount of friction already felt like nirvana. He was so incredibly turned on, his body craving any kind of touch that would drive him towards release.

Ellie lifted herself up, causing her erect nipples to gently tickle his chest, and his dick jerked against his stomach. She nipped the crook of his neck before she spoke against his skin, still groggy from just waking up.

"I haven't brushed my teeth."

"Not important at the moment," he said, grabbing her around the rib cage and in one swift motion, pinning her underneath him. His mouth immediately landed on her left nipple, biting and sucking to get her riled up. Her back arched up against him, and this was his cue, planting kisses from her navel to the start of her pubic hair. Everything about her turned him on. She spread her knees open for him as he hooked his arms on under her ass, drawing her close with kisses up and down either side where she's already glistening wet. Her groans sent something carnal to his cock, aching at how hard he was. He just had to hold out a bit longer.

"Oh my god, Cyrus. Uhn, fuck," she huffed with his first taste. Sweet, sharp, and *Ellie.* Coffee and gardenias had nothing on him anymore. This was his new favorite smell. He took all of her in his mouth, sucking her fully as his tongue drove the action, melting into the delicate folds. Her stomach spasmed under his palms, now holding her in place to monitor her breathing. Whenever her breath hitched, he'd try again, driving her wild before she couldn't stay still or keep quiet. "Yes, yeh, Cy— Cy— oh my *ah*, Cy—"

He felt every one of her pelvic muscles clench around his tongue, and with one in the bucket, he couldn't hold back anymore.

"Condom," he breathed, getting up from the bed to run to the bathroom (why the *fuck* didn't he bring them to his nightstand?), and in record time he was back in his bedroom, unable to look away from her body on full display. Her eyes weren't on his, though, they were following his bobbing cock as he walked back to the bed. She reached for him instinctually, kissing the base of his shaft before giving it a lick up to the head. As much as he wanted *that*, he pushed her away, kissing her neck and lining himself up.

Before he pushed in, their eyes met. "You okay?"

"Yeah." Her face said otherwise.

Something was off.

"You sure? We can wait a little longer. You ready?"

"Mhmm, yes."

His hand was back on his dick, centering himself up before thrusting in. It would have been ecstasy, pure pleasure, if Ellie's face didn't contort as soon as he was more than an inch inside.

He was... fine in that department. Nothing like a porn star, but definitely not below average either. Something wasn't right.

"El, you okay?"

Her clenched fists opened with her eyes. "Yeah, just give me a second."

"No," he said, pulling out and flopping beside her. "We can wait. I can go down on you again."

Ellie tried to laugh, but it felt like a cover up. "I mean, I won't say *no* to that. That was the best head I've ever received."

"Well, if I'm up against Tyler."

"Stop! Don't say his name!" she chuckled, and luckily this time it felt genuine.

Cyrus ran a few fingers in her hair, kissing her cheek. He whispered against her jaw, "What's going on?"

"It's really nothing. I'll get used to it."

Used to it?

"That's not really how sex should feel, El." She hid her face into his armpit, and he let her stay there for a bit before making her speak. "Ellie? Come on, talk to me."

"I've never really liked anything inside of me. It just doesn't feel good."

"Okay, then we don't have to do that."

"Oh my god, we can. It just won't get me off."

It was obvious she was irritated. He started caressing her arm, the one exposed from where she still had her face pressed up against his pec. "El."

She groaned, and not the good kind. He was losing his erection and starting absent-mindedly tugging at himself, hoping that this conversation wasn't ending their morning together. The condom was starting to feel uncomfortable.

"Can we just pretend this never happened?"

"Uh," he paused. "Like do you want to get up and get dressed?"

"No! It's fine. Let's go back." She kissed his sternum and moved down to place another one where his hip met his thigh, then again the head of his dick where it rested near his belly button. She looked at him with a curious expression. "Okay?"

"If you want to," he chuckled, trying to be casual when in reality he wanted her lips on him more than anything. "But I think we're going to have another conversation about this later."

With a heavy nod and lowered eyelids, she put his entire head in her mouth, and even with protection, her tongue flicked back and forth to create nothing but complete euphoria. She grabbed the base with one hand and started removing the thin piece of latex that separated them.

"Tastes bad."

He nodded. "Um, I'm clean. I got tested ah-after the last time I had s-sex" — he gasped with the new raw touch — "four years, *oh*, ago."

She hummed around him, and this time he lost control and accidentally forced his hips up, plunging his length deeper into her mouth. It only further encouraged her.

How did he find her? How was this real life? He'd never been so turned on by someone he felt so completely safe with. Not to mention someone who was just as enthusiastic as he felt. With a dramatic sucking noise, she used her spit to help jack him off, kissing him everywhere she could reach.

"Fuck, El." He could feel the pressure building, and she picked up the pace to match his involuntary thrusts. "I'm gonna, gonna cum. Oh gah," he gasped and soon his own stomach clenched as Ellie released him from her mouth, causing his load to paint his stomach in white ribbons.

For a second, he forgot where he was, who he was with. But then there was Ellie, gently caressing his hip, coaxing him down from his high. She leaned forward to place a kiss in his mess. Delusional from the erotica that unfolded in front of him, he groaned.

"I'm so fucking hot for you, Ellie," was all he could get out before her wet lips were on his.

This was secretly one of his favorite things, a hidden kink discovered when he was with other guys. It bled over onto any sexual encounter that consented to it. Some people hated it. Ellie and Cyrus were not those people. She hovered above his mouth, inches away from his face.

A single strand of spit, cum, whatever, connected them.

"I can't wait to do that again."

"Me either," he whispered into a smile as she placed delicate kisses on his jaw, then trailed down to his neck. The heat dissipated around them until he couldn't stand it anymore. "Is that my new name then? 'Cy'?"

"Shut up," she collapsed onto him, laughing. "I never want to leave this bed."

"I mean, that's always an option."

She looked up at him with an unamused expression.

Right, because they were adults. She probably had to get up and head back to the farm, but if Cyrus had his way, they would stay here the rest of the day, weaving in and out of the pleasure they'd now created. The world didn't need exploring when their bodies were newly discovered works of art, and he was set on becoming a connoisseur.

CHAPTER 15

Ellie

What started off as a standard journey back to Meriden from Wakuta, quickly turned into a drive of shame, causing Ellie to spiral into second guessing herself and the choices of the morning.

During the first few minutes, she caught herself smiling at nothing, grinning at the memory of Cyrus's hands and mouth and skin. *God, his skin.* There was something addictive about it, tasting of salt and body wash, smelling of some sort of cologne he kept in his bathroom. Probably something expensive.

By mile 10 on the highway, the thought of him compromising sex for a blowjob crept into her mind. Embarrassment ignited in her stomach sending heat to her cheeks and ears. She had to get over this. Even if it was Tyler's voice, the words stung in her subconscious, *"So are you just gonna be a virgin the rest of your life?"* It was a dumb thing for him to say, bullying her into something that eventually made her feel wrung out and used. But with Cyrus, she felt zero pressure. That, of course, grated against everything that Ellie worked towards, always trying to make everyone around her feel comfortable. Usually at the expense of her own comfort. Case in point.

At the exit, tears prickled her eyes. She couldn't actually think that Cyrus was someone that was going to date her for the long haul. He was leaving soon. He was never meant to stay in Minnesota. And how the hell was she going to explain this to everyone in the neighborhood?

"Oh, yeah, Cyrus and I are dating, but only for summer. Then we'll all never see him again."

So here she was, sitting in her truck, clutching to what was left of her dignity after a glance in the mirror showed her eyes and nose were red with emotion. Her head ached. Her body felt heavy. It could have been from the twelve hours of rest she got by accidentally falling asleep before 9 PM on a Saturday. Or it could have been regret.

As she walked through the front door, her dad sat at the kitchen table reading the Sunday county paper as WCCO Radio drawled in the background.

"Oh, morning Ellie. Well, I guess it's technically afternoon," he smiled. "How was Cyrus?"

The question threw her off. She panicked. "Um, good. Fine. Uh. Is it that obvious?"

Doug lowered the paper, giving her a smirk over his reading glasses. She froze.

"How long has it been? If you don't mind me asking."

"Um, just a few weeks. Actually, wait. It's only been one week I guess."

"Whatever you say."

"What do you mean, 'Whatever I say?'"

"You couldn't stop talking about him, Ellie," he chuckled. "You gabbed on about him for an hour his first day here."

"That's because I was annoyed with him."

"Funny way of showing it, taking him shopping, inviting him to Community Nights, having him up here for lunch. Have you figured out what you're doing when he leaves?"

Her mouth hung open, piecing together just how long she potentially had feelings for him and what the hell she was going to do about it. She didn't have an answer about the future.

"Well, anyway," Doug continued, interrupting her inner monologue. "I hope he's treating you right. You being careful?"

No, she wasn't being careful.

"Where's mom?"

The burn was already creeping up her throat.

His brows furrowed with the quick change of subject. "With the Kerns, why?"

"I'll be upstairs," she got out before running up the steps, tears itching in her eyes.

She plopped down on her bed and cried. The kind of guttural cry that scratched her throat and clenched her stomach in a dry heave. What *was* this? What was she *doing*? Cyrus was leaving in a matter of months to return home to a life she had no connection to. There would be no reason for him to even think about Meriden and her farm once he was back in New York.

She needed someone to tell her what to do, to shake her straight and tell her to stop. Someone who knew everything about her relationships, or lack thereof.

Seconds later, Hannah picked up.

"Hey Bellie!" It was the name that derived from years of revisions: Elizabeth, Ellie Beth, to Ellie Bellie, Bellie Bean, Bellie

Bug. Now just, Bellie. Hannah was the only person that could use it.

"Hannah, I think I'm doing something really dumb," her voice cracked from crying, high pitched and breathy.

"Oh, doubtful. What's going on, Bug?" Her voice was soothing. Some sort of big sister magic. "Is this about wanting to move out? You can always come here for a bit. I know how Mom and Dad can get."

"No, it's not that. It's a stupid boy, Hannah."

"I see," she dropped her tone. Hannah hated Tyler. He was the reason they fought more than anything else in high school, well outside of what sisters normally fight about, anyway. "Is it this Cyrus guy mom keeps talking about?"

"Yeah, him."

"New York, lots of money, weirdly loves gardening, and is getting his PhD like some nerd?" So mom really had been talking about him.

"Yes," Ellie cried some more. "We had sex."

This was Hannah's cue. "Shit, Ellie. What happened? Did he do something? Are you okay?"

"I feel so broken," she started. She continued to tell her everything about last night, the meal, the dessert, the loneliness Cyrus had experienced, the revolutionary orgasms, and of course, the lack of *actual* sex.

Hannah cut her off. "Ellie, you had sex. Stop. How many times have I told you that a penis in your vagina isn't the only kind of real sex?" Ellie was crying too hard to answer. "What did he say to you? How did he react?"

"He was perfect! He said we didn't have to, but I'm sure he was disappointed. What if he never wants to touch me again?"

"Ellie," Hannah had her mom voice on. "You're spiraling. He sounds kind of nice. Like, maybe you aren't doing anything dumb. And maybe that's scary?"

Ellie whimpered. That wasn't what she needed to hear. "He's leaving at the end of August."

"Well that, doesn't necessarily, ahh. Shit." Ellie finally calmed down a bit, glad to have gotten her point across. Everything about this was a terrible idea and what was worse, Cyrus was wonderful. "Well, you know that Florence was still finishing up school in Minnesota when I proposed. And that it was only eight months into us dating."

"Yes, everyone knew you were perfect for each other from the get go, thanks Hannah."

"No! Not everyone. Flor was scared shitless. There was no guarantee that she'd find work in Seattle. Which made us getting engaged that much more important to me."

"Hannah, I'm not getting engaged, Cyrus and I have been together for—"

"I'm not saying that! I'm trying to give you advice, Bellie. What I mean is, you both have choices to make and right now it maybe sounds like you have a choice to choose each other. Just choose each other. It's as easy as that."

"It's not, though."

"It could be."

"It can't be! He has a whole life back in New York. I have the farm. What are we supposed to do?"

Hannah sighed over the phone. Ellie was always too stubborn for anyone else's advice. "Flor would say you're being such a Taurus right now."

"Tell her that Cyrus is a Pisces," she chuckled, going along with the bit.

Hannah's voice muffled with a yell. "She says that's a good combination."

"Hmm. Dumb."

There was a pause, long enough to change the subject.

"Did mom tell you I'm coming home for Dad's birthday?"

"What, really? No! When did you decide that?"

"I just told mom this morning, and when I asked her to hand the phone to you, she said you were with Cyrus," Hannah poked.

"Are you bringing the kids?"

"Yep, Florence, too." This was exactly the kind of news Ellie needed today. She hadn't seen Emelia and Leo in months. "So I'll see you in a couple weeks, Bellie Bug."

"You literally are forbidden to call me that around him."

"Hmm, if you two last that long."

"Hannah!"

She laughed over the phone and they hung up, but not before Hannah got a final word in, "Lean into it, Ellie. And don't let yourself get in the way."

Easier said than done.

*　　*　　*

"She loved broccoli as a kid. What kind of child prefers broccoli over chicken strips?" Doug laughed into another bite of stir fry.

The topic of Ellie's childhood was brought up at the dinner table, after Cyrus agreed to finally stay to eat with them one night. Ellie may have told her parents about the "eating alone" comment and they all but berated him when he was getting ready to leave. It was a few nights after her call with Hannah, which gave her strength and stress now that *choosing him* was kind of always top of mind. Partially because Cyrus was always top of mind, and usually about ten feet away from her. They kissed in the morning, chatted in the field before lunch, and kissed some more in the afternoon. It was all a bit surreal.

But here they were, eating dinner as a family and laughing as if they had been eating dinner together for years. Ellie's stomach hurt from the laughter and from the nerves. But not enough to miss out on stir fry night.

"So she really has always had a good head on her shoulders," Cyrus remarked, kicking her foot under the table. Great, now they were playing footsie.

Martha picked up where Doug left off. "I don't know about that. Remember when you found the abandoned newborn kittens in the old granary?" She turned to Cyrus. "We didn't sleep for a week. Hourly feeding, constantly washing the sheets. She wouldn't let them out of her sight."

Cyrus cooed, "Aw, what were you, seven? Eight?"

"Try sixteen," Martha answered. More laughter.

Ellie placed her head in her hands and she felt Cyrus grab at her shoulder.

"Honestly, I wouldn't expect anything less." He smiled at her as if she was the only one in the room and she wished it were true.

Martha also seemed to notice the gooey eyes, and she jumped in again. "Say Cyrus, we're having a bit of a party here for Doug's sixtieth. Would you want to come to that?"

"Oh, Mom. We should probably ask Dad that, it's *his* birthday."

"What day?" Cyrus asked, already taking his phone out to check his calendar.

"It's two weeks from this Thursday. Ellie's sister, Hannah, is coming." Martha's eyes sparkled; Hannah always was her favorite. "She and Florence are bringing Emelia and Leo. Oh, I can't wait."

"Are you sure, Dad?"

"Huh?" Doug finally looked up, his fork halfway to his mouth. "Oh, of course! Cyrus is welcome here anytime. Who else are we going to share your embarrassing childhood stories with? Hannah knows 'em all." With a comment like that, it was probably going to be hell, but Ellie couldn't stop smiling.

During their goodbyes in the driveway, Cyrus kissed her as if they hadn't seen each other all day, shielded by the garage and his car. It would have been PG until his fingers roamed up the front of her shirt.

"Hey, hey," she said, straightening her clothes and holding his hands so they wouldn't retaliate. "You'll be here all night if you start."

"Hmm, that wouldn't be the worst idea." His mouth attached to her neck, kissing down her shoulder and holding her close. The pressure of his embrace felt good, reassuring. They stayed like that for at least a full minute, recharging from the day.

"Are you okay with me coming to your dad's birthday?" asked Cyrus, his voice muffled into her sage green corduroy jacket.

"Yeah. Hannah wants to meet you. Do you feel weird about it?"

"Not even a little. And *that* I feel weird about."

Ellie took a deep breath and stepped back. "Same."

CHAPTER 16

Ellie

She wanted to push it away. Ignore it and pretend it ever existed. But her feelings for Cyrus were like the silver maple tree on the farm, begging to be noticed. The details of their summer blanketed her mind like the helicopter seeds that sprinkled the lawn each spring, touching every surface and blowing wild on windy days.

It started off like every weed does, annoying and determined, breaking through even the most concrete of surfaces. Soon enough it developed a few leaves, and those leaves turned the sunshine of his smile into life. Beautiful, blooming life. With every lunch at the house, morning kiss, private moment making dinner at his apartment, the seedling developed roots, securing itself to her day-to-day. If she let it grow any longer, who knows what it would destroy in its wake? Who knows what fruit it would bear?

Cyrus was doing everything right, working at the farm until evening, assisting with the height of a July harvest. Markets were his favorite place. He could never help but list everything on the stand.

"Cilantro, basil, parsley, thyme, rosemary, sage, oregano, and that's just herbs alone! Swiss chard, kale, romaine, heirloom tomatoes, beets, radishes, zucchini, patty pans, kohlrabi, cucumbers, bell peppers," — at this point, Ellie was usually laughing — "sweet peppers, jalapeños, red onions, white onions, spring onions, carrots, holy shit, El," he would say and like clockwork he'd count on his fingers, "that's almost twenty five different vegetables." Helen was almost as excited as him when the tomatoes filled half the stand.

It was true the farm was in full swing. It kept Ellie's mind busy with the hustle and bustle of constant physical labor. August was soon approaching and her inner monologue wouldn't shut up. *He's leaving soon. Long distance won't work. He hasn't even mentioned it.*

The best distraction was him. His lips, his touch, his kisses, under her shirt in the shed, after lunch and before Community Night. Whenever they had a moment alone, it felt like they could exhale. Each moment pretending they were anything else but lovers exhausted Ellie to no end. But as much as Cyrus was all consuming in her mind, she still couldn't talk about it. Not yet, at least.

After another Saturday market, Cyrus had some big deadline for his doctorate, and Ellie had a birthday party to attend for a newly turned three-year-old, Andrew Kern. Loretta asked where he was, and immediately Ellie felt the significance of Cyrus's presence at Community Nights. It didn't feel like a Meriden gathering without him anymore. She held back tears watching

Andrew blow out his candles, but it might have also been for the fact that Felix and Noah held hands the entire night, and Marisol was showing. Time stopped for no one, not even the people she loved. Roots sank deeper. Another ring formed beneath the bark.

They also hadn't had a chance to talk about the pest buzzing in Ellie's mind, like a wasp ready to sting without abandon. After the market the following Saturday she, in fact, loved Cyrus. It came to her during a heated moment in bed, bare and vulnerable and spread open in every way possible for Cyrus to abuse.

He never did.

"I'm not going to hurt you, El," he promised recklessly. "I'll chuck the box of condoms, I'll only use my hands, my mouth. It's fine. I never want to pressure you into anything." They were fighting. Laughing, naked, fighting.

"You'll get bored!"

"You don't get to decide that for me."

"Cyrus!"

"No more talking. Three minutes," he scolded, smiling into his kisses on every inch of skin he could find.

Her laughter poured out easily and by the second orgasm, tears began to fall, her body coaxed into a climax with words that would never sound the same out of anyone else's mouth.

"It's okay, El. Let go. I got you. You're okay."

She loved him. It would be the biggest secret she kept. The deepest, most inner thought that would never see the light of day.

Silver maples revealed the truth of nature. Majestic and wild, soft and tender, but the growth is uncontrollable. War or acceptance, those were the two options. As each day passed, new branches touched the corners of her life. The root system surfaced. Cyrus was spreading faster than she could manage. And all Ellie could do was sit in the shade as he kissed her on the open mouth, tasting of peppermint and honey. Acceptance turned sweeter and sweeter everyday.

It nearly became too much, but then Hannah was pulling into the driveway, steady and ready to hold her together on a dark, misty August evening. Her arms wrapped firmly around Ellie's shoulders.

"You have no idea how happy I am that you're home."

"Jesus, Bellie Bug. You're wound up tighter than a drum. What's going on?" Ellie might have been shaking.

The soft voice in her ear was all it took for tears to flood her eyes. She wiped them away, determined to hold it together in front of their parents. Hannah jumped into action.

"Alright, Flor, you have the kids tonight." Martha already had Emelia hoisted up on her hip as Leo waddled towards Doug. "Sister night in the shed! No ones allowed except Bellie Bug, myself, and the bottle of Merlot I smuggled in my suitcase. Deal?"

"We don't even get a hello?" Martha whined. Hannah obediently hugged her with a huff while Florence winked at Ellie and opened the trunk, fetching the Merlot.

The wine was a twist off, and they didn't have cups, but it wasn't the first time this exact scenario took place in the shed. In fact, it was exactly the third time. The first was when Hannah came out to Ellie in high school, the second was during Ellie's final breakup with Tyler, and now, it was all about Cyrus. Ellie never liked owing someone a favor, but Hannah had one on her after tonight. The two of them sat side by side on the workbench. Their feet dangled in sync.

"Alright," Hannah started, taking the initial swig from the bottle. "Tell me everything."

"Cyrus is leaving in two weeks. And I feel like a fucking soldier's wife—"

"Dramatic, but sure."

"—who has to say goodbye to someone who I may never see again." Ellie took the bottle from her, chugging two large gulps but instantly regretting it with a shudder. "And we haven't talked about anything. I don't know how he doesn't talk about stuff like this, about his *future*. What goes on in his head all day?"

Hannah rolled her eyes. "You'd be surprised by how little men think about anything."

"Hannah."

"I'm just saying, in my experience, they don't even care if you're a lesbian, as long as you're down to fuck."

"Cyrus isn't like that." She paused, needing to defend him. "At least, he hasn't seemed like that."

"Mhmm," Hannah hummed, taking the bottle from her. "And where is he tonight?"

"I told him to stay home. He wanted to be here, but I wouldn't let him. I needed to talk to you."

"And he listened?"

She chuckled, "Yeah he tends to do that now. It's weird."

Silence fell briefly. The only sounds were the whir of the walk-in cooler and the two passing the dark green bottle back and forth, taking sip after sip. It was all going to Ellie's head. Her shoulders relaxed where she didn't realize there was tension.

"Did you ever consider long-distance with you and Florence if she didn't get a job in Seattle?"

Hannah leaned back on the workbench, eyes wandering in thought. "No, I don't think so. I mean, our relationship had so many of the red flags people talk about with queer couples, like don't marry your first girlfriend, and don't move in together within the first year. But we were roommates, so it took that out of the picture."

They both laughed and repeated, "*Roommates.*"

"I just knew. All of the weird firsts were a little out of order."

"That's how I feel with Cyrus," Ellie said, lying back completely. The rafters needed to be dusted, there was so much crap up there. "He's already met our parents, he knows what I do for a living, he's met half the county at the farmer's market. Plus, he knows the entire neighborhood. All before having our first kiss. It's all backwards."

"Or you could look at it this way. He passed all of those tests, and you still want to bang him."

"Ew!"

"No. Not ew. Aw," Hannah laughed. The comfortable silence fell again before Hannah broke it in two. "If it makes you feel any better, Florence said no the first time I asked her to marry me."

"Uh, what?" Ellie sat up.

"Yep. I didn't tell anyone, for obvious reasons. It only took a day to change her mind. It was everyone else in her head that told her it was too soon. That's what she told me while she begged me to take her back. I thought we were over."

"And you're just telling me this now?!"

"I figured you're a little in your head. You always get in your head about things you care about. And I know you care a lot, Bellie, but you should try to listen to yourself on this one."

"Listening to myself feels harder."

"Well, yeah. That's the point." She took the half empty bottle and offered it to Ellie. "Do you love him?"

Ellie swallowed another sip, now edging from buzzed to drunk. "I'm not answering that."

"So yes."

"No."

"Who are you lying to, me or yourself?" She leaned over Ellie, whispering with the grin of the Cheshire Cat. "It's okay if you do. Remember? It's all backwards."

Cyrus

"Congratulations, Cyrus. Or should I say, Dr. Lexington."

"You're shitting me," Cyrus said back, not believing Brad's words.

"Nope. Got the verbal confirmation from your committee today. Email should be coming sometime tomorrow."

Thank god Ellie forbid him from coming to the farm tonight, he wouldn't have been able to keep it a secret. And that's exactly what he intended to do, at least for the next twenty four hours. The truth was that he technically had to fulfill the work contract until August 26th. And per Brad, his induction would be in an informal ceremony the week after. Since it was over the summer semester, it would be an intimate gathering, a precursor to the actual commencement for all PhD recipients in the Spring.

This was really it.

This was the end of his education.

What the *fuck* was he going to do?

As if she could read his mind from thirty miles away, Ellie called.

"Hello?" His voice was groggier than he meant it to be.

"Hiii, oh crap. Did I wake you?"

"A little." He looked at his bedside clock. "It's after eleven, what are you doing up?"

"I just, uh, wanted to talk. I may have had like, three glasses of wine. Hannah's here! The kids are, too. You'll get to meet them. Are you coming to the farm tomorrow? Wait, you'll be at my dad's thing. Sorry." She was rambling, but he couldn't hide a smile.

"It's okay. Back to your earlier statement. Did you say you've been drinking, El?"

"Um, Hannah brought a bottle of wine. We drank it in the shed. I just, like, needed to talk to her. I missed her so much."

He could understand that. Maren and Aurora used to hide out in their rooms late into the night. Back when things weren't so complicated. He really needed to call her back. He yawned into a question, "What did you two talk about?"

"Uh, like, sister stuff. I don't know. Um," she giggled. She sounded like a thirteen year old. "I told her a little about you."

"Ahh, you were talking about me, I see."

"I mean, not the whole time." *Sure, El.* "But a little, yeah." She giggled again and Cyrus couldn't help himself.

"Do you have a crush on me?"

"Stop!"

"You do, don't you. Oh my god, El. Can I tell you a secret?"

"Cyrus." She stifled her laugh into the phone, and a warm tingle spread through him.

He whispered, "I have a crush on you, too."

"Okay." He fought a full blown laugh. She continued to surprise him at every turn. "I can't wait to see you tomorrow."

"El, that's the most sincere thing you've ever said to me."

"Not true."

Cyrus paused without knowing where to take the conversation. He just wanted to stay on the line. She was talking again before anything got awkward.

"Do you sometimes feel like you have to put up with me?"

"Nah, I got my own shit. Yours is funnier."

Another pause.

"I wish you were here." The sincerity kept coming.

"Hmm, I wish I was, too. But, it's almost midnight and I have to be at a farm by seven in the morning. My boss is a hardass."

"I'm not your boss!"

He laughed, "But you stand by the hardass statement."

"No comment."

He chuckled and hummed. "Goodnight, El."

"Goodnight, Cy."

He gasped at the nickname, but she hung up before he could poke at it. How the hell was he supposed to fall asleep now?

CHAPTER 17

Cyrus

The bluest August sky welcomed him to the farm a few minutes before seven in the morning. Cool, dewy, and smelling of freshly cut grass, it really was one of the most beautiful places he'd ever seen.

Ellie popped out of the house in sweats, still not in her work clothes. "Cyrus! Come inside," she yelled from the front porch and waved him in.

The scene in front of him was straight out of a storybook, the kind that he read as a kid but never quite experienced himself. He was met with a house smelling of maple syrup and coffee, alive with the sizzle of breakfast sausages in a cast iron skillet. A five year old ran between a woman at the stove and Martha at the kitchen table, showing off a drawing with red and blue crayon strokes. A toddler-aged boy sat on another woman's lap, a female lookalike of

Doug, who was filling up his coffee at the counter. Ellie was beside him, pouring hot water into a mug with a tea bag before handing it to Cyrus.

"Good morning." She placed her cheek on his shoulder.

"Hey you." Their brief moment faded as her dad walked past Cyrus and gave him a pat on the arm. "Happy birthday, Doug."

"Thanks, Cyrus." Doug raised his refilled coffee mug with a bright smile.

"Everyone, this is Cyrus," Ellie announced.

"Cyrus!" The woman at the breakfast table was up first, opening an arm while moving the young boy to her hip. "I'm so glad to meet you." She wore denim overalls and smelled like sandalwood. This had to be Hannah.

"Hannah, right?"

"Yes, well done. This is Leo," she grabbed the boy's pudgy arm and waved it. He stared blankly before diving into Hannah's neck, terrified of the stranger. "He's pretty shy this morning. Didn't get a great night's sleep in the new space." She winked and pointed to the stove. "That's Florence, my wife. And Emelia is running around here somewhere."

"She currently has her face in my crotch," Florence piped.

A blonde head of curly hair poked between her legs, right under her butt.

"Hi," the tiny voice said.

Florence twisted around to speak to him. She had a short blonde bob, high cheekbones, and big green eyes.

"Nice to meet you, Cyrus. This is exactly how Emelia always is, so I'm not even going to apologize for her."

He laughed into a sip of tea. Lemon ginger today. Delicious. Ellie's hand slinked around under the fabric of his overalls and his chest constricted with emotion. This was all he ever wanted.

"So, we should probably head to the field after we eat. Does anyone want to pick vegetables?"

Ellie's question was obviously for Emelia, and she took the bait, hanging off her mom's sweatpants. "Me! Me!"

"Em, if you pants me in front of my in-laws, I swear to God," Florence laughed, shifting her attention from the pan to her daughter. She knelt down to eye level. "Did you bring farm clothes like Momma asked?"

Emelia's curls bounced as she nodded vigorously.

"Alright, head upstairs to change. I'll be up in a minute to help." Emelia turned around and with a love tap to the rear, Florence stood up to finish the sausages. "These are probably done, you guys ready to eat?"

Cyrus was amused by the entire exchange, but jumped in to help Ellie set the table, chatting a bit with Hannah and learning that even if she didn't look the part, she worked for a huge tech firm in Seattle that specialized in gaming software. Her title was Head Programmer, and she got into the business because of Florence, who was a digital artist at the same company. Before that she worked in e-commerce and wanted to die. *Relatable,* Cyrus thought.

The pancakes were better than any restaurant he'd been to in New York. Granted, he couldn't remember ever ordering pancakes at a Michelin star restaurant before, but something about them hit the spot. They paired perfectly with the sausages and scrambled eggs that Florence made.

"The secret is to put maple extract in the batter. Makes everything taste like it's supposed to," Florence divulged, right before Emelia's little hand crept up on his shoulder. He flinched with her sudden appearance.

"Are you and Ellie married?" she whispered in his ear, loud enough for her mom to hear every word. Florence put her hand over her eyes, barely hiding a rub to the temples.

"No, we're just dating right now," he whispered back, shielding his mouth from the room.

"Why?"

"Because I love her," he answered just below a whisper and felt his body exhale. It was the most honest thing he'd felt in the last week.

"Oh, that's good!" the five year old practically yelled, disrupting the unspoken agreement between them. She proceeded to run around the table to Hannah.

"Momma, can we go pick vegetables now?"

Ellie raised her hand to answer. "Absolutely. Let's head out!"

Everyone but Florence and Martha followed them to the field, and within a few hours the pick list was complete, albeit, with a few less snap peas, cucumbers and carrots that served as snacks throughout the morning. Emelia and Leo were amazed, dunking their hands into the soil as if it were magic. Leo had a particular affinity to the worms. His eyes brightened while watching them squirm in his miniature hands and twirl around his chubby fingers. Cyrus watched on with a smile, taken by the same curiosity that got him into botany.

"They act like we never take them outside," Hannah noted to him, chuckling with upturned eyebrows. "We literally have a garden in our backyard."

With the extra help they were able to fill the cooler, eat lunch, wash, pack the produce, and box it up for CSA shares all before 4 PM, giving them plenty of time to clean up and prepare for Doug's party that night. In a sacred moment of peace, Cyrus and Ellie were the only two upstairs, showering last and changing for the festivities.

The entire time under the spray of water, he was in his head. He wasn't going to make it 24 hours with the news of his doctoral review accepting his research. He had to tell her. After putting it off for as long as he could stand, he needed to know what was going on in her mind.

Cyrus walked into her room wearing a towel and found Ellie in an off the shoulder sage dress that flowed down to her ankles. He couldn't help himself, and kissed the bare skin as she finished her makeup in the mirror.

"Well, hello," she whispered, reaching for his jaw to properly greet him, tasting of toothpaste and smelling floral. He moved to the bed, watching her put the final touches on her blush.

"How was the shower?"

She must not have noticed how nervous he was. "It was fine," he chuckled. It was anything but.

His clothes were laid out next to him, but he refused to get dressed. If he could focus on her for a few more minutes, maybe it would be easier for him to bring it up, especially if he was rejected. His lack of movement got her attention.

"Everything alright over there?"

He wiped his eyes. He could blame it on the shower.

"Um, I found out that my dissertation was accepted. My final presentation was a little over a week ago, but I got the news yesterday. So, I'm finally getting my PhD. The official email came this morning."

On cue, Ellie rushed over to him, pushing him back on the bed with a full body hug around his neck. "Cyrus! That's amazing news!"

His arms squeezed her tight, afraid that this would be one of the last times.

"Yeah, and um, I know you don't want to talk about it, El. I know we've been putting it off, but I wanted to ask you something."

She sat up, her face looking pale, even through the summer glow and the blush she had applied.

"Okay." She swallowed.

"My last day on the farm is soon," his voice caught. What the *fuck?* Out of every scenario he made up in his mind, he never thought he would start crying. "And I was wondering if you wanted to come to New York with me. For my induction ceremony. It's the first week in September, a Friday. And maybe we could fly out the weekend before. There are some friends I want you to meet, and then we'd take a rental up to Ithaca. I know it's a busy time here on the farm, but I can't imagine you not there now. And," he stopped. A fucking tear streamed down his cheek. Ellie wiped it away before it traveled to his chin. "And, I don't want to say goodbye yet."

"Me either."

"I can pay for your ticket, I can pay for everything—"

"Cyrus, no. I can't have you do that."

"Ellie, please. Come with me. Just for a week. And then we'll figure it out."

"The farm," she whispered, struggling to land on an actual answer for Cyrus. "I don't even know what an induction ceremony is."

Panic set in. Embarrassment enveloped his senses, his tongue stuck to the roof of his mouth, his vision blurred with tears. He was too much. This was too soon. The obsession and addiction led him to this, falling head over heels for someone who didn't feel the same way.

"Yeah, you're right." He cleared his throat. "It would be a lot. It's okay. This place needs you, I can't take you away—"

"Oh goodness, Cyrus."

"But, if you came with, y-you—"

"I'm coming with!"

He tried to find his way in her hazel eyes. "Wait. Really?"

"I'll just need to ask around to see if someone can harvest. But Felix has been doing great working markets, and my mom and dad can probably step in. Oh, Cyrus," she whispered, kissed him, and pushed away the damp hair clinging to his cheekbones, "how could you even think I'd say no?"

"You didn't answer right away, I thought you were being nice! We haven't talked about anything."

She stood and clenched her fists in her classic Ellie's-mad-about-something-but-is-still-smiling stance. "You never brought it up!"

"You, early on, said that you didn't want to talk about it because you didn't want to overthink it," he said as a matter of fact. He poked her belly from where she stood in front of him as he sat on the bed.

"That was over a month ago!"

"Well, I hadn't heard anything different." His hands reached out to her waist, inviting her back into his space to plant kisses on her cheeks and chin and forehead. "I can't wait to spoil you rotten."

"Cyrus!" She pushed away from the sincerity, laughing at the onslaught of pecks. "You're not paying for my ticket. I'm very serious."

"Uh huh, yes, you sound serious."

He kissed her fully this time, pulling her into his lap and letting his hands run free up her back. The scent of gardenias filled his nose as it bumped against hers, shifting for the best angle to bring their mouths closer together. Her tongue teased him, licking his upper lip before diving in for more. Their responsibilities for the day slipped away as Cyrus's hand pulled down her dress, exposing her nipples while Ellie undid his towel, palming his cock with just the right amount of pressure. Just as he latched onto a patch of skin on her sternum, footsteps outside the door broke them apart. Thank god for the squeaks of an old floorboard.

"You guys almost ready? We could use some help in the kitchen!" It was Hannah.

Ellie took the lead. "Yeah, yep! We're changing. Out in a minute!" She turned back to Cyrus, grimacing and laughing silently.

"If you two are having sex, I'm telling Mom."

"Hannah!"

Cyrus laughed and fell back on the bed, now sporting a full blown boner that was destined for desuetude.

"We should probably get going," Ellie whispered, putting herself back in the dress and going over to the mirror.

He pointed at his erection. "And what am I supposed to do with this?"

"Think prudish thoughts. Toe fungus, the smell of a rotten tomato, Helen's blue eye shadow."

"Alright, it's gone."

She burst with laughter.

They were out the door and down the stairs in record time, helping in the kitchen with a pasta dish, grilled chicken, and a tomato salad full of basil and balsamic vinegar. Similar to all the other Community Nights on Thursdays at the farm, this one included all the neighbors, plus some new faces that were staples in Doug's life it seemed. Ellie introduced him to them all. Rick, an old farmer friend who helped Doug with equipment during the financial crisis. Mary and Bruce, a couple he graduated with at the University in Wakuta back in the day. Isabelle's grandfather who played cards with Doug back in the '90s.

The trio was on the stage once more, playing old Eagles tunes that Doug must have requested, since he was singing along to every word. Felix and Noah held hands under the table, Cyrus noticed, and so he did the same with Ellie, only they were less discreet.

He didn't mean to be so forward with it, but when the band played "Take It Easy," Cyrus grabbed Ellie and dragged her up to where others were dancing on the grass, swaying to the music.

"This song was written specifically for you," he joked, holding her waist in one hand as their fingers intertwined in the other.

Even with an eye roll, her free hand hooked under his armpit as they spun around, bouncing with the upbeat harmonies of Lance and Jason. The lyrics were a little too on the nose. Cyrus tried to focus on Lance's keyboard solo and the smell of Ellie's hair. The song nearly finished, and he stepped back to twirl her under the twinkling lights in the maple tree. She smiled and kissed him for all to see, and it symbolized how he felt, open and free.

Ellie stepped away to refill the cooler with waters, and a gentle hand brushed his hip just as he lost himself in the breeze.

"Hello, my precious pumpkin," Loretta greeted. His eyes popped open and he wrapped an arm around her shoulder, nearly a foot shorter than his. "You taking care of her?"

"I'm trying to."

They watched the two new lovers, Felix and Noah, dance like it was some big joke, holding hands but bumping into other couples, laughing and hugging and laughing some more. They both chuckled before Loretta turned to him.

"She'll never just be yours, you know. She'll always be our sweet Ellie."

A scratch developed in his throat. "Wouldn't want it any other way."

"And Cyrus," she whispered, standing on her toes with a gentle pat on his back, "you'll always be ours, too."

His emotions only let him respond with a teary nod before she was off with a wink. He put it away before Ellie's eyes found him across the yard just as opening notes of "Shower the People" by James Taylor played from the trio. He felt the magnetic force pull him towards her, reaching out his hand for her to take in an easy slow dance. He held her hand close to his chest, clinging to her waist as Ellie's head rested against his shoulder.

Martha was watching on with a blissful smile, dancing with Doug who was still singing along. Hannah, Florence, Isabelle, and Maya monitored the children, each couple hand in hand, as Emelia and Leo jumped around with Brielle and Grace Ortega. Little Andrew Kern was in on it, too, finding a quick friend in Leo who was the same size.

At this point in the summer, Marisol was showing, swaying with a doting Loretta just out of reach from the dancing crew holding down the dance floor. A dance floor that Jason's girlfriend, Caroline, and Trang avoided like the plague at one of the tables near the food. They managed to stay clear of the chaos but smiled up at the stage, admiring the talents of the people they loved.

And that's really all it was about, wasn't it? People. Loving people. It had never occurred to Cyrus before, but every time he chased his own pleasure from another person or a high at a club, he was really just looking for this. A bunch of people who loved each other, spending time together, even after years of knowing every intricacy, every detail of their lives. What had he been so afraid of all this time? Being known?

The song stopped, and Ellie was wiping his face. He didn't even realize he was crying again.

"You're a little emotional tonight," she whispered, trying not to make a scene.

He chuckled to blow it off. "Yeah, sorry. Didn't realize it would be so weird to be done with school."

"Hey, you don't have to apologize. Can I get you anything? A drink? Some food?"

"Nah, I'm good right here."

Their attention was grabbed by a cake with an alarming amount of fiery candles held by Hannah. Lance found the key and played chords underneath the birthday song as the crowd joined in. It was the moment they were all leading up towards, made better by Ellie grabbing Cyrus's hand and squeezing it tightly.

The night still smelled of grass and dew now that the sun had set, mixed with the smoke of the blown out candles. It was the perfect night, and all Cyrus could think was, *where was he ever going to find this in New York?*

*　　　*　　　*

Ellie didn't end up coming home with him that night, which was expected. Instead, he stayed at the Somers', trading in a night with Ellie for a slumber party on the couch with every kid over the age of five in the neighborhood. Emelia, Grace, Brielle, Felix and Noah all took turns giggling and screaming at every noise around them, making sure to keep Cyrus from even one second of sleep the entire night. The girls were obsessed, piling onto his stomach, putting an assortment of Ellie's old clips and bows in his hair, and trying to get him to admit that he was ticklish. Which he had, several times. They still needed to prove his word.

Like a traitor, Ellie did nothing. He hadn't seen her laugh like this, so he let the kids torture him until they tired themselves out, sometime after one in the morning.

Felix and Noah were still awake, in whispered conversation with Ellie and Cyrus, acting all grown up as the adults in the room. Felix wasted no time in telling Noah about Cyrus, hoping to help his boyfriend.

"Cyrus is bi, too. He likes girls, just like you do. He's dating Ellie," Felix whispered, trying to coax Noah into talking. "Which I would like to say, I called, like two months ago."

Ellie smiled, lifting up slightly from where her head was in Cyrus's lap. "Noah, do you think you're bi?"

He nodded. "Yeah, I've had crushes on girls at school. But now that I want to be with Felix, I feel like no one is going to believe me, and we have camp this week, so everyone will see us together. They'll just call me gay."

"And there's nothing wrong with that, we've already established, thankyouverymuch," Felix corrected.

"I know! I know. Cyrus, was there ever a time where you weren't sure that you liked girls? Felix said you dated a boy for five years."

Pausing in thought, Cyrus stilled his fingers on Ellie's scalp. "Uh, it's different for everyone. But I always put it like this. Noah, do you have a celebrity crush?"

He nodded "Zendaya. And Shawn Mendes."

"Okay, true," Cyrus responded. Ellie giggled in his lap. "So, did you stop thinking Zendaya was pretty because you're dating Felix now?"

Noah looked shyly at his boyfriend, who smiled and egged him on. "No, I still think she's pretty."

"Exactly. Attraction doesn't just go away once you're with someone. So to me, that's why I consider myself bi. It doesn't depend on who you're dating right this second."

"That makes sense," Noah finally admitted, smiling back at Cyrus. "I've never thought about it like that."

Felix beamed. "Told you he was cool."

With a chuckle, Cyrus looked to Ellie to see if he said everything right, but she was fast asleep, as usual. He played the parent, telling the two teenagers that it was *actually* time to go to bed, and thankfully, they listened, nestling under the covers while facing each other.

"Hands where I can see them," Cyrus quipped.

They both instantly brought their hands out of the blankets, noses scrunched. Muffled laughter fell into their pillows.

Cyrus was a teenage boy once. And because of that, he knew that saying goodbye to Ellie was one thing, but saying goodbye to Felix would be that much harder. Hormones and big emotions sat at the surface, making every one of life's changes feel punchy and out of his control. If Cyrus had someone like him growing up, he'd never recover from saying goodbye.

So he was going to put it off until the very last minute.

*   *   *

The drive back to Wakuta the next day put Cyrus in a foul mood, made worse by an impromptu phone call the minute he walked through the door of his apartment. He knew he should give Ellie some time with her family, but it was hell knowing he had his own on his tail.

"Hi Cyrus, I'll patch you through." It was Angela again.

A click, a rustle. "Cyrus?"

"Dad," he answered, trying to sound normal.

"Did you have any news you'd like to tell me?" John's tone was accusatory. It reminded him of the days after his and Ian's first trip to Paris. He'd accidentally spent $5k in three days. That wasn't even why he was mad though, instead he scolded him for not using the right credit card that earned points overseas. Not, *hey, how'd the trip go?* Or, *we'd love to meet your boyfriend that you took to Paris.* Only the credit card thing. But Cyrus hadn't used his dad's credit card since Joe's Farm Mart.

"Um, news? I don't think so?"

"Really." It sounded less like a question, and more of an interrogation. Had his dad learned about Ellie? How could anyone have told them? "I just got off the phone with the Dean. I figured you would have already contacted the New York county court to get your name changed to Dr. Lexington."

"Oh, right. Yeah, my committee accepted my research. Commencement is next spring."

"And your induction is in two weeks."

Cyrus fought a sigh, even though his shoulders sank with disappointment. "Yeah, it is."

"Well, your mom and I will be there." *Fuck.* "It'll be nice to see you since you blew us off for the 4th."

"I told you, the farm was too busy to take time away," Cyrus bit back. It was partially true. On the actual 4th of July, Ellie insisted they take the afternoon off and have a barbeque before driving to Wakuta to watch fireworks with the rest of the Meriden crew.

"Yeah, you can tell that to your mom. Maren and Adam might come, too. Should be fun—"

"Why are they coming?"

"Because she's your older sister and she wants to see you." *Bullshit.* "They're going to make a trip of it, visit with a few of Adam's clients in Ithaca. I figure I'll take some Cornell folks out to lunch and listen to them beg." *There we go.* "We could take the jet back to Manhattan for dinner."

"*Dad.* Don't start."

"Fine. We'll stay in Ithaca and go to that French place downtown after the ceremony. I'll have Angela set it up. Five of us, right?"

Cyrus's itinerary with Ellie was dissolving with every word his father said. "This is kind of short notice. I might have plans."

"With who?" Interrogation again.

"With, with someone I've been seeing."

There was a pause. Long enough for his dad's judgment to settle in.

"What's his name?"

"El-Ellie," he stuttered. "And she's a girl."

"Hmm. Bring her with, then."

Before Cyrus could list all the reasons why that would be a terrible idea, his dad hung up. He threw his phone on his bed, yelling with frustration. This was not how any of this was supposed to go. Ellie didn't need to be exposed to his mom and dad, let alone his alcoholic sister and her brown nosing, spineless husband.

In retaliation, he opened his laptop and picked the two most expensive first class tickets to JFK, and pulled out his wallet. If Ellie had to deal with John and Gina Lexington, then John and Gina Lexington had to deal with a three thousand dollar credit card bill. That's how the game worked, and Cyrus was going to play it until he won.

CHAPTER 18

Ellie

"You're flying to New York in *first class*?!" Hannah took a swipe at Ellie's forearm at the dinner table.

"Cyrus invited me," she said, looking around the dinner table shyly. "It'll be nice to go with someone who knows the city. He says he wants to introduce me to his friends."

"Must be nice," Hannah hummed, raising her eyebrows.

Martha said the other thing everyone was thinking, "Things are pretty serious with you two, huh?"

"I don't know about that. I think we're going to try to figure it out or something after New York. But yeah, I like him a lot."

They all went back to eating, and luckily Emelia changed the subject to something about unicorns and how they eat glitter, rather than poop it out. A common misconception.

The next day, Cyrus came to the market as promised, giving Martha and Doug a morning off to spend with the grandchildren before Hannah and Florence took off that evening.

The busyness that came with just two people manning the stand during the height of summer harvest kept Cyrus and Ellie occupied. They managed to sneak in a few kisses and touches here and there, and it was cute until Cyrus put his hand in her back pocket and pinched until she shrieked. It made her laugh, but she pushed him away whenever he got close. That was, until later in the night, alone in his apartment, where she let him touch her all over. And over. *And over.* Saying goodbye to Hannah and the family was hard. Harder than expected. Luckily, Cyrus was there to piece her back together.

Time was moving faster than Ellie could handle. Every moment was the last of something; the last time harvesting carrots together, the last transplants of lettuce, even the last Monday, Tuesday, and so on felt sacred to Ellie in a way that she couldn't vocalize, or else she'd spiral and never stop.

The worst of the lasts was Community Night. The neighborhood buzzed about Ellie and Cyrus leaving for New York, but cheered them on in a way that felt genuine. Most folks had caught wind of their trip, and since they were openly kissing at Doug's birthday, their relationship, too. She also overheard Martha gushing about Cyrus to anyone who would listen. Maybe she liked it. Maybe if everyone else noticed him sink his roots into Meriden, they could all mourn the eventual loss together.

Before the band settled in, attention was quickly diverted from their travel plans to a glowing Jason and Caroline the minute they stepped into the backyard.

Loretta was the first to speak up, "Well aren't you two smiley tonight. Caroline, it's so good to see you." She leaned in for a kiss on the cheek, while Caroline juggled the flat bakery box she arrived with.

"We have a bit of news," Jason hinted.

Caroline made her way to the table filled with a smattering of egg rolls, enchiladas, and macaroni salads. The neighbors gathered round as Caroline and Jason made an effort to remove the lid together. Underneath was a frosted white cake adorning two wedding rings and silver lettering that read, *"She said yes!"*

The small crowd gasped and cried with excitement and congratulations.

"No way!" Maya was the first to cheer, running to Caroline in a bear hug that turned into a circle with Isabelle, Marisol, and Keather grabbing at her bejeweled left hand. Something clicked in Ellie's head. Lives were constantly in a state of beginning, middle, and end. What felt like a beginning for Jason and Caroline also aligned with the end of the summer. A new season approached. Different, but necessary.

Cyrus stepped up to Jason, patting him on the shoulder with a tight smile. "You finally did it!"

"Wait, you knew?" Ellie looked between the two.

"Cyrus was accidentally the first person who saw the ring. Ran into him in Wakuta the night I picked it up. What was that, two weeks ago? Thanks for keeping it close to the chest, man." They hugged and a tinge of sadness and guilt punctured Ellie's stomach with the understanding that she wasn't the only person Cyrus made an impact on this summer. Nothing would feel the same with his absence.

As folks continued to congratulate the happy couple and mill around the food table, Ellie and Cyrus ended up sitting with a cheery Felix and Noah.

"We missed you at the market, Felix. How was camp?" Cyrus asked, further driving the pain in Ellie's stomach. She wasn't hungry anymore.

Noah's eyes brightened.

"It was really good. We came out," Felix touted, matching Noah's grin. They shared a proud smile.

"Did anyone give you a hard time?" Cyrus asked.

Noah was more animated than Ellie had seen in recent memory. "No, that's the best part, Cyrus! One of our counselors has a boyfriend, too."

"Hell yeah, boys!"

"Can Noah come to the field next week, Ellie? It's the last week before school starts." Felix had his fists close to his chest, practically begging. "We can work with Cyrus!"

"Oh, um," she hesitated, glancing at Cyrus who looked about as guilty as she felt. "We're headed to New York this week, Felix. Cyrus finished his research and his work study program is done. I thought you knew."

"You're leaving?" he asked, eyebrows turned up.

"Well, yeah, my work out here was temporary. My last day on the farm is tomorrow," Cyrus joined in.

Felix turned to Ellie, his face dropping with disappointment, waiting for her to tell him something different. "Is he serious?"

"Felix, it was always set up like this. Remember? His contract is up when the summer is over, and next week is already September."

The waterworks began. "But how can you just leave? The whole neighborhood knows you. What about us? What about Noah?"

At this point, a few others had glanced over with the commotion, and Trang got up from her table with Lance. Noah remained uncomfortable at Felix's side, with a hand on his forearm as he stood from the table.

"Felix, I'm sorry, I should have told you sooner—"

"Sweetheart, he'll still be in touch. You can call him, or email. He just won't be at the farm," Ellie tried.

"Leaving us to go back to New York! Why did you even come here in the first place?!"

"I'm not—"

Before Cyrus could finish the thought, Felix ran. Stormed out between the tables and down the hill to the shed as Ellie rose from the table with a clamor. Trang chased her, but she put her hand out, signaling that she could handle this if Trang let her. With a nod, she followed Felix into the shed.

She found him sitting up on the workbench with his head in his hands, not much different than when she found him here three years ago, when he was first developing feelings for Noah. Not just friend feelings, but romantic, big feelings. Something about the shed always brought out the truth.

"Felix, I thought you knew."

He looked up at her with red rimmed eyes. "Why is he leaving?"

"I..." She shrugged. "He's done with his program, I don't know what else to tell you. I'm sad, too, Felix." She hoisted herself up next to him, offering an arm for him to fold into. "But, he lives in New York. He has a whole life there."

"But what about us? What about the life he has out here? Noah thinks he's like, the coolest person we've ever met. He's so nice, and he talks about things no one else will talk to us about."

Ellie reached out to hug him, letting him cry into her shoulder. "I know, Felix. I know."

"And what about you? Doesn't he love you? Doesn't he want to stay with you? What's the point of dating someone if they aren't going to stay?" He was asking the questions that she had been asking herself all summer. "You're not leaving, too, are you?"

"I'm not leaving, Felix," she confirmed. "We're coming back to Minnesota after New York, Cyrus has to pack up his apartment before he heads out."

He nodded, finally calming down enough to take a deep breath. "Do you think he's mad at me for saying what I said tonight?"

"It's nothing that a good 'sorry' can't fix."

Felix sat back up, wiping his eyes and looking off to the drawings on the wall. He was thinking about something, she could tell.

"I'll be the only person who's out in school, I know it. And who will I be able to talk to?"

"Hey, not the only person." Ellie put a comforting hand on his knee. "You have Noah, right? You have each other. Remember that. As long as you two have each other's backs, I think you'll be able to handle anything. And your dad is at school, so he can get the other teachers to support you." They bumped shoulders. "And you'll have me and the farm. And Meriden. We're all here for you, Felix." He fell into another hug that lasted for a few deep breaths. "You ready to go back out there?"

She felt a nod against her shoulder, and they eventually jumped down from the workbench, walking arm in arm back to the yard.

"Is the bitter melon ready?" Felix asked, barely looking up with how tall he was now.

"Yeah, it was in your share this week."

He broke away from Ellie without a word, running to his mom. Trang almost managed to hug him before he was squirming away and talking a mile a minute.

Their table had been cleared, and Noah returned to his parents, looking as dejected as Cyrus, sitting alone. Ellie approached him with a gentle hand on his shoulder, and Felix was back.

"Cyrus, I'm sorry for yelling at you."

"No, it's me who should be sorry—"

"Are you free for dinner tomorrow?"

Cyrus looked up at Ellie, as if he'd find the answer in her eyes. "Uh, I think so, yeah."

"Do you want to come over for dinner? My mom's going to make bitter melon soup. Maybe I can invite Noah! One sec," he muttered the last bit to himself before running to his mom again then moving to the Ortegas.

"Does he mean just me?" Cyrus whispered to Ellie.

A shrug was all she got out by the time Felix was back.

"Okay, Mom said Noah can come, too. Wait, Ellie, do you wanna come?"

She chuckled, "If you'd like me to."

"One sec." Felix was off again.

The silent conversation Ellie and Cyrus were having with each other now included Trang from across the backyard as Felix ran back.

"Okay, my mom said you both can come. Dad's gonna get papaya salad. It's really spicy. I'm going to go tell Noah."

He was off without another word.

*   *   *

The Khang house was straight out of a West Elm catalog. Strikingly sleek, modern, and yet full of life with the collage of colorful Felix originals on every wall. Themes of Vietnam interspersed along photographs. Although, most notably, the house smelled of pork and cilantro, welcoming Ellie and Cyrus into the kitchen that opened up into the dining room. Ellie had spent many weekends here, back when Felix was in grade school and the Khangs were new to town. It surfaced bittersweet memories full of uncertainty and hope.

Ellie watched Cyrus take a look at the artwork, shaking his head at each framed masterpiece. "I didn't know he could draw people, too? These are incredible."

"He's incredible."

"These aren't even his most recent." Trang followed them in the living room while Lance stirred a large pot at the stove. "I don't know who he got it from, definitely not me."

Rapid fire thuds on the carpeted staircase signaled that Felix was descending from upstairs and had company.

"Is the soup done yet, Mom?"

Trang nodded, but Noah nearly bumped into Felix on the steps with the sudden halt. "Cyrus!"

"Hey, you two," he smiled widely.

Lance shouted from the kitchen, "Soup is just about ready, boys! Felix, you wanna set the table?"

Ellie jumped in to help. She couldn't stop herself from overhearing Trang talk with Cyrus and Noah, all held up in conversation by the wall hangings. From the sounds of it, some were photos taken in Vietnam when Trang was young, others were of trips back home to visit her grandparents before Felix was born, but most were his artwork framed in matching white-stained wood. They hung near a sketched portrait of a teenage boy running in a field of wildflowers. His smile was bright and resembled Noah's.

"Felix showed me a drawing of some monarch caterpillars early in the summer, he said they were his favorite."

Noah nodded. "We caught some in the pasture last summer."

"Well, I'm sensing a pattern. He likes to draw his favorite things."

Ellie glanced up at a wide-eyed Felix, who was pointedly not looking up from the large bowl of rice he had just placed on the table. She looked back at Noah who had his face in his hands, but his smile was still visible, matching the one on the wall. Everyone in the room went a bit silent, relishing in the awkward cuteness of the two.

"Aaanyway," Felix giggled. "Wouldn't want the rice to get cold."

Trang chuckled with smiling eyes. "Let's eat!"

Felix did the honors of explaining every item on the table, both for Noah and Cyrus. Ellie had eaten this exact meal plenty of times, with the same perfectly cooked white rice and produce from her garden; green onion, cilantro, and this year, bitter melon.

"And then," he continued, peeling plastic wrap off a bowl of what Ellie knew was papaya salad. A savory and distinctly fishy smell filled the table. "My dad made a special trip to the cities to get papaya salad from Hmong Village. Have you ever had it, Cyrus?"

Cyrus's eyebrows raised. "Sure have, but only Thai style. Is this Laos style?"

Lance nodded, seemingly happy Cyrus knew the distinction. "It's the only kind I buy. There's a lot of fish sauce in there, so don't feel bad if it doesn't do it for ya. Same for you Noah."

Noah had already piled his plate with some. His head snapped up. "The smell isn't as bad as Felix said it would be." His chopsticks wobbled in his hand, even after Felix showed him how to hold them, but he managed to get a bite secured and slurped the thin matchsticks of papaya into his mouth.

Every adult seemed to watch with bated breath, while simultaneously putting in an effort to avert their gaze. Finally, he nodded at Felix while he crunched away.

"Wow! It's really fresh. Kind of spicy."

He grabbed his water glass to wash it down, and Felix seemed to exhale. Cyrus, with a lot less of a production, noted the same before ladles of brothy soup filled their bowls. The table filled with easy chatter, mostly sadness that the summer was coming to a close. Noah and Felix in particular, with Lance potentially taking the lead in dreading going back to work.

"So Trang," Cyrus spoke up during a lull in conversation. "Have you guys always lived in Meriden?"

She and Ellie exchanged a smile. "No, I've only been here about ten years. Before that, I grew up in Wakuta. My parents and my younger sister moved from Vietnam when I was about six years old."

Cyrus nodded and Lance took over, "I was born in St. Paul. My parents moved here in '76 and still live in the Twin Cities, but I went to college down in Wakuta."

"Is that how you two met? In school?"

Lance opened his mouth, but shut it again and cocked his head with a hum.

"I can share that story," Ellie chimed in, already laughing. "Lance was in a *band*."

"Felix, cover your ears."

"I know how it goes!" Felix pushed. "Mom was a groupie."

"How many times have I asked you not to use that word?" Trang interjected. "I met him at a party he was playing at and then went to *one show*, Felix. You make me sound like I dropped out and followed them in a van."

"To be fair, you *almost* did that," Lance teased. Trang wasn't amused. "But, our drummer transferred to the Twin Cities campus, and our guitarist ended up dropping out of school altogether. So we disbanded, what, my Junior year?"

Trang nodded. "It was my first year in school and I was still living with my parents. He'd rented a house with about six other guys, and I thought he was the epitome of adulthood. I don't know how you all even survived."

Felix and Noah exchanged a grin that went unnoticed by everyone but Ellie. She hid her chuckle into her napkin before turning to Cyrus to change the subject. "What do you think of the soup? First time, right?"

"Really?" Lance asked, dropping his spoon into his bowl. "This is your first time having bitter melon soup?"

"Yeah! It's great, it's... bitter. Hah, but the pork and cilantro taste great. The papaya salad is fantastic with it."

"I think Ellie's melon makes it taste better, Mom."

"I agree."

"Hey, I can't take all the credit. Cyrus helped prune and weed all summer."

Felix shot up from the table. "Wait! I almost forgot!"

The group stilled as Felix thumped up the stairs and moments later ran back with a piece of paper in his hand.

He lifted the drawing to reveal a shiny chrysalis of a monarch, transparent and dark, showing the burnt orange markings of a butterfly ready to break out and fly off. Noah craned his neck to see Felix hand it off to Cyrus.

"I found it on one of the apple trees!" Felix's smile matched Lance's, a proud dad through and through. "You can have it. Maybe you could hang it up in New York. That way you'll always remember us in Meriden."

Cyrus nodded, silently reaching out to hug Felix, placing the drawing aside. Like a switch, Ellie's eyes watered and her throat clenched. This is what she would miss. Not just Cyrus, the kisses, the company, the partnership. She would miss the way the neighborhood loved him. Especially two kids who saw themselves reflected in his identity. Ellie wasn't alone in the waterworks, they embraced longer than anyone could keep a dry eye for.

"Well then, heh," Lance cleared his throat, causing the room to relax with the broken tension.

"I'm really going to miss you, Cyrus."

"I'm gonna miss you, too, bud." Cyrus patted Felix on the back as they split apart.

On the car ride back to Wakuta, Cyrus kept wiping his eyes. Ellie could've said something, but it was obvious he was deep in thought, staring at the details of the drawing held in his hands as if it was his entire world.

CHAPTER 19

Cyrus

He should have been excited to go to New York. And he was, but Cyrus didn't realize how much anxiety came with being back in the city for the first time in three months. He had also come to enjoy everything about Minnesota, or everyone in Meriden, more specifically. Even his routine. Getting up early, watching the sun rise on the way to the farm, and the anticipation of Ellie. First it was seeing her, then hugging her, and eventually kissing her every morning for the past three months.

The best part about New York was that it was providing six days of uninterrupted Ellie time, something that they usually didn't get between CSA pickups, farmer's markets, and spending meals with her parents. He was also looking forward to introducing her to his friends in the city, ones who he hadn't seen since he moved to Minnesota, and before that, he rarely saw more than once a month.

School had taken up more of his life than he realized, now that he was on the other side of it. Moving to Ithaca was good — *no, necessary* — for him to get back on track, but it cut him off from a world he used to thrive in. Late nights, good food, and good company. He'd have all three on this trip.

Ellie and her parents were waiting in the driveway on the drizzling morning of their flight. His goodbyes to Doug and Martha were much more dramatic than needed. He felt loved all the same.

"Text us when you land," Martha requested, petting Ellie's hair after a smooch to the face. "And text us each night to let us know you're safe."

Doug wrapped her in a tight hug. "Take lots of pictures!" They moved on to Cyrus as Ellie put her suitcase in the truck and got into the driver's seat.

"Thanks for everything you guys," he lowered to kiss Martha on the cheek. "I promise I'll take care of her."

"Why don't you give us your cell, just in case," she said, pulling out her phone. Cyrus punched in his number and texted himself. Ellie rarely had her phone on her anyway, and would probably forget to send a nightly check in.

He walked around to the passenger seat to join Ellie in her dark green pick-up and they rolled out with Cyrus's hand nested in her lap. Where it was supposed to be.

She took a deep breath before smiling at him. "Here we go!"

"Next stop," he put on his largest, most boisterous train conductor voice, "Newww Yooork!"

She laughed and he relaxed a bit. Even if his insides felt like mush, at least she'd be with him. And he would be able to tackle anything as long as he knew that.

The road between Meriden and Minneapolis consisted of one main highway, Interstate 35. Ellie pointed out towns that made up her childhood, a speech meet there, her sister's volleyball game there. At one point she told the story of driving up to a concert at the Xcel Energy Center with her friends, then stayed the night with Hannah at the U of M campus, a first taste of freedom and alcohol.

"Unfortunately," she said, "the bar we went to is closed now. I would do anything to go back in time and be a little more stupid as a teenager. I was always so afraid to live." She looked at him with regretful eyes. "I mean, I know it's good that I didn't. Sorry, that was a dumb thing to say."

He rubbed his hand on her knee. "No, I get it. There's a bit of me that's thankful I got all that shit out in my youth. But, if I could do it over again, I would probably live a little less, if you know what I mean."

"Right." There was a pause, long enough to notice, but not to be awkward. Things weren't awkward with them anymore. "Funny how it all happened," Ellie said. "Because here we are."

She grabbed his hand and kissed it repeatedly, on the knuckles, on his palm, and then delicately on his wrist, sending a shiver up his spine. If he could, he would stop traffic to tell her how much he loved her, but the cars sped on and life continued.

Traveling with a new partner is always a test, and since Ellie hadn't ever been in a premium first class before, let alone first class at all, Cyrus felt he had a duty in sharing all his little rituals upon arriving at the airport. Chocolate covered pretzels from an airport convenience store, a large bottle of San Pellegrino, the day's paper. Nestling into a couch in the VIP lounge his dad's credit card got him into. Things he only did when he was traveling.

It was alarming how much Cyrus loved watching Ellie get wined and dined. He happily let her choose the window seat and when the flight attendant handed out the complimentary sparkling wine, her eyes widened.

He passed, but chuckled, "Maybe don't get used to this. It's not how flying is with me normally. Not when I buy my own plane tickets, at least. I'm just glad it's not a jet, that's a whole other experience."

"You've been on a jet? Like a private jet?"

"Oh, Ellie." He scratched his eyebrow, trying not to encourage her excitement. "My dad owns three."

"Three..." she trailed off, looking out the window at the tarmac.

The rest of the passengers filed in, filling the plane with luggage and body odor and side eyes as they passed the first class cabin. At one point in Cyrus's life, he relished in it, but now his stomach settled with guilt and discomfort that was all too familiar. Maybe this was a bad idea.

Ellie faced him again. "You said we're getting dinner tonight. Who are we meeting with? Please tell me they're not some rich friends of yours with a yacht or something."

"No, no yachts. We're meeting up with my old coworkers from a restaurant group I worked for."

"During your master's?" He smiled and nodded, realizing that Ellie was starting to piece together his past.

The cabin closed and soon the plane was preparing for take off. Up until this point, Ellie hadn't expressed any concern about flying or fear of planes, but it was always a gamble during take off. Old Cyrus usually was asleep by now with the help of an

Ambien, but that was before. Now, he could squeeze Ellie's hand, ask her for a kiss, and hopefully his stomach would settle.

The pilot's scratchy voice announced their departure overhead, and Ellie smiled up at Cyrus. "Can't believe this is actually happening." He tried to smile back but must have failed. "Are you okay?"

"Uh, well," he chuckled, but his chest wouldn't let anything out. "I kind of hate take off and landing."

She immediately reached for his hand and as if she could read his mind, shifted over to kiss his cheek after wrapping her fingers around his jaw. Instant relief.

"Tell me about your friends in New York. Talking sometimes distracts me if I'm nervous. Oh, and take a deep breath."

"How are *you* the one that's consoling me right now?" he sighed. She smiled. "Okay, so there are three of them you'll meet. There's Rosario, or Rosie. He's an executive chef at a Spanish restaurant in Chelsea." The plane sped up, and he locked eyes with Ellie. "And there's Matteo. He's wild. He runs the community gardens that a bunch of high end places use for ingredients." The stomach sink of lift off. Ellie's hazel eyes. Her reassuring smile. *Focus.* "And then Ray, who owns the restaurant that we're going to. We're gonna stay at his condo."

"So *he's* rich."

"Uh, moderately, but not born into it. He worked his ass off."

She squeezed his hand and he finally felt present again. "What's this place called?"

"Du Soleil."

Outside the oval window, the city beneath them turned into a miniature scene, cars racing by shrunk to ants, as the saying goes. They were gliding over trees, shining lakes, and skyscrapers that turned into neat squares of varying shades of green and tan. And Ellie was witnessing it all with bright eyes.

When they landed, she held onto his hand again but he felt just fine. Her smile didn't fade from the time they deplaned to when they took a cab to Ray's condo, conveniently placed three blocks from Du Soleil, and two blocks from Central Park.

While it was fun to see the city through her wide eyes, the pit in his stomach painted everything with strokes of regret. It all clicked right back into place, the hustle, the fast walking, the punchy cab driver. The cigarettes, the booze, the bumps. It was in his bones. Cyrus was back in New York.

CHAPTER 20

Cyrus

"Cyrus fucking Lexington," a familiar voice greeted them in front of the off white building that Cyrus had once called home. A black flat awning covered the entrance where Ray stood, holding the door open for him and Ellie to bring their luggage through. Not without a massive bear hug.

"Ray, goddamn, it's been way too long, man," Cyrus half laughed, half said. Ellie smiled at them, and suddenly he was nervous. They should've talked about how he was going to introduce her. *Girlfriend? Partner? Date?* "Uh, and this is Ellie. She's the owner of the farm I've been working at this summer."

"Hi, nice to meet you," she extended a hand, but Ray wasn't like that.

He looked at Cyrus with a wink. "This isn't a networking gig, bring it in." He stepped forward to give her a crushing hug, and she backed away with a frazzled chuckle. "So you're the infamous farm owner. Well, hey, here's the key. I'm due in the kitchen in twenty minutes. Make yourself at home. You know the drill." With a pat on the arm, Ray was off, halfway jogging down the street.

The lobby looked the exact same as it always had. That's the thing about New York. There were pockets that changed every weekend, storefronts leased with the seasons, new restaurants that closed within six months, and then there were places that stayed the same decade after decade. The lobby of 660 Park Ave was one of them.

He grabbed Ellie's hand and motioned to the elevator as she took in the space. Marble floors with specks of green and gold shined in the late afternoon sun, and everything seemed to be glowing.

When they finally got to Suite 1100, Cyrus took a breath before opening the door, knowing that memories would come flooding back to him. Ellie followed closely behind, *oohing* and *ahhing* right on cue.

Ray had done so much with the place. Growing up in New Orleans, Ray brought his Creole and French influence everywhere he went. The rich wooden panel ceilings matched the hardwood floors, contrasted by muted cream walls with plants growing in every corner. Mostly herbs, but Cyrus found a ficus peeking from the living room and a dragon tree spiking up over the TV.

He jumped into gear. "So this is the living room, then the kitchen is connected." He led Ellie through an archway that opened up to a kitchen that didn't scream restaurant-owner, but was cozy all the same. "Then Ray's room is the one upstairs, and ours is right here around the corner, across from the guest bathroom."

At last, he released his suitcase and plopped down on the bed. They made it.

"Ooh, we should text your parents. Come here," he said, pulling his phone out to send Martha a quick picture of Ellie sitting up on the bed with a tired smile. She looked as exhausted as Cyrus felt, but it wouldn't be the last photo he'd be taking this trip.

"Thank you for doing that. I would have totally forgotten." She nuzzled into him on the bed once he joined her. "How long until your lavish plans for dinner?"

"Not lavish tonight, just special. Later this week, however," he teased, "we're going to the MoMA. There's a photography exhibit I've been meaning to see. Matteo raves about it. *And* Rosie managed to snag us a reservation at Per Se." He couldn't wait to start recreating old New York memories with her. Maybe then he could start loving this city again. Or rather, maybe it would start loving him back.

She hummed in response and he looked down to find her eyes closed against his chest. He tickled her ribs under her shirt as she squirmed and screamed.

"No falling asleep on me. Up, up, up!"

Ellie

On the walk to Du Soleil, Cyrus wouldn't let go of her, battering Ellie's temple with kisses over and over until she laughed too hard to stand upright. He was in a good mood, and it was obvious it was because he was back in New York. The second they landed, he was alive, his vibrant energy radiating as they entered Ray's condo. This was where he thrived and the realization cut through her heart like a dagger.

There was no way he was leaving this. And she couldn't let it get to her this trip. These may be the last few days of their relationship, and if Cyrus showered her with kisses in the middle of a busy sidewalk in New York, she would cherish every last one.

They strode up to a wide walnut door that stood out against the light beige brick and carved stone arch framing the entrance. Two giant flowering hydrangeas welcomed them, but as soon as Ellie finally had the wits to look up, she noticed the lights lining the awning were off. In fact, the whole front foyer was dark.

"Uh, Cyrus?"

He spun around. "Yeah?"

"Are we sure this is open today? Everything looks dark."

His look of surprise melted into a grin. "It is indeed closed today. But, that's why we're here."

He reached for her hand again and squeezed as she followed him inside. Ray, the same burly, bald, black man came into the main room from a swinging door and pointed at the bar before returning through the still swaying doors. She noticed two people sitting at the bar, who turned towards Cyrus and lit up.

"Cyclone!"

"Oh here we go," Cyrus laughed.

"The Lex, back in the city again," the voice of a petite man with flipped out hair just above his shoulders greeted Cyrus first with a hug on his tippy toes. "And who's this?"

"This is Ellie. My... my Ellie. Are we doing girlfriend?" he asked, brushing a hand down her back.

The question threw her off and she wanted to pinch his nipples through his dark grey shirt right in front of them, just to make him as embarrassed as she felt.

"We can do girlfriend," she chuckled.

"Oh my god, hi Cyrus's girlfriend!"

She laughed into a hug with the same flipped-out-hair-man before moving to the taller one who had yelled first. He was covered in tattoos, rocking a nose piercing, and wore a beanie lightly placed on his dark short hair.

The smaller one introduced himself as they all sat at the corner of the bar, "So I'm Matteo, I'm sure Cyrus has told you all about me." She widened her eyes at her *boyfriend*. "Or not! Great, great. Rosie?"

"I'm Rosario," the man with the nose piercing said, taking the other seat closest to Ellie. "And I hope he hasn't said a thing about me."

"You guys suck." Cyrus laughed and nestled a hand on Ellie's thigh. It kind of lived there now.

Ray came swinging out of the doors with a carafe of water and four glasses expertly held between the fingers of one hand.

"I'm playing waiter tonight since our front of house staff has the day off. You guys know what's coming. I'll bring out each course, a tasting card, and I want your honest feedback, alright?" He nodded at the four of them. Ellie was stunned into silence. "And if this sways your decision at all, we're testing out wine pairings, too. Haven't quite nailed them. Ellie, do you drink?"

She appreciated the ask. "I do, yes."

"Cool. Rosie, I got some new mocktails coming on the menu next month. Our mixologist loved creating them."

"Suena chévere, amigo," Rosario said with a smirk, taking a sip of the newly poured water.

"Cyrus, are you drinking these days?"

"I'm not, thanks for asking."

"Roger. I'll be back with the first course. Salad course. Watermelon, toasted pine nuts, pomegranate balsamic reduction, arugula" — Ray pointed at Matteo and they both winked — "and torched feta. Be right back." He bustled into the kitchen again.

"Is it okay that I'm having the wine?" Ellie whispered.

He blinked slowly and nodded into a smile. "'Course. Enjoy yourself."

She placed a comforting hand on his, proud of his decision and thankful for his confidence in doing exactly what he needed for himself.

Matteo wasted no time in asking how they'd met, and Ellie smiled up at Cyrus while he explained their first few weeks on the farm, at each other's throats in a different way then they were now. He left that last part out, but Ellie was having a hard time concentrating on anything but the smooth, kissable skin on his neck.

She realized he had stopped talking and was looking at her after mentioning the farm. "Right! Yes, I run a produce farm. Heirloom varieties, permaculture-ish practices. Oh, and I hear you run community gardens?" she asked Matteo.

"I do! So he's mentioned me at least." They all laughed again and Ellie felt in on the joke.

"And you're an executive chef?"

"Finally got the title," Rosario answered, sticking his tongue out between his teeth.

"What's the restaurant called?"

"Pintxos."

Rosario was not a man of many words.

Cyrus chimed in, "A pintxo is a small plate or snack in Spanish. Like tapas? Have you ever had tapas?"

Ellie shook her head. "I've heard of them. Andrés talks about them sometimes, but that's Spain, not Mexico, right?"

"Which is why my title means everything to me, ah amiga?" He smiled for the first time. "I bring a certain Mexican flare."

"And they're better off for it," Matteo piped in, and Cyrus nodded in agreement.

The first course landed at their place settings, followed by two wine options, one white and one light pink.

"Alright, so this is the first time our sommelier and I have disagreed. She thinks the Roscato is too sweet for an opening wine, but I think it sets the palette up nicely. Otherwise, there's a White Burgundy that's dry and oaky. Enjoy!"

"Wait, can't you join us, Ray?" Cyrus asked, waving to stop him.

"Hardly. Got our new General Manager here. Getting him all trained in." The next moment he was gone with the breeze.

"Who's the GM?" Cyrus asked curiously.

Rosario answered after Matteo gave an apologetic look with a full mouth. "Names Rick. He was the Maitre D' when we were here."

"Ah, sure. Always was a kiss ass." They nodded in unison.

Ellie forked into the first few bites of the salad, watching Cyrus do the same. It was plated like a piece of artwork onto a stark white glazed plate, thick as earthenware. The watermelon brightened against the deep brown balsamic reduction, matching the char on the creamy feta. Her first bite was orgasmic.

"Holy shit," she moaned involuntarily.

Cyrus lowered his voice as if they were the only two in the room. "Try it with the wine. Which one do you like better?"

She took a sip of the white wine, bursting with tartness and a cream-like undertone. Good, but nothing life-changing. Matteo's shrug mirrored hers.

They took another bite, chasing it this time with the pinkish hued wine, and her mouth awakened with sweetness that matched the pomegranate balsamic reduction, not overpowering it in the slightest.

"Your faces just lit up," Cyrus bubbled. "That's the one, huh?" He looked at Matteo, rolling his eyes in ecstasy. Yeah, that was the one.

A few more courses revealed themselves, dish after dish, along with wine pairings for each. Foie gras, tartare, a vegetable fricassee, which Ellie mentally translated into duck liver, raw steak, and stewed vegetables in her buzzed mind. Things weren't really making sense to her anymore, but that didn't stop the food from tasting like heaven.

Another dish came out, looking like caviar topped onto yogurt and an egg yolk. Green chives sprinkled about. She followed Cyrus's lead and scooped the concoction with the white spoon they were given and slowly chewed. It tasted like fancy sour cream and onion chips. Or dip, in this case. With a mild and fresh fishy flavor underneath.

Cyrus was a little loopy, too, but he held up better. "Well? Thoughts, El?"

"I want potato chips with it."

Matteo perked up. "Yes! I was just thinking it needs a crunch."

"A crostini, if we're being traditional," Rosario answered.

"Hmm. I don't know. I think I want a kettle cooked potato chip. The really crunchy ones."

"Write that down!" Cyrus leaned over to watch her pencil work on the tasting note card and she locked eyes with him when she was done. His smile was so dopey.

A few sips and cleared plates later, Ray finally came out to enjoy a drink with them, allowing a perfect opening for Ellie to ask, "So how do you all know each other?"

Cyrus's arm was around her chair now, his thumb making gentle circles on her shoulder.

Matteo raised a fluttering hand first. "I'm happy to share how I met Cyrus."

"Matteo," Cyrus warned.

He bulldozed through. "Picture this. I was in the *heat* of my early twenties—"

"Matteo, I swear to God if you say anything weird."

"I would never. Anyway, it's the middle of August, and we're at the hottest club in Greenwich. I got in because I convinced the bouncer I was Ricky Martin. Had his headshot up and everything, which was ridiculous. I'm twenty years younger than him. Anyway, I later find out Cyrus got in because he bribed said bouncer with two grand."

Ellie was on the verge of laughter, brushing her cheek on her shoulder and subsequently on the back of Cyrus's hand.

"We lock eyes on the dance floor, wild and free, then proceed to make out like teenagers—"

"*Matteo!*"

"Relatable," Ellie got in.

"—and hook up that night in his gorgeous Park Ave condo."

Laughter boomed in the empty restaurant.

"And how was it?" Ellie asked, wanting to egg Matteo on. She'd never seen Cyrus blush like this.

"Eh, seven out of ten. Hot but not really memorable." He waved his hand dismissively. "Anyway so, he makes me breakfast in the morning, asks me where I work, and at the time I was part-time at a community garden in Brooklyn, where I lived. He wouldn't let me leave without promising to show him, so we took the train and the moment he saw it, he was obsessed."

Ellie laughed again, leaning into Cyrus's warm and soft shoulder, glad he was laughing, too.

"He came to the garden every day that week, and I, of course, took that as interest in me. So I asked him out the next weekend. He gently lets me down and I proceed to meet Arie, my now husband, at the same club. I always tell him, if he wouldn't have rejected me, I wouldn't have found the love of my life. Anyway, we stayed in touch and he connected me to the restaurant group that was looking for a garden manager. And snap, just like that, full-time job with one phone call." He sat back, pleased with himself.

"And Rosario?"

The tattooed man chuckled, downing the rest of his water. "Well, I don't know Cyrus like *that*."

"*Oh my god.*" Cyrus put his free hand over his face, stifling a laugh while shaking his head.

"But, we met right back there. I was workin' here as a fuckin' saucier." He pointed at the swinging doors before making a jack off motion with his hand. At this point, Cyrus buried his bright red face into the palm of his hand. He was positively humiliated.

"Cyrus was working for free like he does. I was an alcoholic outta the womb, in and outta the joint since middle school. And well, we started drinkin' after shifts, and that turned into partyin' and tryin' to outrun the morning. Next thing I know, he's grabbing me by the shoulder one day, saying he's going to rehab and he'll pay for my spot if I promise to go through with it. Saved my goddamn life, this fuckin' prick."

The mood shifted and smiles faltered, but somehow Cyrus remained intact while his fingers fiddled with his water glass. "You saved mine, too, don't get it twisted."

For the first time since meeting him, Ellie noticed a slight hint of a New York accent. Maybe she was imagining it with her buzz. Or it could have been the harshness in Rosario's. Either way, it was new.

"He's gotta way of doing that," Ray started, swishing around a finger of whiskey he had left in his lowball. "Worked for free for almost a year. Sold me his condo when he moved upstate. Wouldn't take a payment until I paid off the restaurant."

Cyrus' smile fell, and his heavy eyelids opened to Ellie, who had her mouth agape in shock. "It was my dad's. Money makes money."

The bitter taste of regret crept up Ellie's throat. Every judgment she had towards him had been proven wrong time and time again. She knew his past was questionable, filled with secrets that were his own to keep, but at every turn, he made a decision that benefitted someone else. Sure he had his selfish tendencies, but with that always came self awareness. Even if he needed a prodding.

When they got back to Ray's condo, a little more giggly and wobbly than before, they couldn't keep their hands off each other. Kisses and caresses in an unfamiliar bed, after familiar routines that they'd learned about each other in the last month.

They settled into their system, facing one another with intertwined hands when it was finally time to sleep.

"Did you have fun tonight?" Cyrus asked, checking in.

Ellie kissed his knuckles. "Mhmm. I didn't realize how full I would get from a tasting menu."

A moment passed, and Cyrus took a breath. "And my friends?"

"Are you nervous I didn't like them?"

"They're a lot. It's an interesting bunch. Sorry about Matteo."

"He was great," she chuckled. "I love them because they love you." *And I love you.* It was time to admit it, at least to herself.

"Yeah, they helped me through a lot." He wrapped an arm around her waist and she twisted to align with him as the little spoon. "I can't wait to show you New York."

His voice soothed her into sleep, and even with the steady breath on her neck and hand holding her tight to his chest, the only thought her mind provided her before she slipped into unconsciousness was:

This is going to hurt like hell when it ends.

*   *   *

They spent the next few days hand in hand, eating the best croissants Ellie had ever had in her life, strolling around Central Park with hot beverages, and nursing slight headaches from travel that made them lazier than usual. This was a vacation, after all, and Ellie planned to sleep in as much as possible. When hunger struck, they explored street vendors in lower Manhattan, and even though her mind was occupied every second, she couldn't help but think about the farm, asking for photos of the harvest and progress of the succession plantings from Felix. Of course he was glad to provide updates, usually taken with a cameo of Noah or her parents.

Cyrus, on the other hand, was flourishing. He pointed out places that mattered to him, his first kiss (Washington Square Park), his childhood home (a high rise on 5th Ave), and the NYU campus. It was all here, compact and important to not just Cyrus, but the rest of the world.

She couldn't tear him away from this, it was his home. How selfish would it be to ask him to stay in Minnesota? To tell him she loved him? His eyes lit up showing her his favorite gelato spot, and she knew this was exactly where he was meant to be. And she was meant to be in Meriden. Even if the gelato was the best thing she'd tasted in all of her twenty-seven years.

"You alright?" Cyrus asked, back at Ray's empty condo their last night in the city. He caught her mid-thought as they dressed for Cyrus's planned night on the town.

"Yeah, just a little overwhelmed I think. Processing it all." She tried to smile, but her stomach hadn't really stopped hurting since the afternoon.

"Here, let me zip you up." He motioned towards her dress, a tight grey sleeveless number that almost reached her knees. She didn't want to wear it, but it felt necessary for where they were going. First to the MoMA, then to another fancy tasting menu at some high end experimental American establishment that Cyrus had said at least three times today. *Purse? Or Parlay?*

She ran her hands down the front of her hips, uncomfortable with the way the dress accentuated her femininity when she was usually in work clothes. In the mirror, she watched

Cyrus put on a big silver watch and button his shirt. He didn't look like himself either.

"I don't want to wear this," Ellie blurted. Cyrus froze and met her eyes in the mirror.

"Okay, do you have something else?"

"No, I mean, I don't want to wear a dress."

He cocked his head. "What about that green one you wore on your dad's birthday?" She shook her head. "Why not? You look great in that. You look great in *this*." He was in her space now, a hand wrapped around her hip where she had hers a moment earlier.

"I didn't bring it. I didn't think I should wear something like that if we're dressing up."

"Because we're in New York?" She nodded, full of concern. "El, we don't have to dress up if you don't want to. I just thought it would be special. You know, working in the dirt all summer. The two farmers clean up pretty nicely." Her neck tickled where he nibbled at it. "I can change, though."

"What? No! I didn't mean *you* change." But he silently undid his work, shucking the button up for a light knit sweater and trading slacks for a pair of dark jeans. His watch was thrown in his accessories bag without thought. Ellie felt terrible. "I'm going to look ridiculous in a dress next to you."

"Please, this sweater is a vintage Yves Saint Laurent."

She huffed, mentally debating what to do next. Her fists clenched at her side.

"You, my El, are the most stubborn person I know."

"You make me stubborn." She only said it to throw off the use of *my El*.

"Something tells me you were like this before you met me."

With a grunt, she lifted her curly hair off her neck. "Can you unzip me?"

"Ooh, Ellie. Before dinner?"

They both laughed, and there he was again. She pushed down the thought that it felt like he was compromising everything for her, even if it was just his clothes for the night.

Cyrus

As much as Cyrus would have loved dressing up and hitting the town with Ellie looking like a curly-haired Audrey Hepburn, her high waisted Levi's hugged her in all the right places, plus she had on a matching black spaghetti strap tank top that was doing it for him, covered up by her corduroy sage jacket.

For some reason, Cyrus was starting to feel nervous, knowing that at some point tonight he wanted to talk to Ellie about their future and needed to know where she was at. And yes, his motives for taking her to the MoMA were two fold, he wanted to see the photography exhibit first hand, knowing it would mean the world to him, *and* he wanted to treat Ellie to something she'd never done before. So when her eyes widened and her hand tightened around his in the lobby, he knew he'd made the right decision.

"It's so sleek. And modern," she whispered.

"Well, this *is* the Museum of Modern Art." She smacked his stomach playfully and he grabbed her hand. Luckily, it was a weeknight, meaning the crowds had dissipated.

"Since we're here after hours, it's only open for members who live in New York City, and I still have a Manhattan address on my license." He raised and lowered his eyebrows repeatedly until she smiled.

"You said there was a photography exhibit you've been meaning to see?"

"Yeah, let me show you the classics first."

They perused the greats; Vincent van Gogh, Salvador Dalí, Jackson Pollock, pausing at *The Lovers II* by René Magritte.

"Look, it could be us," Cyrus said, pointing at the two covered faces kissing.

Ellie looked at it, really looked. Her eyes danced across the folds of the white fabric, over the man's suit and woman's pale red top. The more she gazed, the more he couldn't wait to hear her thoughts. That was, until she opened her mouth.

"Huh."

"What."

"Who are they?"

"Whoever Magritte wanted them to be." She looked back at him, hummed, and shrugged her shoulders. "Alright, you. Let's head to the photography exhibit," he conceded. Maybe she didn't like surrealism.

He intertwined their fingers once more and led her to an empty room with walls full of black and white photography. Portraits, landscapes, city scapes, and ruins hung in pristine rows. He took a deep breath knowing these photos meant so much to him when he was younger.

"Peter Hujar. He was a photographer who died in the '80s, but his work didn't get a lot of recognition before then, even though it was phenomenal."

They paused on a pleasing strip of pavement, winding up to the sky. *Road, West Virginia Trip.*

"This one is really pretty," Ellie spoke.

"Mhmm."

"Is there any significance to where it was taken?"

"I don't know. He has a few photos from West Virginia."

She nodded and led him to the next picture, a crisp view of grass on a beach. *Grass, Port Jefferson, NY.* They moved further down the row until they saw portraits of people, raw and vulnerable in the nude.

"That is a naked man," Ellie whispered.

"It is." A giggle bubbled out of him.

"That is a naked man urinating."

"El, my god. Isn't it interesting though? Think of the timing on the photo, he had to get it quick." He pointed at the next one, a naked man sitting back on a chair, staring straight into the camera. "Look at the eyes, they're so relaxed and open. I don't know, I like to imagine what that studio was like, or what Hujar's relationship to them was to make them feel like that."

Ellie furrowed her brow again, this time trying to put a lens on how she was viewing it. It was wrong, all wrong. He thought that she would like this more.

Her shoulders tensed. "Sometimes art makes me feel dumb. I don't know what I'm supposed to think about when I look at it."

Ah, that's all she had to say. Cyrus pulled an arm around her, holding her close to his chest.

"From my own experience, art shouldn't feel like a puzzle to solve. If you think about it, photos are just a way of capturing something in time. I think that's what Hujar was doing, capturing life. He was gay, watched people die of AIDS before he did himself, but he wasn't afraid to take photos of people on their deathbeds, or of men he loved in a time of hate."

"That's devastating." She removed herself from under his arm. Cyrus followed her as they continued walking down the line and landed on Hujar's most prominent work. "Is he crying?"

"No, he's having an orgasm. Read the title." Ellie didn't really react, but eyed him with suspicion. "I'm serious! It's one of my favorite pieces."

She was still silent, so he grabbed her hand.

"What I was trying to say is, art, photography, all of it, is about humans. What we love, what we cherish, how we want to live. And it's so beautiful the way you love people, El. Your parents, Felix, even Helen. You're always so welcoming, and you listen when others talk. Rosie said that you made him feel like he wasn't being judged, and he gets so guarded with new people all the time." He took a breath. "That's what art is. To me. It's humans falling in love and needing to say something about it. Even if it's hard to look at or painful or, or short lived."

As he was speaking, her eyes flooded, ready to overflow with the slightest movement. Something had been sitting at the surface. She didn't respond to him, only continued to stare into his eyes.

"I love you, El. I am so in love with you, it feels like art." He didn't plan on saying it tonight, but the words spilled out of him. It was the only thing that made sense after he rambled on for the last five minutes.

"*Cyrus.*" Ten seconds of silence felt like a lifetime. She buried her face into his shoulder as he wrapped his arms around her back, hiding his panic until she spoke again, barely above a whisper. "I love you, too."

Every one of his muscles relaxed. His eyebrows dropped, the tension in his shoulders released, even his back straightened. He couldn't help but laugh. "I *love* you."

"I love *you*," she chuckled back.

Elizabeth Somers loved him.

And if they were in love, nothing else mattered. They'd figure out the rest eventually. He had loose ends in New York, she had a life in Meriden, but this was a promise. A confession. There was love, real love. The summer wasn't over yet.

"Can it just be us tonight?" He realized they were still in an embrace, and he stepped back to grab her hands. "I don't even want to share you with the wait staff. Let's skip dinner."

"What about our reservation?"

"Fuck a reservation. I just want you tonight. Let's get a hotel."

She squeezed her fists on his chest and crowded into him again. "Room service?"

"I'll do you something better. Let's order pizza."

"Okay, I actually love you," she said it again. And he felt like he was flying.

CHAPTER 21

Cyrus

"What does it say about me if I told you this is the best pizza I've ever had in my life?" Ellie asked. Her elbows sat up on the edge of the bathtub in their hotel room while Cyrus dropped his robe to join her. Someone had to be decent to answer the door.

"It means that you've barely eaten today and it would also mean you have correct opinions about pizza. This is my favorite pie in town, and I would say my opinions are true." He stepped into the scalding tub. "My god this water is boiling. You don't do anything half-assed, huh?"

"No. Are you just realizing this now?" she joked, pulling him into a kiss. She tasted of garlic and tomatoes in the best way possible.

"I shouldn't be. Hand me a slice."

There they sat, eating pizza in the bathtub, careful not to bring the greasy meal over the water and ruin the pristine layer of bubbles that smelled of citrus and pine. Cyrus may have splurged on the hotel room, charging it to his dad's credit card with little to no regret, seeing as they'd be in the same room in less than 48 hours. He still hadn't told Ellie that his parents would be at the ceremony, but now was as good a time as any.

"So, Ellie," he began and she blinked a few times at him. Her eyes had been locked on his lips for about a minute and without warning, she waded over to lick the corner of his mouth. "El."

"Sorry."

"You're very distracting right now," he chuckled.

She walked her fingers up his chest. "Well, we're naked. And in a bathtub. And maybe we could take advantage of that."

His hand wrapped around her jaw, pulling her up into a luxurious kiss that quickly turned sinful as her tongue swept over his. She latched onto his neck while his fingertips pinched at her nipples, causing her to gasp at the sudden sharpness in his touch. Every brain cell stopped working as his eyes caught a glance of her naked, wet body rising out of the tub. *Fastest boner ever.*

"Cyrus?"

"Turn around. Lie back," he strained to get out. She complied without thought.

He didn't even realize this was his fantasy, but watching his hands run down her body in this point of view sent him straight into ecstasy. Ellie's eyes followed his palms down her front, squeezing at her breasts before caressing her upper thighs, stopping at either side of her entrance. He always knew how to make her beg. Her hips thrusted up involuntarily and he finally gave in.

After all this time, he knew exactly where to touch, to tease, to pause and release. Fingers plunged into her while his other hand worked her clit into ecstasy. Watching his deft knuckles from her own perspective was some intimate form of porn that activated every nerve ending in his body. His hardness dug into her back, the softness of his breathy voice brushed against her ear.

"You're so fucking hot. I love you, El."

"Cy—"

His favorite moniker. She tried to reply, but her body was too busy convulsing. Her knees squeezed together with the intensity of the orgasm and he smiled against her neck. "Atta girl."

The pizza may have grown cold, but the bath was still heated. He shamelessly chased friction against her back.

"Cyrus?"

"Yeah?"

"Can we try?"

He knew exactly what she meant, but he was unwilling to flirt with the option. He kissed her neck to soften the blow. "No."

"But don't you want to? I understand if you do."

Sure, he had thought about it, dreamed about it, jacked off about it. But seeing as he had a beautiful woman lying naked on top of him, he didn't need to do anything about it right now. "Sweetheart, I don't even have a condom."

"Then we could—"

"No. Stop that thought."

She lifted herself up, twisting to face him while her hands delicately skimmed over his thighs, pushing the water around with a soft trickling sound. His skin tingled.

She blinked slowly. "What do you want?"

"This. You. I want *you*, El."

"You have me," she whispered on his lips and kissed him with such vigor he forgot about anything else.

*   *   *

The five-ish hour drive to Ithaca was way nicer than Cyrus remembered. Probably because he had Ellie there, holding his hand, laughing at his jokes, and driving. It took five minutes of him white knuckling it in the rental car before she insisted on taking the wheel. He didn't even try to be polite by arguing.

When they pulled into the winding driveway north of town, he watched Ellie's eyes widen. The house he had somewhat called home for the past three-ish years came into view. It wasn't necessarily somewhere he had any sentimental feelings towards, just a quiet place to study and sleep when he wasn't in the lab or at some research station. But through her eyes, it was a two-story French Country mansion, because well, it was.

"You live here?"

"Before you roll your eyes, this is my dad's, not mine. Real estate is a very lucrative investment if you ask him," Cyrus said as she drove the rental car up to the garage door. He jumped out and punched in the code so she could drive onto the sealed concrete inside.

The house smelled like it always did. Sheetrock and new carpet, a little musty from the last three months of vacancy. It brought back the grey memories of becoming a recluse, isolating himself from his old friends and refusing to make new ones. Anything to stay clean after his stint in rehab.

"Um, Cyrus, did you actually live here?" Ellie questioned. The kitchen was nearly empty and the walls were bare.

He was busy disarming the security system. "Yeah, for the last three years."

"We're gonna have to talk about buying furniture. Where is everything?"

"I guess it never really felt like home." He put his hands on his hips and looked around. "My dad has a key, so I never wanted anything here that I actually had any attachment to. It's weird to have you here," he admitted, stepping towards where she was setting her suitcase down.

"Weird good or weird bad?"

"Weird scary. Worlds colliding and all that."

She wrapped her arms around his waist, instantly soothing him. "Are your parents going to be there tomorrow?"

It was about time. He released a heavy sigh. "Yeah, and I'm sorry in advance for anything they say."

"They can't be that bad."

With his eyebrows raised, and a tilted head, he asked the only thing that would comfort him in the moment, "And do you promise to still love me if they are?"

She kissed him and he hoped that was her answer.

CHAPTER 22

Cyrus

For the second time in a week, Cyrus zipped the dress he knew Ellie didn't want to wear. Only this time, she didn't whine her way out of it. Cyrus wore the same turtleneck from the first time they met, under a suit jacket, with his hair swooped across his cheekbones. It was getting too long, but he kind of liked it. He was tanner than he'd ever been, too. As he was scrutinizing his appearance, he caught Ellie in the reflection of the mirror.

"You're staring."

"I am." She blushed. "You look very handsome, and I'm really proud of you."

"So cheesy." He probably blushed too, but was too focused on getting his lips on hers before they left the house. It was the only thing loosening the pit in his stomach.

Cyrus grabbed her hand when they entered the old red chapel. He unbuttoned his suit jacket with a plastered on smile, and with a final deep breath, squeezed their palms together.

"I'm right here," she answered.

They passed the threshold into a warmly lit atrium with ceilings fifty feet high and stained glass windows that illuminated the floor in a kaleidoscope of colors. At least Ellie would hopefully be entertained by the grandiose of everything. A booming voice rang out.

"Cyrus! Or should I say, Dr. Lexington." Brad approached him with a handshake that turned into a hug. Good ole Brad.

"It's been too long. How have you been?"

"Busy as ever with the start of the school year." His advisor looked over at Ellie and her smile stiffened. "Don't tell me, is this Ellie? Sorry, Elizabeth, right?"

"Call me Ellie, hi," she said, shaking his hand firmly.

"Heard a lot about you. That farm of yours is pretty special. Sounds like you are, too."

Cyrus beamed. "Ellie, this is Brad, my advisor. And Brad, yes, this is also my girlfriend, Ellie."

"There it is!" Another pat on Cyrus's arm. "You look well, my friend."

Cyrus' smile fell slightly. "Are my parents here yet?"

Brad's smile faltered, too. "I did see John, yeah. I think he's talking to the Chancellor."

With a tense nod, they broke off and Cyrus's hand was back in Ellie's, providing the only comforting thing in the room.

"Hey Cy? When's the last time you saw your parents?" she asked.

He tensed. "Uh, not last December, but the one before that."

"So it's been over a year?"

"Yep," he exhaled.

It was his younger sister Aurora's birthday. She had just started her post-grad program at Harvard that fall, and their parents flew to Cambridge after Cyrus moved her in, excited to network with an Ivy League. Things went to shit over dinner when Cyrus made a comment about the impact of hoarding real estate that quickly descended into a screaming match about their private jet usage and the environmental effects. They fought back with accusations of altruism and rehab brainwashing him. In the middle of the restaurant. Specifically on course three of an eight course meal.

Since then they'd made up, er, well, since then Cyrus had "apologized" and "said he was out of line" when in reality he meant every word he said. He called the restaurant to actually say sorry about causing a scene and found out the owner was a friend of Ray's. The wait staff heard the whole thing. A week later he received a packed cooler in the mail of osetra caviar and two 8 oz. filet mignons. It was nice to have insider connections behind the world his dad lived in.

Now, almost two years later, he approached his father and a man who Cyrus recognized as the Chancellor. He got nothing more than a stoic nod.

"Cyrus, there you are," his dad said, speaking louder than he needed to. By the looks of his near empty glass, he had been indulging for a while, and not just in schmoozing. "Congratulations to the next Dr. Lexington." He pulled him into a hug, effectively breaking Cyrus's hand from Ellie's. He latched back on without thinking.

"Thanks, thanks, yeah." He never knew how to take his dad's empty flattery. "This is Ellie, Dad. The owner of the farm.

And my, uh, my girlfriend." *Why was that so uncomfortable to say?* Ellie gave him an uncertain glance before smiling at his senior.

"Nice to meet you, Mr. Lexington."

Fuck.

"It's Dr. Lexington, thanks," Dr. Jonathan Lexington said cheerfully, but Cyrus knew he was pissed. He kicked himself for not warning Ellie about this.

"I'm so sorry, I didn't mean to offend. It's nice to meet you, Dr. Lexington."

He blew her off. "Well, Cyrus. After this, we rented out Café Cent-Dix. Your brother came up as well."

"*Oliver* is here?" What the actual hell was going on.

"Don't sound so alarmed. Does it surprise you that your family wants to celebrate you getting your PhD?"

Before he could come up with some snarky response he'd regret later, Brad approached them, whisking the Chancellor away and motioning for Cyrus to follow him inside the small auditorium connected to the atrium.

His dad was still eyeing Ellie. "Mhmm, well. I'm sure we'll get to know each other over dinner. See you in there." He nodded them off as Cyrus led her inside the auditorium.

"You couldn't have told me he goes by Dr. Lexington?" she asked, shaking out the hand Cyrus had been holding.

"I'm so sorry, El. But, who cares? His degree is honorary. He paid for it, he didn't earn it."

"But it's your dad!"

He didn't have time to explain every way she could insult his dad's ego in the next two minutes, so instead he kissed her on the mouth and backed away while rubbing her arms.

"It's going to be fine. We'll smooth it over during dinner. Love you, okay?"

"I love you too, but you can't hold my hand that hard. You're going to break a finger."

He had been a little tense.

During the ceremony, he tried to focus on his breathing, but his brother kept smirking at him, chewing gum of all things and looking like he was about to call him a slur. Maren was terrible, made worse by her tool of a husband, but Oliver was by far the most destructively horrible person who shared Cyrus's DNA. Why he was here was completely lost on Cyrus, and his mind only went to worst case scenarios. This entire thing was supposed to be about Cyrus celebrating his PhD, but he couldn't help feeling like he'd done something wrong.

He looked up further in the seats, and there was Ellie, sitting alone with her hands in her lap. They locked eyes and for a moment he felt relief and safety in knowing she would be there in case anything awful happened. That comfort quickly turned into foreboding with the realization that now there was another person his family could aim their condescension towards. The air in his lungs turned stale and his throat stopped working when he tried to swallow.

The last of the graduates were congratulated and after a final speech from someone who was doing way cooler things than Cyrus, they were able to leave the stage. Each graduate descended and happily met with significant others, family members, and faculty waiting to congratulate them. Cyrus, however, stumbled down and ran out of the nearest set of doors, disappearing from view.

Fuck, he needed a cigarette.

Ellie

"Cyrus!" she yelled after him in the hallway, trying to run in her stupid high heels. She watched him push a door open that took them to an outdoor courtyard and into the dark evening. When she finally caught up with him, he was pacing the length of a patch of grass. "What are you doing?"

"I needed some fresh air."

Irritable. That was the only way to describe how he looked. He shucked his jacket and threw it in the direction of Ellie, where she picked it up and brushed off some dead grass.

"I can't believe my sister and my brother are here. This is so fucked up."

"I, um, I'm sorry." She didn't know what else to say.

"No, you shouldn't be apologizing."

"Cyrus, hey." She approached him, placing her overly air conditioned hands on his cheeks. His eyes closed and he brought his hands to press into hers. "At least they're here, right?"

After what felt like minutes he responded. "No, it's the opposite. Something's happened. I have no idea why they're here. Why now?" He stepped out of her reach. "They're pricks who have no consideration for others and live off making themselves feel better than other people. And they're sucking me into dinner tonight because they can, because I spent Dad's money and this is how it works. We should have never come to New York."

It was hard not to take that personally. New York seemed intrinsic to who Cyrus was. If he didn't want her seeing that, what else did he want to hide?

"I guess I just don't understand why we have to go to dinner with them if they make you feel like this."

He held his hands out in a pleading gesture, which only aggravated her further. "Because I, he paid for our plane tickets. And he's paid for my schooling. It would look, he'd cut me off."

Realization settled over her. Ellie understood to an extent that Cyrus was a bit out of sorts, tired from the drive yesterday, out of routine from traveling, and thrown off by the addition of his brother attending a somewhat unimportant acknowledgement of graduation, but this was the thing that she knew was always settled at the core of Cyrus. He didn't want to feel guilty about spending his dad's money, or rather, he didn't want to lose access to it. No reasonable person would. And he was willing to go through all of these treacherous hoops to keep it.

She bit her tongue with what she really wanted to say.

"Then let's make the best of it. I'll be right next to you. You can hold my hand. Squeeze as hard as you need to." She put on her most reassuring smile, hoping at this point it didn't look forced.

Cyrus stepped closer and kissed her fiercely, momentarily removing the emotion in her throat. "I love you so fucking much, El."

*   *   *

Ellie later found out that not only did Cyrus's parents reserve them a table, they rented out the entire restaurant for dinner. As the staff waited on them hand and foot, she learned that Cyrus's older sister's name was Maren, her husband was Adam, and the younger brother (the youngest of the four Lexington children), was Oliver. That's about as far as they got before Cyrus clenched her hand and his parents took over the conversation. Up until this point, Cyrus' siblings were complicated, abstract ideas and now she was sitting across from two of them at a dinner table.

"So, Cyrus, what's next?" his dad asked.

Cyrus glanced in Ellie's direction. "Uh, nothing of note at the moment. Still seeing what's out there."

His mom deflated slightly, but Maren beat her to it. "Cyrus, come on. How do you not have something already lined up?"

"Maren," Cyrus tried.

"You've had all summer to look. Adam had three offers before he passed his Series 7." *The hell was a Series 7?*

Cyrus nodded with his eyebrows raised and didn't look up from his menu. "Well, he was interning for Dad."

Before Maren could rebut, the waiter came around to get their drink order, which seemed like it would have been a normal, everyday occurrence. It was not.

"We'll do a bottle of the Chateau d'Yquem Sauternes—"

"Mom, that's a dessert wine—"

"Oh here we go."

"—shut up, Ollie."

"Stop calling me that, Cyrus."

The waiter paused. The dust settled.

Dr. Lexington broke the silence. "And I'll do a double of the Elijah Craig Barrel Proof. Splash of water."

"Same for me," Oliver was next, then Maren.

"I'll do a bottle of the Dom Rosé, and he'll have a glass of the Tua Rita, that's a Merlot, right?"

"Yes," the waiter nodded. Adam seemed fine with her ordering for him and all Ellie could think was, *so it was* that *kind of relationship.*

On to Cyrus. Ellie held her breath. "I'm good with water, thanks."

The whole table looked at him.

"Me too," Ellie followed his lead. In a weird way it felt like she was taking his side in some unspoken argument.

The waiter escaped unscathed.

Oliver was the first to speak. "What, are you completely sober now?"

"Why does it matter to you?"

His mom chimed in, "We're celebrating, sweetie. Have a glass of the Chateau. You too, Ellie."

"That's okay," Ellie said. Anything to deflect from their focus on Cyrus's beverage. "It's his choice, and I'm driving, so."

"It's one glass," Maren pushed.

"Just let it go! I'm fine, honest."

Oliver eyed him. "Huh, how long are you gonna keep pulling the rehab card?"

His dad rolled his eyes, but didn't look up from his menu. "Yes, we all know about your time at the horse ranch, Cyrus."

With that, Cyrus's grip clamped harder on Ellie's fingers and she felt a swell of anger in her throat. These people were awful. *Why was Cyrus trying so hard with them?* He would have never taken this much bullshit from anyone else.

His mom's focus turned back to Ellie. It hadn't really left after the, *"it's his choice,"* comment. "So, Ellie, is it? Cyrus says you're the owner of the farm he's been researching at this summer."

Cyrus's hand somehow tightened, but she had a hard time knowing what he was trying to communicate.

"Uh, yes. It's a produce farm. It's a part of a CSA, and we sell at the farmer's market, too." She tried to smile, but swallowed instead.

Cyrus began with an artificial sweetness, "CSA stands for Community Supported Agriculture, so people pay for a share upfront. It's like a shared risk investment."

John took interest in that. "And how is this funded? Who pays for the shares?"

"Uh, mostly it's the folks that live around my neighborhood in Meriden, where our farm is. A few in Wakuta pick up at—"

"Wakuta is a big college town in Southern Minnesota. It's where I was hosted to do my research with the U of M," Cyrus added. She didn't know if she was relieved or annoyed that he kept finishing her thoughts.

"And this is how you make your living?" his mom asked, straddling curiosity and confusion.

"Ye—"

"Yep, and she was awarded a pretty substantial grant this last year, which is why I got funded to do my research."

John nodded at Cyrus. "Was this a federal grant? State, private?"

Ellie finally answered where Cyrus couldn't. "It's a national grant from the Tellema Foundation." When she looked at Cyrus, he was still watching his dad, as if he was looking for approval.

"Have you heard of them?" Cyrus asked.

"Oh yes. Their endowment is quite impressive. They're funded partially by the USDA. Interesting..." he trailed off as their drinks appeared on the table. Ellie was the only one that managed to make eye contact with the staff, thanking them silently with a smile and a nod.

There was something itchy about the entire exchange, and Ellie couldn't help but feel scrutinized for the way her business operated, made more obvious by Cyrus's need to be her mouthpiece to get Daddy's approval. She'd written the damn grants, she knew how to talk about her farm with the elite. She could handle herself just fine.

"Are you all ready to order?" the waiter asked.

Cyrus's dad answered for the table. "A few more minutes." His eyes were back on Ellie. "So does your family come from a line of entrepreneurs?"

Cyrus finally looked at her, but rather than comforted, she was being tested. "Um, kind of? My dad operated a corn and soy farm for nearly thirty years before the recession."

"Ah, yes. That hit farmers hard if they had poorly managed investments." *That didn't feel good.* "Where did you learn to run a business then?"

"Dad, we don't have to ask about her qualifications," Cyrus tried to say light-heartedly. His tone was night and day from how he spoke to Oliver.

"Well, if you were associated with this business, it's good to know their financial standing."

"Dad—"

"I'm sorry, *Dr. Lexington,* but our financial standing is not really your concern."

Cyrus's head whipped around to face her. "*Ellie.*"

He'd gone pale. Why wasn't he defending her?

"Look, I didn't mean to pry, I just was curious what school you attended to obtain a degree in business."

"*Dad—*"

She bit her tongue and spoke through her teeth. "I didn't go to school. I went straight into the field."

"Corn or soy?" Oliver asked, smirking at Maren. This had to be a joke. People weren't actually this rude.

Ellie looked at Cyrus for help, but he looked more lost than her.

His mom was talking now, "Listen, Ellie, we don't mean anything by it. You seem to be successful in your field— Oliver, stop that." The youngest was still sniggering with Maren, obviously hellbent on acting like a 12-year-old.

His dad spoke up, because of course he did. "I bet you were glad to have someone there who's qualified to teach you a thing or two about a hobby farm. But you called it early on, Cyrus. Nothing you couldn't handle."

"Cyrus told us you were a little, how did you phrase it? 'Rough around the edges,' I believe?"

His mom kept going, but Ellie didn't hear it. She was stuck on that last part. *Rough around the edges.* Cyrus had said that. To his parents no less. His parents that he supposedly hated. About her. Someone he supposedly loved.

And what the hell made him qualified to teach her anything about running her own farm? And *handle*?! Ellie Somers didn't need to be *handled.* If anything, Cyrus had needed a handling or two.

"We're not a hobby farm. And it was my understanding that Cyrus had never worked on an actual farm before coming to Minnesota, something that I've been doing almost my entire life," she scoffed.

Immediately, Cyrus extracted his hand, and finally she felt the blood rush back to her fingers. She could feel his eyes on her, probably full of hurt and disbelief, but she focused on the place setting in front of her. She couldn't look at him. Not while she said, "And Cyrus, I'd love to hear you try to explain your way out of what you meant by *rough around the edges,* but I'll save you the trouble. I'll *handle* myself and leave you guys to it. Excuse me."

She gathered her belongings without looking up and made her way to the front door where a doorman nodded at her politely before she exited. She knew she was causing a scene. She didn't care. Anything to get out of this stuffy, overpriced, pissing contest of a restaurant.

With a deep breath of fresh air in her lungs, tears formed as she took in the unfamiliar streets before her. Everything irritated her, the tightness of the dress around her thighs, the pinch of her toes in her high heels, the smell of exhaust and concrete baking in the sun. People whizzed past her, and the noises got to be grating and too loud.

Every worry and insecurity from the first time she met Cyrus in that fucking turtleneck zoomed around her like the cars passing with every second. She couldn't believe he had the audacity to kiss her with the same mouth that shittalked her to his parents.

They probably laughed at how uneducated she was. Laughed at how simple her life seemed. *Hilarious.*

This was how it ended, in some fancy restaurant on an unfamiliar street in a town she didn't know and in a state she'd never been in. With Cyrus clinging to his money and Ellie clinging to her pride. This was all a game to him, all the degrees and pieces of paper he'd gotten for fun. Her farm was a case study. *Look at how the other half lives, isn't it funny?* She refused to let Cyrus make her the butt of some joke for a second longer.

His voice caught her mid spiral.

"Ellie, what the fuck was that?" He reached for her arm, but she twisted away.

"Don't touch me," she cried, tears dripping from her chin.

"El—"

"I wanna go home."

He paused, closing his eyes and exhaling with a bite. "Fine, I'll drive you back to the house. I don't—"

"No, I want to go *home*. Not some empty house of your dad's that you don't take care of. I'm getting on a flight or a train or anything. I'll take a bus if I have to. I'm getting my things, and I'm leaving. We're done."

He stared at her, mouth hung open. He blinked once, twice, three times. "Ellie, please. We can talk about this. Let me grab the keys to the rental."

As much as she didn't want to talk about anything with him, he was right. She needed the keys to the rental and then she needed to get the hell out of here.

CHAPTER 23

Cyrus

When Cyrus went back into the restaurant to grab the keys, his family sat unamused, which thrust his confusion right into anger.

"Thanks a lot, guys."

Maren smiled around a sip of her wine. "She can't take a joke."

Oliver sneered into a laugh and Cyrus wanted to hit him.

"You two can truly, and I mean this with every fiber of my being, fuck off indefinitely."

"Cyrus James!" His mom stood up from the table, wobbled, and pointed her finger. "You do not speak to your siblings like that."

He met her outburst. "I'll speak however I want to!"

"Glad we rented the place out so you could have your tantrum in private this time."

"Stop giving me reasons to, Dad, and maybe I could calm the fuck down for once." He turned to his mom. "Why would you say that to her? I swear to God, if you've just messed things up for us, I will never speak to you again."

"You sound like Rory," Oliver said, shooting back his $50 glass of whiskey.

"The fuck does Aurora have to do with this?"

Maren's eyes flickered to their mom. "Why don't you ask Aurora that."

"What's that supposed to mean?"

This was just like them. Secrets shared between glances, silent conversations that made him feel insane. They always seemingly had the upper hand in any social situation, when in reality they were just plain mean. Trust didn't exist in a family like this. Ellie was right. He didn't have to put up with this.

His keys dug into his palms. They acted as the only thing keeping her from running rogue and leaving the premises. A fleeting thought of her not knowing how to hail a cab pinched in his stomach before it formed fully. *Did he really think she was that helpless?*

"Rory got herself knocked up," Oliver finally spit, albeit a bit slurred. "And what's worse, she wants to keep it."

His mom collapsed into the chair with a soft sob as his dad buried his face into his hands. This was why Oliver came tonight. This was why his family made such a to do about coming to his ceremony. He wasn't the black sheep of the family anymore.

Fucking disgusting.

"Don't contact me again. Any of you," he finalized before his feet were dragging him towards the exit.

He couldn't deal with this at the moment. Luckily Ellie was still outside, and minutes later they were speeding down the winding road that led to the house, both silent and raging with emotions that clashed and shattered with each mile. The car was barely in park when she rushed out and slammed the driver's side door shut.

"Ellie!" He chased her up the cobblestone driveway.

"How could you say that to them? How could you think that of me?"

"I don't think that of you."

Tears already formed in her eyes, making them sparkle in the late evening dusk. "So you didn't actually say that I was 'rough around the edges'? Or that I was 'nothing you couldn't handle'?" She used air quotes wildly. "What did you say, then?"

He lowered his head. He was either going to lie or break her trust by telling the truth.

"I did say that—" she turned and bolted towards the front door, but stopped short since his keys were still gripped in his hand. "But it was before I knew you! Really knew you. And my dad was cornering me, asking if I was liking Minnesota, and if I told him the truth, he wouldn't have understood!"

"Open the door."

"Ellie, please." *Fuck* he was crying now. "You have to believe me. I've never once thought you were anything less than brilliant and dedicated and the most thoughtful person I've ever met."

She had taken off her heels, but refused to look at him, standing there at the door while tears fell from her cheeks. "I need to get my things."

His eyes scanned her, hoping to find a crack in her exterior where he could climb in and make a home, settle in and start a life. But she remained stiff as a board. With a soft sob, he shuffled through his keys, unable to make anything out with the state of his emotions. He may have imagined Ellie's eyebrows knitting together, and a sharp inhale that sounded like a sniffle, but seconds later she ran through the door.

All he could do was sit on the edge of the bed, watching her put away the last week they'd spent together, book ending the best summer of his life.

"We can talk about this, Ellie. I love you, that's all that matters, right? I told you my family is the worst. I warned you about this."

"No, you warned me that *they* would judge me. Not that *you* would be the one to put things in their head about me. I could've handled anything they threw at me tonight, because I knew they didn't have a clue who I was. But to know that their words came from *you?*" Her face collapsed. "I thought I could trust you."

"You can. Please, I'm so sorry, El—"

"Don't call me that," she cried, high pitched and breathy. "This was never supposed to last. You have your research, I got a farm hand. You can go back to being the rich city boy you've always been, and I can go back to being someone who lives in the real world."

"That's absolutely not fair." He somehow found the energy to yell. If this was his last plea, he needed her to know this. "I told you from day one that this wasn't some fling. My parents are fucked, and my relationship with them is complicated, but that's what it is, *my* relationship with *my* parents. Not all of us come from families that dish out love for free. It's always been a transaction with them, and the fact that I'm at a place where I can say that and not want to destroy myself is a fucking miracle. I live in the real world too, and the consequences are a lot more real from where I'm standing."

She started off measured and quiet, gaining speed and volume like a thunderstorm in the distance. "You are all the same. You think everything is more important because of your zip code. All you seem to care about is clout and esteem and things that don't matter to us *at all* in places where we're just trying to get by!" She was screaming now. "I don't *care* about any of this, Cyrus, I never claimed to. I don't want to think about the Ivy League or have someone pity me for where I live. And I especially don't need your parents shaming me for not getting an arbitrary degree that would've put me into debt. At least my decisions are my own."

Fuck that.

Rage collected in his chest for her calling him out, and he fought every instinct not to fling his self-hatred back at Ellie. How did they get here? How did it come to this? If Ellie would just *listen* to him, he could explain everything, but at this point, he had nothing more to say. Nothing productive, at least.

She frantically finished packing, reaching behind her to grasp uselessly at her dress. Cyrus was still beyond pissed, but caught on to her dilemma instantly.

"I can unzip you."

"No," Ellie mumbled, moving to the adjoined bathroom in a thinly veiled act of indifference. The door slammed shut.

"Ellie, just let me help you, I know you can't get it off by yourself," he yelled through the barrier. Everything Cyrus knew about Ellie told him she was suffocating under the fabric.

A ripping noise tore off like an alarm.

"Ellie, come on! So you'd rather destroy something beautiful than let me in and take some goddamn help."

Finally the door opened and she came out with the ripped dress covering her half naked body, red in the face and dark in the eyes. She paused after quickly poking her head through a golden yellow pocket tee. Her eyes wouldn't meet his, but the room silenced with understanding.

"Not just with the dress though, huh?"

She grabbed her pants and continued dressing before tossing the tattered fabric in the nearest bin.

"I don't need your help."

Those last five words were final. So final, that ten minutes later the rental car was gone and so was Ellie. And now Cyrus was left in a French style three bedroom, three bathroom mansion alone, with nothing but his shortcomings as a son, a brother, and a lover to fill his mind.

He had to leave. He packed up as much as he could in his suitcases, looked around the room for the few things he knew he couldn't live without, and grabbed the scissors from the kitchen drawer. As if on cue, he saw a car pull up, and it wasn't the taxi he called. *Great*. What better finale to end the fireworks of today?

"There you are. Cyrus, listen," his dad spoke the minute his key opened the door. He wanted to stand up to him right away. He wished he would have had the balls, but he froze. "We just want what's best for you. You know that."

"But you're not—"

"And sometimes you don't know what's best for you, dear," his mom somewhat garbled.

"Like going to rehab?"

His dad groaned, "Here we go again."

"And Ellie seems like a pretty enough girl, but Cyrus, honey, she's not quite what we were hoping for."

"Hoping for. Like how you weren't *hoping for* Aurora to get pregnant out of wedlock."

His mom smiled with eyelids so heavy, it was clear alcohol wasn't her only vice tonight. "Aurora has made her decisions—"

"And it's about time I made some of mine."

His dad held out his hands in a futile attempt to calm the room down. "What your mom is trying to say is, we hoped for someone a bit more... ambitious."

"Ambitious how, exactly? Ellie runs her own business, and she's sacrificed her entire adult life to help her parents because they *love her*. I've never seen the kind of dedication and work she has and, and she's everything to me." He'd never meant it more, even in the aftermath of the explosion. "Being back here has done nothing for me. All it reminds me is that there are people like you who made me do half the shit I did when I was so fucked up."

"Cyrus—"

"But with her, I finally feel worth something. It's not fair that you've had this long of a hold on me, and the fact that you're leaving Aurora exactly when she needs you most. I want absolutely nothing to do with you. Leave me the fuck alone." He wiped his face frantically. How did those tears get there? How did his voice get so loud?

His mom met his volume. "This doesn't have to be such a production."

"Great, then here's how this is going to work. The credit card is destroyed, and I'm leaving the house." He pointed to the small pile of cut up plastic on the counter. "I don't want you in my life if this is how you treat the people I love. Cut me off, dissolve the trust, anything. Sue me if you need to, I don't care anymore."

His dad genuinely looked offended. "Oh, please, Cyrus. You're our son not a fucking client. You don't want our help, fine, but it doesn't have to be like this."

He grabbed his overstuffed suitcase as his taxi pulled up. "Yeah well, you're right, it doesn't. But your decisions have been made, too," Cyrus spit and got in the car, hoping to never feel this small ever again.

CHAPTER 24

Cyrus

He took a bus. A *fucking bus* to Manhattan. And if that wasn't enough, Ellie hadn't responded to any of his texts or calls all night. A summer's worth of choices rattled in his head, questioning their own morality and most importantly, the choice he had in front of him.

He'd been staring at an empty lowball and a bottle of Redbreast with dizzying focus for the past hour. His tears were drying on his chin, making his face itchy and damp, causing his entire body to shiver. The entire experience felt familiar, dangerous, and invasive. He just wanted this feeling to end. The desperation, the deprecation. He couldn't do anything to change the past, all he could do was react to it.

His memories were catching up with him. This was worse than when Ian broke his heart at twenty one. He was ten times as fucked up when Clara left him, but this felt twenty times more real. Put all of the morning-afters into a jar, bottle it up and smash it into his chest and maybe it would resemble how his heart felt at the moment. And damnit, he'd kill to just feel *good* again. To feel loved. To have someone look at him the way that Ellie did.

What if he never saw those hazel eyes again? Heard the song of her laugh? Inhaled that fucking scent? *Coffee and gardenias, coffee and gardenias, coffee and gard—*

"Cyrus, what the hell are you doing?" Ray's voice boomed in the high ceilings of his condo. It jolted him back to reality, back to the glass in his hand and the bottle at arm's length. He didn't even hear the door unlock.

"I didn't open it, I swear."

"You scared the shit out of me." Ray slowly approached, watching Cyrus closely before swiping the bottle of whiskey, cracking the seal, and pouring it down the drain. All Cyrus could do was stare blankly ahead, listening and crying at the liquid streaming down the drain.

"What are you doing here? It's half past bar close," Ray asked, now calmly pulling up a seat next to Cyrus at the breakfast table, still unsure of his movements.

"I don't know. I've just been sitting here staring at that fucking Redbreast for hours."

"Yeah, haven't seen a bottle of that in a few years. Used to be your go-to."

"I'm sorry I didn't text you first."

"Cyrus, you're always welcome here, but buddy," he whispered, leaning over to silently ask for eye contact. "Why are you here? Where's Ellie?"

"She's... gone... met my parents," he attempted. "I fucked up. I'm such a shit partner. And my sister. Aurora. She's having a fucking kid. I'm going to be an uncle and the only family that baby will ever know." His head landed in his crossed arms.

Ray placed a hand on his shoulder, shifting Cyrus to lean into his stocky chest, heaving sobs that he didn't know could exist within his body. It was surprising to know that Ray could be like this, since for most of their friendship, Cyrus was the cut-the-bullshit, voice-of-reason when Ray needed support, financial or culinary. Ray let him cry for a bit longer, but soon Cyrus felt a rough pat on his back and strong hands pushing his shoulders up.

"Alright, time to talk."

The story spilled out of him, the good, the bad, the Ellie. He was so naive when the summer started, unsure of what he was getting himself into and unprepared for how much he would fall in love with the farm and its owner. Then his parents, squeezing their way into his life and forcing him to say hurtful things about someone he barely knew at the time.

"I'm going to stop you right there," Ray interrupted. "I don't think you were forced into saying anything. You're in control of your mouth right?"

Ray was right. *Fuck.* "I'm such an ass. I messed things up so bad."

"You've messed things up worse. And what did you do about it?"

"You already know the answer to that." The answer was rehab, months of rehab.

"And you apologized to the people you loved. You fucked up, fine. Say sorry and move on. Next."

Cyrus shook his head. He wasn't getting it. "I shit-talked her to my parents, the most judgemental people on Earth. I called her 'rough around the edges.' Like, she knows I said that about her *to them*."

"Diamonds are rough around the edges in nature, still diamonds. That's barely an insult. Either way, say sorry. Easy. Next?"

It wasn't easy, anything but. "Ray, stop. I don't even know where she is right now. She won't answer my calls or texts."

"You know where she lives?"

"Okay, you're actually sounding a bit insane," Cyrus chuckled. He wasn't crying anymore, and smiled at the realization that this was exactly what Ray was trying to accomplish.

Satisfied with his work, he sat back in his chair. His devilish smile turned somber. "What's going on with your sister?"

He told Ray everything he knew, what little of it he got from his family.

"Have you called her?"

Cyrus answered by lowering his head and picking at his fingernails. They were almost completely clean now, the remnants of the farm nearly gone. Ray slapped his palm on the table to bring him back.

"Well, tomorrow is a new day. I'll be upstairs. Liquor cabinet is locked. Don't do anything dumb. I care about you too much."

Cyrus let the silence settle after the last of Ray's steps ascended the staircase. For a moment, he tried to convince himself that he could just sit here for the rest of his life, forget all about Ellie and Aurora and his fucking parents. But his mind landed on Ellie. She wouldn't treat someone she loved like this. He flung himself up and made his way to the spare bedroom.

A familial voice picked up on the third ring.

"Cyrus? Hello?"

"Rory," he started, but lost his voice.

"Oh my god, it's the middle of the night."

Goddamnit, why was he such a fuck up? A shuffle lasted long enough for him to catch his breath. "Shit, Rory, I'm so sorry it's late. I just found out today. I would've reached out."

"Yeah, why are you calling at 3 AM? Is everything okay?" He didn't deserve her.

"No, it's not. I didn't know you were pregnant."

"Oh. Who told you?"

"Oliver. He and Maren came up with Mom and Dad. We had dinner last night after my PhD ceremony."

"Cyrus! No one told me you'd graduated. I would've come."

"I'm really, *really* glad you didn't."

"That bad?"

"Yes," he bit. They sighed in unison. "Rory, what's going on?"

"Ah, well. How long do you have?"

"I mean, fuck. You probably want to go back to bed."

"I actually woke up starving," she chuckled and he loosened his shoulders. As terrible as Oliver was, Aurora always had a special place in his heart. Even if she did grow up following Cyrus around constantly before he went off to college.

"So I met this guy at a party this spring." Her mouth was full, but she spoke as she chewed. "We hooked up. We were drunk and well, miracle of life and so on."

"When did you find out?"

"In May. I called you, but you never answered."

A wave of grief washed over him. He hated himself. Hated what drinking did to him.

"Rory, I'm—"

"Actually, it's a funny story. It was also on our third date. I liked him, so I asked if I could see him again after the party. Didn't quite know just how much I would be seeing him," she chuckled dryly. "He took me to the drugstore, helped me with the pregnancy tests, and actually drove me to my first appointment. And, um, he dropped out of UMass last semester to code full time. He's like, so smart. But you know, all Mom and Dad saw was a no good bum who got their daughter pregnant. His name is Kyle." She paused to chew some more. "I love him, Cyrus." It sounded like she meant it.

"Rory, I'm so sorry I wasn't there. I'm supposed to be your big brother."

"Hey, hey Cyrus. Don't cry." And now *she* was comforting *him*. He couldn't stop messing things up. "Weren't you in like, Manitoba?"

"Minnesota," he gave a wet chuckle.

"Oh, right."

He sniffed to even out his breathing. "Are you okay? Did Mom and Dad cut you off?" Maybe he was asking for her, maybe he was asking for himself.

"He shut off my credit card if that's what you mean. They keep saying they'll pull my tuition, but I've been keeping an eye on it. They haven't yet and it's been months. It's still being paid from the trust fund. I think Dad's too proud and Mom's too emotionally invested. She said Maren and Adam have been trying for months. Did you know that?"

"No, I didn't."

"This whole thing is," her voice caught. "Why is our family like this?"

"I have no fucking idea, Rory. Do you need money? I have some of my own saved up—"

"Absolutely not. Kyle is helping pay for everything. We're gonna be fine." Of course she was going to be fine. She was Aurora fucking Lexington. He'd never been more proud of her and had never been more disappointed in himself for not calling sooner.

"H-how far along are you?"

"About twenty six weeks."

"What does that mean? Can you send me photos?"

"Of a black and white blob with a nose? Yes."

"No. Of you. And Kyle. And the blob with a nose. Everything. Do you know the gender?"

"I think it's a boy, Kyle's convinced it's a girl. I don't care, I'm just so excited." She finished chewing something crunchy and the mood softened. "Hey Cyrus?"

"Mhmm?" Was all he could get out.

"It may be the hormones talking but, I really miss you. I really, *really* want this kid to have some kind of family in his life, and you're the only one who's reached out who hasn't scolded me. I know we haven't talked as much since everything happened with Mom and Dad, but you were right. Even though I didn't say it at the time. All they care about is showing off their money and it's obvious that you never fell for it. If you ever need anything, I'm here. I love you, you know."

An unfamiliar relief seeped into his veins, sinking into his chest, full of guilt and determination. Aurora may not have known, but that's exactly what he needed to hear.

"I love you, too. Photos, you promise?"

She did, and after they hung up, he swallowed his pride. His tattoo caught his attention. Maybe it was because he'd been studying one all summer, but the faded black lines didn't match the uniform sugar maples that scattered Central Park in New York. It matched the one in Ellie's yard.

The idea might have been a bit insane, but damnit, maybe that's exactly how he felt.

CHAPTER 25

Ellie

The thing about crying in airports is that no one really pays attention to it. The crowds of people were too busy focusing on their luggage rolling behind them, getting through security without being berated, and making it to their gate in time for departure. Just like Ellie had been, until she missed her connecting flight from DC to Chicago, extending her nine hours of travel to a solid fourteen.

The travel time could have given her an opportunity to think, but all it did was make her more and more angry at herself. In the chaos of mourning a relationship, being in a state she'd never been to, and booking her first airline ticket by herself, she had inadvertently selected a flight that had not one, but two layovers. Immediately, when she realized the mistake, she took out her phone to dial Cyrus. Her finger hovered over the call button for a moment until she realized what she was doing.

So here she was crying in the O'Hare Airport, the third airport she'd cried in within the last 24 hours. A five hour car ride in the rearview mirror, two hours of security lines at JFK, and a forty minute layover in DC that turned into four hours in a terminal with nothing but a closed coffee shop. She realized this might have been the dumbest decision of her life. In fact, it was preceded by a series of the dumb decisions that got her here, including meeting, kissing, and falling in love with Cyrus Lexington. Each one more stupid than the last.

In a way, that's what got her into this mess, right? Even if she didn't ask for help, or didn't accept it, she'd come to depend on Cyrus. His sturdy trunk for support, his roots to ground her, his branches to provide shelter and comfort, rain or shine. Just like the grandeur of the silver maple at home. She'd never look at that tree the same way ever again.

It didn't hit her until the last leg, finally on a flight to MSP, crying silently as the sun rose outside her window seat. She may never see Cyrus again, never hear his laugh between tomato bushes, a secret that felt like a privilege to know. This is what happened when she let her guard down, took the help of a stranger, and fell in love with someone who was never meant to promise her anything. Of course he was never going to understand why she lived where she lived. How could she have thought he would sacrifice his lavish life in New York City to be with someone like her? Especially now that she knew where he stood. She was a charity case. Something to be *handled.*

She woke up in a daze. Dried tears tightened the skin on her cheeks. The gentleman next to her gave her a smile, as if to apologize for something he had no control over. No one did. Cyrus was Cyrus and there was nothing anyone could do to change that.

The hour drive back to Meriden sped by. Familiar trees and roads kept her company until the turn through Wakuta flushed her emotions again. She'd driven home from this direction on countless occasions, but this time she carried the weight of the summer in her memory. The cars passed and tears traveled down her face, each drop full of hope leaving her body. She cried for the loss after a summer out of a fairytale, enemies to friends to lovers to strangers. Back to how it was always supposed to be.

With all the strength in her, she finally made it to the Meriden County line, the farm coming into view with each mile. Her mom and dad were waiting on the front porch when she arrived, glowing in the early morning sun that cascaded golden beams onto the maple tree that always pulled her back into shore. An anchor. Ellie was finally home.

Everything had been blubbered to her mom over the phone. By the time Ellie collapsed into Martha's arms, both her parents knew that her newly forming tears were mourning the loss of a friend, a lover, and a night's sleep. They shuffled her upstairs where she drifted off instantly, dreaming of pizza and bathtubs, strawberries on fingertips, and maple trees etched into skin. And without warning, all of it was being uprooted in the vortex of a tornado.

*   *   *

She slept through the entire day, only waking to eat a quiet dinner with her parents before falling back into her bed to sleep through the night. The missed calls were there, the unanswered text messages, one more heartbreaking than the last.

Cyrus was putting on an excellent show, but every declaration of love only caused her more guilt and heartache.

By the time her clock read four in the morning, she was wide awake. With the awareness that she hadn't been in the field for an entire week, she got up to shower, make coffee, and change into her work clothes. All with Cyrus suspended at the top of her mind.

She heard footsteps coming downstairs and her mom's soft voice a moment later.

"Ellie?"

She dried off her hands from where she was cleaning her coffee mug. "Hey, Mom."

She was still in her robe, greying hair pulled back and her glasses sitting low on her nose. A vision she grew up with early mornings before school and late nights after working all day in the farm. Home, love, comfort is what she looked like.

"Tyler's mom called last night after dinner," she said. His name made her flinch. Out of all the things Ellie thought would come out of her mom's mouth, that was the last on the list.

"Hmm."

"He's been in Florida for the last month or so. Yesterday was his thirtieth day sober."

Oh. Tears.

"She said that he went down there after Community Night, and she wanted to call to thank you for talking to him, getting him some help." Her mom paused, stepping closer to Ellie to place a hand on her forearm. "And while I thanked her for calling, I think we both know who really helped Tyler that night."

Cyrus.

Of course everything led back to Cyrus. It had all summer.

"Listen, Ellie. My sweet girl. I know what Cyrus said to his parents was hurtful, but I don't think Cyrus is a hurtful person. We all make mistakes, hell, you even admitted you didn't like him at first. But, I wanted to tell you about Tyler because, well. I think Cyrus touched a lot of lives here in Meriden, and I don't think losing that is worth keeping your pride."

Ellie swallowed. It felt like she'd been punched in the gut. Her mom kept talking, now pulling her phone from the front pocket of her robe.

"Cyrus was sending us photos the entire time you were in New York. I've never seen you happier." She placed the unlocked phone with the conversation on the counter and reached up to pat Ellie's wet cheek. "I love you, Elizabeth Mae."

"I love you, too." She sniffed deeply, wiping the sensitive skin around her eyes. It felt like she had been crying for years. "Is Dad here? I'm gonna go to the field soon."

Her mom backed away, not making eye contact. "He was helping someone with harvest or something. I think he should be back soon."

Ellie nodded, her attention drawn back to the screen in front of her that sent her right back to the streets of New York. She swiped through the conversation, a secret back and forth between the contacts Martha Somers and Cyrus Lexington.

"Looks like fun!" and *"She loves the gelato!"* interspersed between candid photos of Ellie in Central Park, laughing in her pajamas at Ray's condo, or holding a cup of coffee. Ellie sitting up on the bed with a tired smile hours after they landed. She didn't even notice he had been taking them. His words rang in her ear. *Art, photography, all of it, is about humans. What we love, what we cherish, how we want to live.* It was time to admit that this wasn't how she wanted to live.

The front door opened and Ellie's dad walked in, heading straight for the coffee while Martha went for the fridge.

"She's alive," he joked, giving Martha a wink and a kiss on the cheek as she poured his cream for him. "You headed to the field?"

It took Ellie a second to realize he was talking to her. She was too transfixed on the cream that Martha had poured. Her dad had no problem taking it, and her mom so freely offered it. It was the smallest thing, but that was the whole point. Love wasn't in the big moments, was it? It was in the daily actions, it was learning the idiosyncrasies of someone else and choosing to love them still.

Love wasn't supposed to be a burden. Maybe it wasn't a burden to Cyrus, either.

"Ellie?"

"Hmm? Oh, yeah. I should take a look at the tracker. Did you keep up with documenting everything?"

Doug swallowed his first sip. "Oh yes, Felix wouldn't let me forget."

With an absent minded smile, she waved them off and left for the shed, still thinking about the creamer. The entire walk over, he was on her mind. Cyrus, Cyrus, Cyrus. It would be the first day back in the field without him. Without his morning hug, their playful banter, secret kisses behind raspberry bushes. Guilt overcame her.

What the hell had she done? Why did she constantly push him away all summer? Not once did she just let herself be loved for more than a moment after a kiss or a night in his bed. Every morning came with second guessing, and for what? He wasn't Tyler. He was Cyrus. Warm, sturdy, *I don't want to hurt you,* Cyrus.

She opened the shed door and without looking up, she knew. As if they could be in the same room unknowingly. There he was, in his Carhartt t-shirt, workman's overalls and her dad's faded Twins baseball cap. In the flesh, in her world. No turtleneck, no sunglasses, no fancy swoop of his hair. Just Cyrus.

"Hey, El."

"Holy shit."

The tears had miraculously halted, but her feet kept moving her towards him, a magnet whose only purpose was guiding her home. Her body gently docked into him, and her head was in his chest before she knew what she was doing.

Cyrus laughed. *Thank god*. There it was, the stupidest, most perfect sound that she thought would never grace her ears again. His hands stroked down her back until he gripped the back of her thighs, lifting her up and around him, only to place her on the workbench. They melted into one another, gentle touches acted as unspoken apologies and promises that this wasn't over. It couldn't be. *Please, let this not be over.*

Cyrus pulled back. "Can we talk?" He looked as tired as she felt, even with the near twenty four hours in bed.

She nodded. "How are you here right now?"

"I took a red eye. Your dad picked me up from the airport."

"*What?*" She leaned back. She'd scold her dad later for not telling her.

"Listen, there's a lot I have to say—"

"No, you don't have to say anything. It's me. It's my fault. I'm sorry, Cyrus. I'm sorry about everything these past three months. I didn't understand how much I was trying to push you away. Especially when you had every right to just come here to do your research and leave, but you didn't! You loved me and treated me right and I," — she took a breath — "I messed that up. I'm just scared, okay? I was so scared, but I can't stop loving you, no matter how hard I keep trying. And I'll understand if you don't want to continue this, if you're here to say goodbye or get your things, especially after I ran away, but I want to be with you, Cyrus. I want every summer at this farm to be with you, and I get it now.

"All this time I was afraid of you loving me because I couldn't control it, but I love you, too, and that's what matters, right? I love you, and it feels like I can't live another minute without *doing* something about it. That's what it's supposed to feel like, right? That's what you said about art."

The entire time she was talking circles around him, his eyebrows upturned in concern, his mouth open ever so slightly, taking in each word. When she stopped, though, his expression neutralized. She braced herself for impact. Words were cheap, she already had acted. And she ran.

"Cy?"

And then he smiled, and for the first time since New York, a glimmer of hope expanded in her chest.

"El," he huffed. "I had this entire speech planned, and you just totally one upped me."

"One upped you?"

He crowded up into her space, mirroring their first kiss. His hands grasped at her thighs. "I didn't come here to break up with you," he whispered, running a finger behind her ear to set a loose strand of her hair back. Her entire body was vibrating. "I came here to tell you that I've decided to come home." *Come* home? Not *go* home? "And I do have to apologize. What I said to my parents about you was really cruel. And I really hope this lands."

He stepped back, digging in one of his many pockets and pulling out something delicate. He unraveled it and a necklace fell into his fingers, sturdy and gold with a pendant the size of a pea of something rocky and jagged. His free hand reached into the collar of his shirt to reveal a matching one.

He took a deep breath, seemingly psyching himself up. "I'm a little rough around the edges, too. But I've been told recently that diamonds, raw diamonds, are rough around the edges in nature. They're still diamonds, though. So," another breath, "I'm just gonna start over. I'm Cyrus. I'm a PhD candid— graduate. I recently moved to Wakuta. I have ten thousand dollars to my name, I'm unemployed, and looking for work in the field of horticulture, specifically at Somers Farm LLC. I have a master's in Botany and Gastronomy, and a PhD in Physiology & Ecology of Horticultural Crops. And my qualifications are I'm in love with you."

She laughed, peering down at the necklace in his hand. Without words, he opened the clasp and wrapped it around her neck. He stood up straight and smiled, but Ellie had an idea. She hoisted herself off the table, knowing that it would be pure luck if she could find what she was looking for in the cooler. It seemed like the universe had been on their side, though, especially since it was high time for the second round of the ever-bearing harvest.

"El? What are you—" She didn't hear the rest.

She popped back out to a concerned Cyrus, running his hand through his strawberry blonde swoop that she loved ever since day one. She could admit that now.

With a wide smile she held up the bright red fruit as a white flag and looked into his sparkling deep brown eyes, somehow growing warmer with every second.

"Do you want a strawberry?"

EPILOGUE

Cyrus

"You ready?" Ellie said, adjusting his tie and smiling peacefully at him. They were getting dressed at a mid-tier hotel in Ithaca, running early, because that's how Ellie traveled when she was in charge of the itinerary. A gold chain hung to the top button of her favorite denim jumper, the small pendant sharp and jagged. Cyrus pressed his tie to his chest, feeling the scratch of his matching one.

He smiled at her in the mirror. "Never been more ready to be done with something in my life. I still can't believe you made me come out to do this."

"It's your commencement! You deserve to have your name read into a big stadium."

"Along with a thousand other people. I won't even be able to see you."

"*Cyrus*," she pressed.

He had her right where he wanted her, fists clenched, smiling widely, her eyes threatening to roll at any given moment. It was the perfect time to grab her jaw, kiss her, and make her forget what she was even annoyed about in the first place. He pulled back and her peaceful smile returned. Mission accomplished.

A knock at their door lifted their moment.

"Yep?" Cyrus answered.

"Just me." *Just Martha Somers,* Cyrus thought, *never.* With the way she acted as the mom Cyrus never had growing up, the modifier was out of place. "I was thinking we should head out, since it's such a big group of us. I want to make sure we can all sit together."

Ellie checked her watch and moved towards the door, opening it to Doug and Martha dressed up in their Sunday Best. "That's probably a good idea. Is the crew meeting us there?" She turned to Cyrus.

The crew included Ray, Rosie, Matteo, and his husband Arie. "Yeah, they're finishing up brunch. Rosie has a friend who runs a spot up here."

"Hi Cyrus!" Felix popped his head into the door frame.

And of course wherever Felix was, Noah was right behind.

"Woaw, you're wearing a tie!" Noah ran off, yelling, "Mom! Should I have brought a tie?"

Cyrus chuckled with Ellie. Noah had taken an interest in every item of Cyrus's closet recently, so it didn't surprise him in the slightest that he'd want to match him on a day like today.

They made it to the hallway, knocking on doors along the way to pick up more and more loved ones. The rest of the Khangs, the Ortegas, Jason and Caroline, all here for his dinky little commencement. Cyrus avoided a punch in the side, laughing at Jason's idea of a greeting. The two of them had gotten close over the winter, partially because his house was as far as Cyrus would drive in the snow, and selfishly because he went through a jar of salsa a week.

"Look at Mr. Manhattan, all dressed up for his little doctorate ceremony."

"PhD, Jason." Cyrus scoffed and made a face at Ellie. "This guy doesn't even know the difference between a doctorate and a PhD." With a push to his shoulder, and an eye roll to a laughing Caroline, Ellie ushered them out of the hall to pile into cars.

They'd decided to make a trip of it, staying in upstate New York for the week before the ceremony, doing tourist-y things that Cyrus had never done before like visiting Niagara Falls, and well, that's about it. Everything else, Cyrus was far too familiar with and had been the designated tour guide for all the best that Ithaca, NY had to offer. Which was more than he remembered when he lived here, if he was honest.

Andrés and Marisol stayed back due to them having a newborn to deal with, Loretta didn't like flying, and Nick admitted traveling with two small children would've been hell. But Maya and Isabelle joined them for a few days before heading back to take care of the ever finicky fungi. Even though this was their last leg, spirits were still up and energy was high.

Ellie pulled the rental into the parking lot adjacent from Schoellkopf Field, the setting for the day's festivities and a place he had never been in all his time at Cornell. He wasn't much of a football guy.

His phone buzzed in his pocket on the group's way to the entrance. "Ah, it's Rory."

"Is she here?!" Ellie asked, full of excitement and anticipation in seeing the only sibling he was on speaking terms with.

"Hello?"

"Hey, Kyle and I are here with James. We're standing at the, oh my god. I see you."

He looked up, and through the wave of people gathered at the entrance, he saw the blonde hair and wide smile. He'd seen her six months prior, when James was born in early December, just like Aurora. Then he saw her again when they flew out to Boston after Christmas. And once more when Ellie begged him to take her to visit Aurora and the baby as a birthday present in late April. That was three weeks ago, and Ellie was still running towards her like a pistol.

She and Martha fought over who could hold him first, but Cyrus won. It paid to be Aurora's brother.

"Kyle, Rory, this is some of the neighborhood back in Meriden. This is Jason and Caroline, the Khangs, the Ortegas, and Ellie's parents."

"It's so good to finally meet you and see those chubby little cheeks in person," Martha began first as rounds of handshakes and hugs took place.

Kyle petted one of James' tiny fingernails and smiled. "Sounds like we'll be crashing a Community Night in the near future."

"Really?" Cyrus cheered. "You know you're always welcome."

"Yeah, we've been thinking of spending some time in Minnesota. And if the farm is as beautiful as you two are always saying, we might have to make it a yearly summer trip."

"Yes. Please, *please,* Rory, you better not be joking," Ellie whined.

"Well, and if everything goes through with the house, by then you'll have the place to yourself," Martha added, still not taking her eyes off baby James.

Cyrus shared a glance with Aurora. He'd already told her about the Robran's decision to move to Rochester, and couldn't believe that Doug and Martha were at a place to part with the farm. But, seeing as neither of them wanted to take care of a three bedroom, two bath farmhouse, everything kind of rooted into place. It was the first time anywhere ever felt like home. He couldn't wait to buy furniture.

Martha got her way, or rather, Cyrus gave in and passed James off to her open arms, holding him close with a gushing Ellie and Trang. Even Brielle and Grace wanted a peek.

Aurora closed in on Cyrus. "Have you heard from Mom or Dad?"

"No." He swallowed. "And that's fine. You?"

"Mom wanted pictures of James, so I sent them." She shrugged. Because she was Aurora fucking Lexington, and nothing fazed her. "Maren and Adam are splitting up, did you hear?"

Cyrus's eyes widened. "You're shitting me."

"Nope. He wanted kids, she didn't. Adam thought she was off birth control for the last *year.*" She grimaced. "Sounds like Mom didn't even know. Maybe we won't be the outcasts anymore."

"Wouldn't that be something," he chuckled. If that day came, he didn't need the validation anymore. Not when his entire future was right in front of him.

Ellie

"Okay, we should probably get inside," Ellie announced, acting as the timekeeper for the day. She stayed behind as Cyrus gave one last kiss on James' forehead before Aurora left with Kyle.

"Hey, good luck," she said, smoothing out a nonexistent wrinkle in his shirt. She just wanted to touch him. "You look so professional. After this can I call you Dr. Manhattan in bed?"

"You don't even call me *Mr.* Manhattan in bed."

She laughed at her own joke. "I know, but I could always start."

"I am begging you not to." Their eyes met and the moment of levity melted into sincerity.

"Do you wish they were here?"

He shook his head, pulling her into an embrace.

"You feeling okay, then?" she asked.

"Yeah." He pressed his cheek against hers. "Because of you."

"I love you."

"I love you too, El."

They kissed goodbye and Cyrus was off with a wave, disappearing in the crowd of other well-dressed graduates in the designated entry point. She followed the rest of the group inside and by some miracle found Ray and the crew. Matteo wore a glamorous maroon jacket that shimmered in the sun, while his husband, Arie, looked effortlessly chic in a thin black turtleneck and dark grey slacks. Ray and Rosie both sat uncomfortable in business casual, but soon were greeting the group with easy smiles and spirited small talk. Two worlds collided, roots intertwining inseparably.

A collective sigh escaped them once they were finally seated. Ellie was at the epicenter, seated on the warm metal bleachers with the mid-May sun shining down on the green field.

Jason leaned over, giving her a side eye. "Heard anything?"

She smiled, not wanting to break Cyrus's news for him until dinner, their pre-planned time to announce that Cyrus had gotten the job at the University in Wakuta as an undergrad full-time biology professor. He'd teach during the school year, then help run the farm during the summer. It was the best case scenario for both of them, and Ellie couldn't believe how it all happened. The universe was definitely on their side.

"We have, but I'll let Cyrus share the news at dinner," she whispered coyly, trying to hide her smile from his wide, understanding eyes.

A scene of chaos developed at the end of their row, catching Ellie's attention.

"Hi, sorry we're late, sorry, sorry," the frazzled voice of Hannah called out. "Emelia didn't want to wear pants this morning, and Leo got sick on the car ride here." She shuffled into the seat next to Doug, giving him a kiss on the cheek before waving to the rest of the group.

Grace Ortega shot up from her seat. "Emelia!"

The now six-year-old released her vice-like grip from Florence's arm and her entire being changed from recluse and pouty, to open and free now that she had a similar-sized friend, while Leo crawled onto Doug and hung on for dear life. The two were similar: quiet, observant, and seemed to laugh at the same things. Hannah and Ellie exchanged a glance, words of love and contentment spoken with a soft smile. It was good to have the family together again.

The commencement began with all the formality of the first ceremony, but Ellie wasn't alone staring at the back of unfamiliar heads, trying to impress strangers. Today, she was surrounded by people she loved. As the graduates shuffled in, Martha pointed him out first, donned in his official doctoral regalia of black and crimson. Important and stately, with what Cyrus told her was an eight-sided graduation *tam* not to be confused with a *cap*.

And like a moth to a flame, an invisible string pulling them together, the anchor of the maple tree etched into his forearm, their eyes found each other in the sea of people, just like they did every other day. Only this time, she was surrounded by family and people who loved Cyrus for exactly who he was. Not because of his name, or his money, but because he loved her like art and she let herself love him back.

The summer wasn't over. It was just beginning.

ACKNOWLEDGEMENTS

It's one big giant cliche to say I don't know where to start, but I feel like I have a pass for this one. I honestly never thought I would be writing a book, let alone publishing a full-length novel in my lifetime. Yet, here I am writing the acknowledgements to thank a handful of wonderful people for cheering me on along the way. (Even if they didn't realize it.)

To Ly. You were one of the first people in my life to ever read a story of mine. Our friendship means the world to me and I am so honored to have a piece of you forever embedded into this novel. Thank you for teaching me about bitter melon soup. Thank you for sharing about your family's garden growing up. Thank you for eating delicious food with me and asking, "What did you have for lunch today?" Thank you for continuing to support me through all of my twists and turns. I am so incredibly lucky to have you in my life, and Ellie is just as lucky to have the Khangs in hers.

To Kendra. Thank you for making me realize that the hundreds of hours in Create-A-Sim was actually just character development, and the subsequent thousands of hours playing Sims was simply story building. You were the first person to ever make me think of myself as a storyteller.

To KaRa Lyn. Your support through these last chapters of my life is unsurpassable. I would not be who I am today without you. I would not have started writing if it wasn't for you. Thank you for listening to me ramble on the phone and for insisting that what I have to say is interesting.

To Whitney. Thank you for your decades of friendship. And for listening to me talk and talk and talk about these books, but not real books, okay maybe they're real books, okay I think I'm going to try to publish them. I love you.

To Jean. Having you read this book meant the world to me. Thank you for the edits, the encouragement, and for caring about this story enough to sit at the kitchen table with me for hours talking about it. I love you so dearly, and I look up to you in every way imaginable.

To Hannah. Thank you for being the first person (ever!) to finish reading this book. Reconnecting with you through writing has been such a joy and I can't wait to see where this next chapter of our lives takes us. Hooray for homecomers!

To my family. Hey, guess what? I wrote a book! Thank you for supporting me in making all of the strange decisions I've made these past couple of years. Who would have thought it would lead me here? I am so proud of where I grew up and the beauty that it holds. Mom, thank you for always showing me the beauty of Meriden even as a child. Dad, thanks for being my right hand man while we tell stories on the Performing Arts Center stage. Thank you for the love, for the shelter, and for trusting me.

To the online community who doesn't quite know I exist in the real world. Thank you for the last two years of encouragement, kudos, and comments.

And to you. If you've read this far, I am so colossally and frightfully thankful for you. I hope you enjoyed escaping into the world of strawberries and overalls. May you always have a sturdy maple tree to anchor you home. (Wherever that may be.)

ABOUT THE AUTHOR

Anna Pollock is a community lover and high school theater director when she's not writing heated and wholesome novels about romance. She grew up in rural Minnesota where she currently resides with her orange and white cat, Kinston. Stay tuned for more stories centered around the hope and heartbreak of loving and being loved as a full human.

Connect online at annarbpollock.com.